Fairy Tales of New York

Fairy Tales of New York

Books One and Two

Kelly Hunter
Heidi Rice

TULE
PUBLISHING

Pursued by the Rogue

Tempting the Knight

Print Edition

The Tule Publishing Group, LLC

ISBN: 978-1-943963-28-7

Table of Contents

Pursued by the Rogue

A Fairy Tales of New York Romance

Kelly Hunter

Dedication

This one's for Amy, Lucy and Heidi because my respect and admiration for you knows no bounds. We may not own Sully's pub in reality but in my mind every corner of it is ours.

Dear Reader,

Pursued By The Rogue is the first in a four book, multi-author series called *Fairytales of New York*.

The stories are connected in a number of ways. Firstly, by four heroines who have been friends since boarding school. Secondly, by an often used setting – an old, family-owned, Irish pub in Brooklyn. Each story also riffs off a different fairy tale. I chose *The Ugly Duckling* by Hans Christian Andersen and promptly set about making my heroine feel ugly and unwanted.

Once Dawn soars, she becomes a successful and highly regarded young woman in the field of medical research. Unlikely, perhaps, but her career trajectory was inspired by the real-life story of the remarkable Elizabeth Holmes and her blood testing company, Theranos.

I hope you like my ugly duckling,
Kelly Hunter

Prologue

Ten years ago, St. John the Apostle Academy, Upstate New York.

DAWN TURNER WASN'T a pretty girl – she only had to look in a mirror to know that.

And now she was ugly on the inside as well.

She crossed the moonlit room and sank onto the pile of pillows and blankets on the floor. She didn't care that her stripy grandfather pajamas stood out in stark contrast to the pretty nightwear of the other three girls nestled amongst the bedding. She just wanted their company on this dark, blood-soaked night. She wanted to talk about little things not big ones. She wanted their laughter and their acceptance of her, regardless of her flaws. Dawn, the scholarship girl, the charity case, the biggest misfit of them all.

It was still a mystery as to why the three other girls in her dormitory tolerated her at all.

Her parents hadn't wanted her. They'd stayed in Australia to study remote outback communities, and when carting Dawn around with them had gotten old and her schooling had become too much of a burden they'd shipped her off to an aunt and uncle in Upstate New York.

They'd called it seeing to her welfare but it had felt a lot like abandonment to Dawn.

Her aunt and uncle – childless and happy about it – hadn't known what to do with her either, so when the scholarship to St. John's had come up Dawn had made her way to boarding school with barely a backward glance. It hadn't taken her long to discover that the good sisters at St. John the Apostle Academy treated her with even *more* chilling indifference.

They'd made it very clear that as long Dawn's grades made the school look good, her presence would be tolerated.

Nothing more.

Big of them, she thought, and then with her next breath cursed herself for her lack of gratitude. She could get a good education here, one she was determined to put to good use. She had a roof over her head and food in her stomach. She'd made friends here.

There was a *lot* to be grateful for.

The three girls who'd waited with varying degrees of impatience for her to join their midnight party – Faith, Mercy and Zel – they *liked* her.

They were the first real friends she'd ever had.

"Is there any particular reason we're drinking stolen altar wine at midnight?" she asked. Not a regular activity – even for them.

"We're celebrating." Faith handed her a tumbler of wine.

"Celebrating what?"

"Us. Our friendship. Sláinte."

Dawn's smile wobbled at the salute she'd heard for the first time six weeks ago at a twenty-first birthday party in an old Irish pub in Brooklyn. Faith came from an American-Irish family; four beautiful older brothers, one grieving father and a dead mother who had lost her fight with cancer two years ago. One of those brothers – the most handsome of them all – had looked at Dawn and smiled.

And thought her beautiful.

Don't think about him, Dawn. Don't go there.

Not so smart at all, the scholarship girl.

Dawn looked at the wine; in the darkness it looked like blood. And there was Faith, waiting for a toast.

"Sláinte," she offered faintly and Mercy echoed her.

Mercy, with her thick Spanish accent courtesy of her Argentinian heritage. Mercy, who'd bonded with Dawn four years ago for reasons unknown. Misfits both. Maybe that was the reason.

Dawn the abandoned, Faith the motherless, Mercy with her elsewhere heritage, and then there was Zel, the final addition to their little group of four lost souls.

Zelda Madison had arrived at the convent school only

last year, orphaned and in possession of an uncaring older brother who couldn't wait to see the back of her. Zel had been abandoned too, and the Sisters in their wisdom had thought Faith, Mercy and Dawn would be a good influence on her.

Wrong.

Zel could corrupt anyone.

"My glass is empty. Why is my glass always empty?" Zel wanted to know. "Where's the wine?"

The wine, yes. Wine, not blood. Good call. Maybe Dawn could drown her sins in it. She set the tumbler to her mouth and swallowed down hard on the thin, sweet liquid.

Don't think. Don't stop. And whatever else, don't confide to *anyone* that six weeks ago she'd lost her mind, not to mention her virginity, to Faith's youngest brother, Finn.

She'd felt so loved.

So very, very beautiful in Finbar Sullivan's arms.

It was a feeling that had ended all too soon.

There was a special Hell reserved for willful, wayward, ugly girls who might just possibly be having a miscarriage or might just possibly be having a really late period.

And Dawn was in it.

Sex without marriage, sin and punishment.

More blood.

"Where did this wine even come from?" she asked.

"Kitchen storeroom," said all three of the girls.

"So it's not consecrated? Good to know." Dawn swallowed what was left in her glass and held it out to Zel for a refill. "Am I pretty?" No. That was a no-brainer. "Wait, let me rephrase. I'm not pretty and I know it, but is there *anything* I can do to make me look more normal?"

"Conformity's overrated," said Zel. "Embrace the uniqueness that is you. And get some clothes that aren't three sizes too big for you."

"I'm going to grow into these clothes. My aunt said so."

"Not any time soon," muttered Zel. "Your aunt needs to rethink that prediction."

"You'd start with your eyes," Mercy interceded firmly. "Gray eyes are unusual."

"Since when?" said Dawn.

"In Argentina they are. I could shape your brows just so." Mercy traced a path over her own shapely brows. "Like a frame. Make people look to your eyes first."

"And away from everything else? Will that work? What about my ears? And my mouth? People are always looking at my mouth." It was overly wide, overly plush. She had a crooked eye tooth, but her parents thought braces unnecessary.

"Probably wondering what you can fit in it," said Zel with a smirk.

"More wine for starters," muttered Dawn. She knew what Zel meant. Finn had liked Dawn's lips on him well enough. They'd made him groan, deep and rough. They'd made him curse.

He'd made her feel wanted.

"Mercy's right," said Zel from the comfort of her classically beautiful features. "Emphasize the eyes. And no more borrowing other people's lipstick. You need your own colors. Corals. Nudes. Pale, not bold. I'll go shopping for you next time I'm allowed out of my cell."

"You will not! I'm not a charity case."

Although technically…

Zel smiled, her halo of blonde hair cementing the angelic look. "Let me rephrase. I am about to go on a lipstick buying binge. Later, when I decide that some of the colors don't suit me, I'm going to see if anyone here wants them before I throw them out. Charity it's not. That's recycling."

Dawn shifted restlessly and wore a stabbing pain low in her belly. She'd been having sharp pain there all night. Maybe it was her appendix. Maybe that would account for the screaming terror.

Please, Lord, make everything be okay. I'll be so, so good.

"Finn wants us to come to a gig he's playing next month at a jazz club in Manhattan," said Faith. "He says he can get us all in to watch."

"*Some of us* need permission to get out of here first," muttered Zel.

"You'll be out of detention by then. Consider it incentive to not push Sister Ignatius's buttons," Faith said. "Be good and you too can come along."

"Would we stay at your place afterwards?" Mercy

asked. Faith's house being a small apartment above the pub Faith's family owned. "Will there be room for us all?"

"We could stay at my place. There's room for a circus there," offered Zel with a dangerous smile. "My brother starts another six-month tour in the Legion next week. We could stay there under the careful supervision of no one at all."

"Dawn, do you want to go?" asked Faith. "Because, if you want my opinion, you're the one Finn wants there."

Did Faith know?

Had Finn told her?

"What instrument will he be playing?"

"Does it matter?"

"No, I—he seems to play everything, that's all." Violin, piano, the bodhran drum. Music spilled out of him no matter what instrument he picked up. "Is this gig a big deal for him?"

Faith nodded and her dark corkscrew curls nodded right along with her, although not all at once and not all in the same direction. "It's his first paid gig. He's so proud. No one pays Finn to play at home. And—" Faith's eyes sparkled, "don't tell him I told you, but he auditioned for Juilliard this afternoon. I'm so proud!"

"We should support Finn." Zel gestured expansively. "And then he'll become famous and the Sullivan pub will become *the* Brooklyn pub for great music, and the drinks will flow, and all will be well in Sully world. Count us in."

Dawn shifted again and let out a gasp.

Faith eyed her sharply. "Are you all right?"

"It's just that time of the month."

"I thought you cycled the same time as me?"

"Not anymore." Dawn set her wine down on the floor and away from the blankets carefully, then toppled over onto her side and drew her knees to her chest. "I can't go to the jazz club next month. Count me out."

"Ask her again next week," Zel said. "Show her another picture of your brother and his violin for incentive."

"It won't work." Dawn rested her head on a particularly nuggety pillow lump. "I'm the ugliest duckling in the world, and he's going to become a megastar musician with a supermodel girlfriend. Possibly you."

"I so need to meet these brothers. They sound so delicious," Zel declared, and laughed at Faith's scandalized expression. "What?"

"My brothers are emotionally stunted, self-absorbed and allergic to cleanliness. I hereby declare them off limits to *all* of you."

"I could teach them how to bathe." Zel had a familiar gleam in her eye. "All of them. All at once. Soap suds *everywhere*."

"No bathing with my brothers! Gimme that wine. I need to get rid of that thought."

"Amen," said Dawn, as she tentatively eased back into a sitting position, never mind that it was a hunched one with her arms crossed protectively over her stomach. "I'm going to go into medical research and invent targeted pain medication that works."

"You're too late." Zel reached for the wine bottle. "It's called alcohol."

"Something that doesn't give you a hangover the next morning," Dawn continued. "Chocolate will be the preferred delivery system. Chocolate coated pain relief."

Mercy nodded enthusiastically. "Can you invent zero calorie chocolate while you're there?"

"Why would I want to do that?"

"For me." Curvaceous Mercy gave Dawn the full benefit of her liquid brown eyes. "You'd do it for me."

"I will. But only for you. You're my best friends. I want you to know that. I'd do anything for you." Except tell them the truth and have Faith hate her for what had happened with Finn, and Finn hate her for turning what they'd shared into a potentially life changing event. "And next week I'm going to be a new me, with shapely eyebrows and a beige mouth and nothing to worry about at all. I'm going to work hard for good grades."

"You always work hard," offered Faith.

"I'm going to work harder. I'm going to make good."

If she could just get through this evening, and then the next few days, everything would return to normal and no one need ever know just how close she'd come to—

Just how close she'd come.

God.

She couldn't even think about what might have been without tears pricking at her eyes. "I need the bathroom again."

She tried to stand up, stumbled, and sat back down with the help of Mercy's steadying hand.

So dumb. Maybe all she needed was more wine.

"No," said Mercy gently when she reached for it. "No more for you."

And then the carved wooden door with its shapely pointed arch groaned open and a shrouded shape stood in the doorway, lit by nothing more than moonlight and steeped in disapproval.

"Sister Ignatius," stuttered Faith, and tried to hide the wine, but it was too late.

Sister Ignatius had eyes like a hawk.

Mercy groaned. Zel smiled brightly up at the nun, nothing but reckless challenge there. And Dawn …

Sister Ignatius wasn't the worst thing that had happened to Dawn tonight. There'd been the cramps and the blood. The blood and the tears.

Tears for no reason at all.

Forgive me, Father, for I have sinned.

I loved.

And I think I lost.

And sorrow had drilled deep down into her soul at the shame of it all, but some small part of her insisted that it was for the best and no one need ever know. She would make amends, *she would*, and one day she would no longer be ugly.

Inside and out.

Sister Ignatius and the altar wine?

That was just the sideshow.

Chapter One

ONLY THREE THINGS in life had ever come close to bringing Finbar Sullivan to his knees. Music, his mother's death, and Dawn Turner's mouth.

His reverence for music was easy to understand. He lived it, breathed it. He'd picked up his first violin at the ripe age of four and fallen in thrall. He'd spent most of his waking hours trying to master the instrument, and he still hadn't managed it, but he was closer than most because music owned his soul.

His mother's death had been a blow. Twelve years on and her absence *still* cast a long shadow over the Sullivan family. His father missed her every day and night, and it was heartbreaking to watch loneliness suck the joy from his old man's life.

As for Dawn …

Maybe his father wasn't the only Sullivan to get hung up on a memory.

Why else would the mention of a woman Finn hadn't

seen since he was a teenager make him utterly unable to feign casual interest as he turned to his sister and said, "Dawn Turner's coming here?"

Faith nodded. "And Zelda. And Mercy. And don't you dare tell me to lock up the altar wine because I've already heard that one from Ty."

Their oldest brother had a long memory when it came to misdemeanors – possibly because he'd had to bail his younger siblings out of so many of them. "Zelda's the Upper East Side model with the money, right?"

Faith nodded. "And you'll not be hitting on her."

"And Mercy's the Argentinian one with the curves?"

"Or her."

"I always did like Dawn best." Nothing but the truth, he thought, and grinned at his sister's glare. "I didn't think you kept in touch with her anymore?" He certainly hadn't, although not for want of trying. He'd called and he'd called.

And then called some more.

"Mercy kept in touch with her and apparently Zel did too."

Was that a hint of hurt he heard in his sister's voice?

Faith shrugged as if it didn't matter, but he wasn't buying her bravado. "And now that everyone's living here in the city, Mercy wants a reunion."

"Is this a good thing?" he asked warily.

"Ask me tomorrow. I'm not exactly the group's success

story."

"You manage the best pub in Brooklyn."

"Says who?"

"Me. Classical music's problem child. Brilliant yet contrary. Knows genius when he sees it. You are a genius pub manager."

"You are so full of shite."

He was and he'd never deny it. Truth was, the pub barely made ends meet some months and Faith seemed stuck here because of duty rather than of love. "You need to start drawing again. Painting. Follow that drum."

"I don't have time."

"Faith …" Finn watched his sister look around the well-worn bar with its soft side lighting and old pictures on the walls. Pictures of the city in the making and of the occasional famous face that had wandered into the bar over the years. Pictures his father and grandfather had collected. Pictures that not one of his generation of Sullivans had added to. Why weren't some of Faith's pictures up on those walls? They were good enough. Stick a price tag on them and watch them sell. "Make time."

"How come you had descriptions for Zel and Mercy and not for Dawn?" Faith asked abruptly.

"What?"

"Zel was the model, Mercy had the curves … You didn't describe Dawn."

"I was getting *around* to describing Dawn."

"You lie."

And usually he was good at it. "Dawn's the smart Aussie with the big gray eyes and a mouth a man could worship." Faith probably didn't need to know how the touch of Dawn's plush, plump lips had been enough to set his body thrumming like a tuning fork. "Heard enough?"

Faith was looking at him as if she'd never seen him before. "I think the question is *do you want to go on*?"

"No, I'm all done. When do they arrive?"

"Within the next ten minutes if they're on time. They're coming over by ferry and then catching a cab. Which reminds me, don't you have a performance this evening? Rehearsal? Something to go to?"

"Anyone would think you wanted me gone."

"Smart boy."

"Man. Smart man." He was twenty-seven, one year older than Faith, second youngest in the family and the youngest of the four boys. None of them were children anymore. "No concert until next weekend. And right now I'm waiting for Gil. Em's got a date, so we're having a guys' night with Disney tunes, gummi bears and baby drums."

"Your neighbors are going to love you."

"They do." Finn rented a miniscule studio apartment off Broadway, one that had been specifically outfitted for performers. Noise reduction paneling in the walls, triple glazed windows, other musicians for neighbors. "Do you know where that little violin I had as a kid is?"

"Pop sold it."

"He would *never*!"

"Maybe it was your second one he sold."

"That one he sold." And all the others that had come after it. Always trading up, always finding the money from somewhere to give Finn the instruments that would take his playing to the next level. These days a Fortune 100 company owned Finn's Guarneri violin and had gifted him exclusive use of it for ten years, five of which were gone.

Finn knew how to share. He knew how privileged he was to have access to the instrument at all. And the day he handed it back a slice of his soul would go with it, never to return. That was the *real* price of the special violins of this world. They collected souls. "Have you seen my first violin lately?"

"It's in the cupboard in your old room. Way up high, behind the blankets."

"You're a good sister. Keep an eye out for Gil for me?"

"Has it occurred to you that I might be too busy with my own friends to keep an eye out for your playdates?"

It hadn't, no. And that was his bad. "Or I can wait here until he arrives and then we can go looking for the violin together. I can wait here and help you keep an eye out for your friends. I can be your moral support. No hitting on Mercy or Zel, I promise."

"What about Dawn? Will you be making your interest in her known?"

Now there was a question …

"If you sabotage my reunion—"

"Wouldn't dream of it."

He wouldn't.

Really.

✦

IT WAS A good thing Dawn had Mercy and Zel in the cab with her. If she'd been alone she'd have told the driver to turn around and take her home. Through the tunnel, take an hour, take two. She'd have headed back to the Soho apartment she'd paid a fortune for and bailed on this school friends' reunion that Mercy had insisted would be good for them all.

At the very least, Dawn should have tried to get the venue changed. Somewhere in Manhattan would have been good. Hell's Kitchen, Little Italy, *anywhere* would have been preferable to an old Irish pub in Brooklyn that was choc full of memories she didn't want to own.

Memories of a night full of music and laughter and Finbar Sullivan's cap sitting jauntily on her head. He'd given it to her between the sets of Irish folk music he'd played with his brothers. Told her she was a pretty girl.

She'd been so starved for love and attention back then.

So very enamored of Faith's fun-loving brother whose passion for music had poured from his fingertips.

So here she was, ten years later, heading back to that

place with mixed feelings. *Surely* he wouldn't be there.

Finbar Sullivan was probably somewhere in Europe right this minute, mesmerizing crowds with the music he coaxed from his ten million dollar violin.

He'd become a concert violinist at some point during these past ten years. A composer, a recording artist, a star of the classical music world – all of those things. Chances of finding him at the pub tonight were slim.

Which was why Dawn had cancelled all her afternoon meetings in order to stand in front of her cupboard in the hope of figuring out what to wear to a reunion with old friends, and possibly, maybe, but probably not Finn.

Who was probably in Berlin, playing with the Philharmonic there this evening.

Or something.

In the end, she'd chosen to wear comfortable jeans, a forest-green silk camisole and a dusky pink jacket that fell to mid-thigh. She'd been to an upmarket hair care salon in an attempt to make her blonde hair fall sleek and straight to frame a face that hadn't grown prettier with age, even if she now had a much better clue when it came to making the best of it.

She looked as good as she was ever going to look and it still wasn't enough to satisfy the insecurity gnawing at her belly. Because apart from the ghost of her first lover to contend with, she was also catching up with Faith for the first time in years.

Dawn hadn't had much to do with Faith after the incident with the altar wine all those years ago. She'd blamed it on her punishments, on her study load, on them being relegated to different dorm rooms and on Mercy and Zel being gone. Anything but the truth.

Truth was, Dawn hadn't been able be around Faith and not think of Finn and guilt and loss. She hadn't had the emotional strength for it back then. Even now, her emotions felt stretched thin.

She'd cut Faith out of her life completely, and Faith – who'd once been as close as a sister – had thought it was because of the altar wine incident.

Dawn had a *lot* of making up to do if she wanted Faith Sullivan to call her a friend again.

The cab pulled up in front of Sully's all too soon and Zel paid the fare as they all piled out.

Trying desperately not to chew on her lip and ruin her understated lipstick, Dawn followed the others into the pub's gaping maw.

It took a moment for her eyes to adjust to the dimly lit interior.

And during that time she knew without seeing that Finbar Sullivan wasn't performing on the world stage this evening.

He was right here.

She knew it by the prickle of awareness that burrowed beneath her skin and nested low in her belly. A sixth sense that she couldn't explain and barely believed in. And then she saw him, and it was as if her world narrowed down to the head of a pin and there was nothing else in it but for a pair of shamrock-green eyes focused utterly on her. There was a body to go with it, long and lean. A mess of shaggy dark hair. A wave of feeling big enough to drown in.

Heartbreak and regret. Longing and insecurity.

Need.

Oh, the need to simply reach out and touch him was still there in spades as Finn focused on her lips for a fraction longer than was polite. And then he blinked, and ruefully shook his head as his gaze reconnected with hers.

She wondered what he saw. If he still thought her pretty or whether the years had put paid to that crazy notion altogether.

In the end it was Dawn who dragged her gaze away from his in order to greet a smiling Faith. In the end it was Faith with her wild brown curls, who threw her arms around Dawn and held on tight.

"Hey, you," murmured Faith. "It's been a long time."

"I know. I'm sorry. Busy years."

She pulled back awkwardly and let Faith study her.

"So sleek and classy," Faith said at last.

"It's the clothes."

"It's your confidence."

If only.

And then Faith let her go and the next person in line to

greet her was Finn, leaning casually against the bar as if it belonged to him and, oh.

Well.

There was a scent she remembered.

Up close she could see the details she'd missed earlier. All those long lines and lean muscles, the five o'clock shadow and the smile that spoke of confidence aplenty and a fine appreciation for others. He'd always had that smile. Even back then.

"Hello, Finn."

"You remember me."

"Seriously?" she offered dryly. "How many famous concert violinists do you think I know?"

Mercy caught her eye and mouthed 'rockstar,' and it was so ridiculously playful and innocent that Dawn laughed and tried for her own sake to push her inner insecurities aside. "Yes, Finn. I remember you."

Faith groaned. "Don't encourage him, Dawn. His ego's big enough already."

"Don't listen to her, Dawn." Finn's voice carried a hint of Irish in it. "Encourage me more."

This was what she'd suffered for all those years ago. A warm and easy welcome from a lover who knew nothing of the heartbreak that had followed their one night together. This laughing reunion. This meeting of adults who'd made their own way, secure in their choices and decisions.

She'd earned this.

"You're making beautiful music these days," she told him. "I even went to one of your concerts once, years ago when you played at the Lincoln Center."

"Did you like it?"

"It was magic," she told him with simple sincerity. He'd cut an impossibly romantic figure against the glitteringly formal backdrop of the orchestra. He'd been dressed all in black and had been so far beyond her reach that he hadn't seemed like a real person at all, but his music had been real enough to wrap around her like a lover and drench her in beauty. "And that's about all the flattery I have for you."

"Pretty sure we can help her come up with more," murmured Zel.

"Goodbye, Finn. Moving on," Faith warned and ushered her old school friends towards a faraway booth. Dawn couldn't help but take one last look as she walked away, still hungry to catalogue the changes the years had provoked. New memories to replace the old.

Better ones.

He was looking down at his hands, shadows playing merry with his eyelashes and the planes of his face. As for those fingers, they were long and strong with immaculately kept nails. A musician's hands; made for wringing every last drop of emotion from an instrument. Or a lover.

Dawn stumbled over the leg of a chair and quickly looked away.

That was probably enough new memories for now.

"What are we drinking?" she asked as Faith stopped by the bar and waved them towards the last booth in a long row of booths set neatly against the wall.

"I have a plan," said Faith. "It involves Guinness for you. That okay?"

Dawn nodded and followed the other two women to the window booth with the ruby red seats and battle-scarred wooden tabletop. There was safety in being squeezed in between Mercy and the wall, with Zel sitting opposite.

Safety in not looking towards Finn at all.

Grasping for anything that involved the here and now, Dawn turned her attention to the drinks Faith set down in front of them. Guinness for her, Faith and Mercy. Something icy and minty for Zel. "What's that?"

"A virgin Mojito. I'm trialing a couple of cocktails for the bar, with and without the alcohol. Zel's my jetsetting guinea pig who's graced the fancy bars of the world. She's going to tell me if this one's any good."

"I feel so loved," said Zel, with a wicked grin.

"Next round is mine," said Mercy. "I'm a one Guinness woman and then I'm switching to orange juice." She glanced at Faith's and Dawn's full pints' and then back down at her half pint. "Seriously, how do you drink that much beer?"

"Practice," said Faith and Dawn nodded sagely and

reached for hers.

"I'm mostly in it for the froth."

"Head," corrected Faith. "And next time – if Pop's not looking – I'll make yours bigger."

"Only if your pop's not looking?" Mercy teased.

Faith nodded, her bright blue gaze encompassing Dawn and Mercy both. "There are rules concerning how much head to put on a glass of Guinness. Commandments, some might call them. Not to be messed with. I value my own head also."

Dawn laughed, and then not two seconds later lost her grip on the glass and narrowly missed spilling the lot. As it was, a good quarter of it ended up on the table. "Good job, genius," she muttered, reaching for napkins to mop up the spillage. "Sorry. I'm nervous. Also a klutz."

"What's to be nervous about?" Mercy reached over and squeezed her fingers as Faith called for a cloth from the barman.

"Oh, you know." Vague was good, Dawn decided. Vague and klutzy went well together.

"*I* know," murmured Faith, as she leaned over and cleaned up Dawn's mess. "Impressing old friends is hard. Try being the barmaid in this equation."

"As if that's all you do here," Mercy said. "Just like all Zel does is stand in front of a camera and look beautiful. Just like all I do is pick grapes back in Argentina."

"Dawn runs her own genetic research company," Faith

pointed out.

"Yeah, but she's a klutz." Zel came on board the conversation with a lazy wave of her hand. "I vote we keep her anyway."

"Exactly." Mercy grinned. "The beauty of old friends is that don't *have* to impress them."

Just like that the years fell away and Dawn sat back and relaxed into the warmth these three other women provided. Reunions didn't have to be a stilted show-and-tell full of awkward silence. Maybe they could just sit here and get to know each other all over again.

Maybe she could dream of Finn now and know that things had worked out for the best.

"Is he still watching you?" Faith asked.

"Who?"

"Finn."

"No," she said, and it was true, for his attention had shifted to a dark-haired boy of around four years old who was running towards him with no signs of stopping. A slender, dark-haired woman followed at a more leisurely pace. Finn crouched down and hugged the kid, picking him up so that they were shoulder to shoulder and head to head.

Finn had a son?

Finn spared a kiss for the woman.

Finn had a wife?

That was …

So …

Expected.

Perfectly normal. And that pang of bitter envy in the vicinity of her heart?

Indigestion.

No children for Dawn and no regrets.

Honest.

"What are you looking at?" asked Zel.

"Finn's son."

Zel turned, so did Faith. Mercy was already facing that way.

"Godson," Faith corrected. "That's Gil. A friend of Finn's died young and his wife, Emmeline, gave birth two months later. Finn had already agreed to be godparent. One thing I will say about my brother is that he took that promise seriously. He doesn't always nail the religious aspects of the job but the male influence and the music … he's all over that."

"That's so sweet," said Mercy.

"Yes." Dawn picked up her Guinness and drank.

Her gaze met Finn's again and held.

Yes, it was.

Chapter Two

FINBAR SULLIVAN HAD a decision to make, and it wasn't a Beethoven versus Mozart type call. He could declare his interest in Dawn to the world – or at the very least to his sister –and set about making something happen, or he could try to ignore the inexplicable hold Dawn Turner had on him and carry on as usual.

Not much of a decision at all.

Two days had passed since Faith's reunion with her school friends. Two days of Gil-loaded activities involving Times Square, junk food and music carefully chosen to suit the attention span of a small boy.

But Gil was back with Emmy now – a small violin in tow, and Finn smirked afresh at the memory of the dismayed resignation on Emmy's face when Gil had shown her his new favorite instrument.

"It's time," Finn had told her simply. "Josef would have wanted it. Gil knows what to do between now and when he sees me next."

"You're not the one who has to listen to him practice," Emmy had murmured on her way out the door.

So true.

"Thank you," she'd whispered and bussed his cheek for good measure. "I know Joey would have wanted music for his children. My son's a lucky boy."

Life was good.

That wasn't to say it couldn't be better.

Finn slid behind the bar and began stacking glasses into the dishwasher. It was always easier to get Faith's attention when he was doing something useful. "So how went the reunion the other night?"

"Not bad. Kind of a testing of the waters and the waters were … warm." Faith's eyes took on an unholy gleam. "Dawn thought Gil was your son."

Finn coughed. "What?"

"I hated to disabuse her."

"But you did. You disabused her, right?"

"What does it matter?"

It mattered. "So are any of your school friends married now? Partners, significant others, children of their own?"

"Mercy's not. Neither's Zel. No partners, no kids."

Finn waited, but nothing more was forthcoming as Faith headed down the other end of the bar to tend one of their regulars. She didn't seem inclined to pick up where she left off when she returned.

Finn heaved out a sighed. "Are you really going to

make me do this the hard way?"

"After your performance the other night? Absolutely. It's what sisters are for."

"She wasn't wearing a wedding ring."

He noticed things like that.

"Doesn't mean much these days," Faith said blithely. "Would you wear one if you were married?"

"You know I would. C'mon. You know what I'm fishing for."

"Brothers," he heard her mutter beneath her breath. And then she took pity on him and reached up and wrapped her hand around his neck and tugged him close. "Dawn's single too, no kids, and if you play her the way you play everyone else I *will* castrate you."

"You don't even know how I play."

"Fast, loose and with a great deal of skill. Don't you have enough other women to dazzle with your charms?"

"Faith—"

He pulled away. He didn't know how to say what he wanted to say. "Have you ever heard a piece of music that you *have* to learn, no matter how difficult? Because you know you're going to want to play it for the rest of your life? That's me when I get anywhere near Dawn. Fast and loose isn't what I want at all."

Not their usual level of disclosure, that was for sure.

He'd managed to turn his sister mute.

He rubbed his hand across the back of his neck, where

Faith's hand had just been. "Forget it."

"Unlikely," she murmured, still staring at him. "What do you want to know?"

"About Dawn? Whatever you can tell me. What she's doing in New York. Whether she's seeing anyone. Whether she wants to."

"Dawn's not seeing anyone, she has an apartment in Soho that I suspect she owns and she's made a lot of money out of medical research and streamlining various genetic tests. Gene mapping. That kind of thing," Faith offered. "She's driven when it comes to her research. Same way you are when it comes to your music. Whether she's looking for a relationship …" His sister looked a little sad. "I don't know. She's successful by anyone's standards but she still doesn't seem to think much of herself."

"Why not?"

"I don't know. So whatever you do, don't make that worse."

"You have no faith."

The pun was too old for her to do more than roll her eyes. "I know. I have bills to pay instead. Would you like some?"

Sully's barely made money. Simple fact. "How did Sully's go this month? Did we break even?"

Faith gave him a nod and a grin. "We did."

"Have you taken *your* wage out yet?"

"Yes."

Good news. Finn knew for a fact that when times had been lean, Faith had often rolled her wage straight back into the business. "You ever think about trying to convince the old man to sell?"

"It'd kill him," she said, and maybe it would.

"What are *your* thoughts on selling it?"

"Why would we?" she countered defensively. "This is our home, Finn. The heart of this family is right here. Our memories are here."

"Do you really believe that?"

"Mom's here," she countered stubbornly, and Finn was the first to look away.

Kathleen Sullivan had run Sully's alongside her husband. She'd lived for it, loved in it, raised a family within these walls. His mother's decisions were stamped here – from the color of the barstools to the pictures on the walls. And Faith, more than any of them, kept the family legacy alive.

But she did it at the cost of her own artistic dreams, and this itched at Finn. Made him feel guilty for not doing more.

"Want us to start playing live music on Friday afternoons again?" That always pulled a crowd and made their father happy. "I'll organize it with Ronan and Case."

"I've already asked. They start touring again next week. They don't have time."

If he could make time, so could they. "I'll use words

they can understand."

Faith bit back a laugh. "Good luck with that. What words are you going to use on Dawn?"

"Music. Food. Company."

"Not marriage, babies and eternal love?"

"Not yet."

Got to save something for the finale.

✦

TEN MINUTES LATER, from the privacy of the booth in the far corner of the pub, Finn dialed the number Faith had given him and set about reissuing an old, old invitation.

He'd made a mess of it last time – or maybe the timing had simply been all wrong.

The fallout from those stolen bottles of wine had been harsh and neither his sister nor her friends had been in any position to come and watch him play his first paying gig.

Anyway.

"There's this jazz club off 8th Avenue and West 51st and I play there sometimes," he began.

"Finn?"

Call it arrogance, but it had been a long time since he'd had to start with his name.

"So, yeah. Let me do that again. Finbar Sullivan here. Wanting to speak with Dawn."

"Speaking," she replied dryly. "Do you always call for a repeat when you don't get something right the first time?"

"Musician," he countered. "You're lucky I don't want to hang up and start from the top."

Actually …

He hung up.

He called back.

She got the first word in before he did. "Dawn Turner speaking."

"Hey, Dawn. Finn Sullivan here, Faith's brother."

"How come you didn't start with *Finbar Sullivan here. Notoriously charming famous musician?*"

"You're messing with the plan. Don't make me start again." Because next time he might mention virginity.

His. Hers.

And the fact that they'd lost theirs together some ten years ago. "There's this jazz club—

"Is this the same jazz club from years ago?" Dawn asked.

"You remember that invitation?"

"I remember that we didn't go." There was something in her voice. Something wistful. "And that you went to Juilliard soon afterwards. Faith was so proud of you."

"Is that why you never answered any of my phone calls? Because of Juilliard?"

"In some ways, yes. Immaturity and insecurity on my part didn't help. Your priorities lay elsewhere – that was very clear. So did mine. I didn't want to complicate our lives."

"Who's to say it would have?"

"It was for the best," she offered quietly, and if this conversation were music it would be a lament. Notes filled with sorrow, and for the life of him he couldn't figure out why.

"A lot of years between then and now," he said.

"Yes. A lot of years."

Moving on. "It's the same jazz club. They gave me my first break and for that I stay loyal. They do good barbeque wings and dirty blues and I'm heading there this Saturday night. You want to keep me company?"

He didn't need the extended silence on the other end of the phone to know that this wasn't going well.

"Finn?" She sounded hesitant. "Why are you doing this?"

"You are the second person today to question my motives."

"Motivation's important."

"How about I say that I saw you again the other day and I wanted you all over again. I'm a free agent so I'm following up on that response. Is that motivation enough?"

More silence. So much for honesty.

And then, "It's not that I'm not flattered by your invitation, because I am," she said quietly, and there was that wistful note in her voice again that he didn't know how to interpret. "But I have motivations too and you need to know them. If I meet up with you it won't be because I'm looking for a relationship. The only reason I date at all is because I like sex. I like sex a lot. I probably have you to blame for that."

So. Well. "And this is meant to put me *off*?"

She laughed, albeit reluctantly. "It's meant to give you fair warning as to who I am and what I want. I'm a bad bet if you're looking for a relationship that's going to lead anywhere. I tell everyone this up front and not as a challenge. I don't like disappointing people. I don't want to waste anyone's time."

"Do people see it as a challenge anyway?"

"Some do," she offered dryly. "It usually takes them around two dates to figure out that I'm unlikely to change my mind. That's two dates too long."

"So … just sex, no ties."

"Smart man."

"Is there *any* kind of general affection involved?"

"Yes. That as well. There can definitely be friendship involved."

"I can work with that." He was sure of it. "Come out to dinner with me on Saturday night."

"I have a fundraising dinner to go to. Part networking, part business deal. There's no escaping it."

He noted she didn't ask him along. "Coffee late Sunday morning, then. I have rehearsal all Sunday afternoon. We can aim for a breakfast place I know in Little Italy."

"Finn—"

"Say yes. I've heard your warning. I'm still interested. Music demands a lot of me. More than most lovers are willing to put up with. Sounds to me as if you might understand."

Silence.

"One last question." And it wasn't just because ego demanded it. He wanted to hear her speak without warning. He wanted to hear an unqualified yes. "Do you ever think about what happened between us at my brother's party all those years ago?"

"Sometimes I do."

Not quite the unqualified yes he'd been hoping for. "I remember your mouth on mine, driving me clear out of my mind. I couldn't get enough of it, enough of you. I remember tightness and heat and trying desperately not to hurt you. I barely knew what I was doing. Neither did you."

"You didn't hurt me," she whispered. "We did okay."

"We did better than okay."

Silence. Heavy and waiting.

Finn smiled and moved in for the kill. "Imagine what we could do if we practiced."

"Finn—"

There was only one word he wanted to hear, and that wasn't it. "Have breakfast with me on Sunday," he pressed. "I agree to your terms. No ties. Friendship only. Let's add good food into the mix. Sunshine if we're lucky. A smile or two. But I need to hear a yes from you. One that doesn't come with reservations."

"All right," she said faintly. "Yes."

"Louder," he murmured.

"Yes," she said more firmly but it still lacked a little something. Like enthusiasm.

"Still not feeling it."

"Yes! What do you want? The *When Harry Met Sally* version?"

Well he did *now*. "See you Sunday, Dawn. Feel free to give me that particular version at the restaurant."

He hung up on her groan.

Before he lost his mind completely and asked her to repeat that a few times as well.

✦

DAWN HAD A good life. She'd stumbled across a genetic sequencing breakthrough in her third year as an undergrad, and had promptly dropped out of university for a shot at setting up her own research company. Venture capitalists had come on board and the end result had been a career trajectory envied by many.

She loved her work and was proud of what she'd been able to set in motion in such a short time.

She had a loft apartment in Soho, in a landmark building steeped in history. Two bedrooms, three bathrooms. A vast, open plan, architect-designed living and dining area and a view through floor to ceiling windows that took her breath away. Wrought iron latticework framed the view through the windows – a leftover relic from days gone by.

Her favorite deli was less than a block away.

It took her ten minutes to get to work.

She'd set her life up for maximum efficiency and luxury aplenty.

At twenty-seven, Dawn had enough money to never have to work again and enough ideas to make that impossible.

She didn't need the complications Finbar Sullivan brought with him. Not her overwhelming attraction to him. Not the worry of letting spill that she'd once thought herself pregnant with his child. She kept other secrets these days.

Darker beasts altogether.

And she wasn't about to share any of those either.

Yet here she was and there he was, with his hair gathered back into the stump of a ponytail and a fancy looking violin case slung across the chair beside him. He stood when she arrived at the table and pulled back her chair.

"Old fashioned," she murmured.

"My father's influence. Not collecting you and getting you here was neglectful enough. I need to make good."

No sooner had she sat down than a waiter arrived with glasses and a jug of icy water. He took their orders as he filled their glasses. Coffee and cannoli for her, coffee and a panino for Finn.

All very normal and easy except for Dawn's accelerated heartbeat and shortness of breath. And the way Finn kept looking at her as if he liked what he saw. All the fashion and makeup advice in the world had helped her make the most of her unusual features but she still wasn't used to people liking what they saw.

"Faith tells me that you and your company are a big deal in the world of medical research," he said.

"I have a lot of good people on board. We specialize in DNA sequencing technology."

"I'm impressed. And daunted."

"You shouldn't be. What you do isn't exactly common. You stand up in front of an audience and perform without music for an hour straight and never miss a note."

"Says who?"

"I read the reviews. They say your music is flawless."

"There's no such thing."

"Perfectionist," she teased.

"And you're not, when it comes to your research?"

Maybe the man had a point. "You haven't performed for a while. What's happening there?"

"New repertoire. I'm recording a concerto by a Finnish composer. What do you know about Sibelius?"

Not a damn thing other than what he'd just told her. "He's Finnish? And … dead?"

"Good call. Melancholy bastard," Finn grumbled.

Dawn felt herself relaxing, she couldn't help it. "Do you get stuck in his moods when you play his music?"

"I do. And then I have to fight my way out."

"Thank you for explaining the perils of Sibelius in a way I can understand."

"I expect the same from you when it comes to DNA sequencing."

Dawn felt her smile fade. "We really don't have much in common, do we?" She watched as his gaze flickered to the curve of her mouth and back.

Okay, maybe they had that.

She reached for her water and sipped as he studied her through narrowed eyes.

"Are you always inclined towards stopping a friendship before it's begun?" he asked finally.

No. This unstoppable determination to present herself in the worst possible light was new. A mad mix of hope that he might still find something about her to like, and deliberate self-sabotage. "Could be I'm trying to spare you."

"From what?"

"Me."

"How about you let me make that call?"

The coffee came, and so did the food. Finn started on his roll with uninhibited enjoyment. Dawn tried very hard to hide her rapture at the cannoli but it was too good not to let her pleasure show. Finn watched her with every evidence of enjoyment.

"I'm a Classic Rock fan," she said by way of more sabotage.

"I have a Led Zeppelin T-shirt," he countered.

She leaned forward, not too much, with every semblance of incomprehension she could muster. "Lead who?"

His gaze narrowed. "Nice try, but I know you don't mean it."

"I have a car," she said, in the hope that he might disapprove. "I've never subscribed to the notion of not having a car. Mine's a purring beast of at least eight cylinders. And it's red."

"Australians," he murmured sadly. "Bet you don't have one in Manhattan."

"It's true, my car currently lives upstate at my mother's place."

"I thought your parents lived in Australia?"

"Faith tell you that?"

"Or you did. Long time ago, though."

"My mother brought my father back to the Adirondacks a few years back. That's where she grew up. Her mother and sister are there. She has support there."

"Support for what?"

"My father's in a nursing home and needs round the clock care. It takes its toll on all concerned."

"Tough times."

Dawn nodded. Finn probably knew about those. He'd had to watch his mother die of cancer during his teenage years. He knew something of bodies that failed. "My mother's a strong lady. She makes it work."

"Do you see them much?"

"More than I used to. Not as often as I should." She offered up more of herself to him than she usually would a new date. Then again, he wasn't exactly new. "We're not that close."

"Faith said they stayed in Australia and sent you to the States when you were twelve or so."

Dawn nodded.

"Why?"

"So I could get a better education than the one they could give me in Australia. I was bright. My parents were teachers. For a lot of years my parents were my *only* teachers. They taught in remote communities – six months here, a year there. We moved around the outback a *lot*. There came a time when my mother thought I needed more than what she could provide."

She knew now why they'd done it. Her father's Huntington's disease had been starting to kick in and they'd wanted her out of the way while they came to terms with what that meant.

Nothing good.

Not for them.

Not for Dawn.

The disease had stripped her father of all dignity and most of his function. Dawn had a fifty percent chance of inheriting it. If she *had* inherited it, she had a fifty percent chance of passing it on to *her* offspring.

To his credit, her father hadn't known he carried the Huntington's gene when he'd married and decided he wanted children. He'd been orphaned at birth. There'd been no record of the disease within the scant family history his birth mother had provided. He hadn't known. And the symptoms didn't usually manifest until people were in their thirties and forties.

These days there were tests people could take to find out early whether they had the disease or not. Dawn's own company now specialized in detecting genetic anomalies.

But she hadn't taken that test yet.

On her thirtieth birthday she would.

She'd promised.

Until then, she didn't want to know.

"My mother and my aunt are coming to visit me in a couple of weeks. They want to see a show," she said lightly. "Maybe a musical. Any recommendations?"

"Chicago's got a good cast at the moment. Good chemistry between the leads."

Dawn felt the rake of his gaze as she straightened in her chair and let her chin come up. Her nipples tightened and her skin began to heat. There was chemistry between her and Finn too. He knew what he was doing to her. He'd always known.

"I like chemistry," he continued. "Hard to find at

times." He dropped his gaze to her lips again, offering her a brief respite from eyes of mossy forest green. "You though … you and I have a lot of it."

"I can only offer general friendship and sex." Again, she felt the need to warn him.

"Oh, I think you can offer a little more than that," he murmured as his eyes grew darkly intent. "I think sex with you is going to be off the charts illuminating. It was before."

Nothing but the truth.

There was that smile again. The one she'd fallen for ten years ago.

She could do this. Create a few new memories of this man and paper over the old ones. Good sex. Great sex. And emphatically no consequences.

"Why don't you drop by my place this evening, after rehearsal?" she said. "There could be food involved. Strictly in service to your sexual stamina, of course."

"Food would be welcome," he murmured. "You would benefit by feeding me. Would there be shower facilities as well?"

"Do you sweat when you rehearse?"

"Blood, sweat and tears," he confirmed.

"I shall make shower facilities available."

"Would there be breakfast in bed?"

"I'm at work by seven." That never changed. "You'll find food in the fridge. The door will lock behind you on the way out."

"Oh, that's cold."

"There's a nice view from the bed. Enjoy."

"Better with you in it." He sounded like a wistful little boy. "Can I bring flowers?"

"No."

"Wine?"

"Yes."

"What kind of music will you have playing?"

"That going to be a deal breaker for you, music man?"

"Could be."

Music all afternoon for him, melancholy and all-encompassing. "With all that'll be playing in your head after rehearsal, I'm wondering whether you might like silence."

He went very still at that. And then very carefully set his coffee back down. "Don't do that," he ordered gruffly. "Don't be that understanding. I can't be just sex if you do that."

"Elevator music it is."

"I hate elevator music."

Dawn sat back and smiled and kicked gently at the chair his violin sat on. "Good."

Chapter Three

SUNDAY AFTERNOON HAD passed in a symphony of sound, different interpretations of the sound, and the occasional thought of chemistry. By the time Finn stood in front of the grand old apartment building Dawn lived in, he wondered afresh what he was getting himself into.

Faith had implied that Dawn had done well for herself, and if she could afford an address like this one, she most certainly had. He wasn't intimidated. He'd kicked around the fringes of wealth these past few years and knew that if wealth was the goal, there was always someone wealthier. If security was the goal, well, this was a very secure and well-situated investment.

Finn owned his apartment; he supposed that was an investment.

He owned violins that he could sell, might sell … wouldn't sell – so he should probably call those an indulgence. Or musical improvement or something.

He had his own resources, no need to feel intimidated.

He wasn't a vagabond. He could match this.

Besides. It was just sex.

He rang Dawn's bell and she buzzed him in the security door.

Thirty seconds later he was in the elevator on his way to the sixth floor, apartment D. He always had liked the key of D.

Dawn opened her door with a smile and ushered him in. Her apartment was jaw droppingly spacious, with a large entry foyer sweeping in to a living area with floor to ceiling windows that looked towards the city. Warm wooden floors and all natural materials completed the air of luxury.

"Do you like it?"

"Needs a piano right here."

"I don't play."

He did. He could imagine playing in this space, working in it, living and loving in it. "Shame," he said and she smiled and moved in close, snaking her hand around his neck and bringing his lips down to hers for the merest whisper of a kiss.

If there was a view to be had from this apartment, he couldn't see it. All his attention was focused on those lips still hovering so close to his own.

He'd dreamed of this too many times not to take what he wanted, sinking into another kiss that wasn't nearly as fleeting as the first. He took his time, intent on savoring her softness and warmth. And then her mouth opened beneath his and he tasted Dawn's particular brand of sweetness for the first time in ten years and that was the end of slow.

With a strangled growl he feasted on her, dropping the wine and the cheesecake he'd brought along, in order to get his hands in her hair so that he could tilt her head just so and sink deeper. He didn't mean to pour his soul into this kiss, just his expertise, but by the time he pulled back, his forehead resting against hers as they shared air in ragged gasps, he knew he had no chance whatsoever of keeping this just about sex.

A nice guy would let her know that.

"There's cheesecake and wine in that bag on the floor." Assuming it was still intact. And then he was kissing her again and this time he pressed in close, letting his body slide against hers, craving the heat and the friction and letting her know in the simplest possible way that his body wanted hers. He shrugged the strap of his violin case from his shoulders and with the last remnants of forethought let it thud softly to the floor.

"That better not be your fancy violin."

It was. He shuddered hard as she dipped her fingers in the waistband of his jeans, near his hipbone, and inadvertently encountered hard cock. "It's meant to be played."

She ran her forefinger across his slit and a bead of precome followed instantly. He was pretty sure he only whimpered in his mind.

"Can dinner wait?" She set her lips to the cut of his jaw and undid the button on his jeans one handed before sliding his zip down and reaching in to palm him. Her hand was firm and sure, a little pressure, a lick of friction.

"Pretty sure breakfast tomorrow can wait if you keep that up."

"What about that shower you wanted, can it wait?"

"No." He wanted her mouth on him, all over, and for that he wanted to be clean. "I need the shower. You're welcome to join me." Her facilities, after all.

She sent him a dark, smoky look. "Follow me."

The shower had a slate feature wall and two spray bars either side of an enormous square shower head and was big enough for two. The tiles were a dark dull gray and the basins were white. The towels were white too.

"Take your time," she murmured. "I'll be in the kitchen."

He seriously thought about playing it her way. And then she put her forefinger to her mouth, the same one that brushed lightly over him, and that was the end of his compliance. He had her against the wall three seconds later as he plundered her mouth, hoping like hell that she wasn't expecting restraint, because his was gone.

She did this to him. Stripped him of control the way she was stripping him of his clothes and he was fully on board.

Her clothes went too, this was equal opportunity urgency, and then her hands were on him and those gray eyes of hers were heavy-lidded and blown with arousal.

Full body-to-body skin-on-skin came with a gasp and the kind of fully honed hyperawareness he'd only ever experienced when performing. When she ran her nails across his nipples his skin turned to goosebumps and his forearm hit the wall behind her. "More."

"Because practice makes perfect and all that. Got it," she whispered and bent her head to his other nipple while she continued to scrape her fingernails over the other one.

Damn, but he loved where her head was at.

Somehow they made it to the shower, warm water coming at them from all over the place and adding yet another layer of sensation to the uncontrollable mix that was him and Dawn.

He wanted to tell her to slow down when she brought his fingers to her center and he found her already slick and swollen but instead he turned her so that her back was to his front, one hand steady on her hip while the other played her with fast strong fingers and his cock found solace against the swell of her ass.

"Lean forward," he commanded gruffly and she obeyed, one hand braced against the tiles and the other clenched around that fancy spray bar.

He kept the fingers of one hand working as he slid his other hand over the sweet globe of her buttock and between her thighs. When he got to her pussy entrance he slid two fingers in and caught his breath when she cried out and clenched around him.

"Finn." Her voice held an edge of panic. "I'm close."

"Wait." She was so tight and he wasn't a small man by any means.

She let loose a sob and took her hand from the wall and covered his strumming fingers with hers, forcing them to a halt. "Hurry."

"Condoms." They were in his bag. He really hadn't thought this through.

"Bathroom drawer," she offered raggedly as he continued to stretch her. "Finn, I'm clean and won't get pregnant. Can't."

"Why not?"

"Implant."

Sex without condoms was something he didn't do, no matter what assurances a woman gave, but the need to bareback Dawn was overwhelming. "No one else gets this while I'm with you, you hear? Only me." He withdrew his fingers and used her slick to lubricate his shaft and then set the tip to her entrance, finding his way slowly and inexorably inside. He stilled at the halfway point. "Promise."

"Promise."

He gave her the rest and she slapped her hand back to the tile and seconds later she was coming on his cock.

He wasn't tender as he pulled back and set up a hard

and fast rhythm guaranteed to get him joining her within a few strokes. He released his hand from her hip, she wasn't going anywhere, and tangled it in her damp hair instead, turning her head and upper body to meet his kiss and that was how he came, eyes closed, mouth crushed against hers and his body straining as he spilled his seed as deep as he could get it.

She put her fingers back on her clit again and he took the hint and pushed them aside and started playing and damned if her breath didn't stutter and hitch and spill into his mouth as she began to contract around him again.

By the time he'd regained his senses they were both leaning against the wall. Dawn had her eyes closed and her cheek to the tiles, her lips a crush of swollen pink and a flush of pink on her cheeks and on her chest.

He gathered her close and held her, just held her as she burrowed into his chest. When he could move he moved her into the spray and picked up the soap and began to wash her back. Urgency replaced by tenderness. A slow movement to follow the glorious rush that had gone before.

"You're uh … *oh.*" He'd reached the base of her neck and she was soapy enough so he set the soap aside and started to massage her there. "A little more … *there.*" She melted against him, so he brought his other hand into play and ran both thumbs down her back, one either side of her spine. "You have *really* good hands."

"They're insured."

"Good call." She pushed against his chest, enough that she could raise her head and study him, with a half smile on her face and her eyes still thoroughly sex blown. "You're a little more commanding than you used to be."

"New repertoire. Do you like it?"

"Do you even have to ask?"

"I respond very well to positive reinforcement."

"In that case, I like it a lot. Feel free to play that particular tune anytime."

"I have other tunes." He hoped. "Maybe until his fascination with Dawn faded there would be only one tune. Hotly possessive and eternally hungry for more of her. "I didn't mean to mess with your dinner plans."

"Dinner's easy," she said. "I cheated and bought lasagna and salad from the restaurant on the corner. I should let you wash in peace. That was the plan."

"Hey, Dawn?" he said as she moved away, seemingly skittish now that dirty deeds had been done. But her eyes lingered and heat flared and he turned full frontal and let her look as he adjusted the spray to land fully on him. "Good shower."

"I always thought it was a bit dark and austere."

Not with her in it. The body of her youth had been slim and boyish. This one had more tone, more curves, a grace that she hadn't had before and her skin glowed alabaster. She'd grown into that face of hers, as he'd always known she would.

She didn't appear to have the faintest idea how stunning she was.

She reached for a towel and turned back towards him, her gaze catching and holding on the flow of water over his body. "I hadn't quite appreciated its full potential. Until now."

He smiled, slow and sure and helped himself to her soap again. "Always happy to help."

She hummed thoughtfully as she toweled herself off and then tucked the towel around her body. "I should see what you can bring to the bedroom. It's a minimalist design kind of space too."

"Yes." He was one hundred percent sure he could bring chaos and passion to that space as well. "You should."

✦

TWENTY MINUTES LATER Dawn found herself sitting on the floor in the living room, sharing a meal and a glass of wine with a man she'd dreamed of for years. They'd bypassed the formal dining table and the breakfast bar for somewhere even more relaxed – the low coffee table in the living room, soft carpet and the lounge at their backs.

She'd tried to stay true to her word when it came to elevator music, but he'd reached for the remote control on her entertainment system and scrolled through her music selection until he found some indie guitar music and set that to playing instead.

"Nice place," he offered as he kicked back, barefoot and tousle-headed and reached for his food. "Good view."

She did have a good view – an entire bank of south-facing floor to ceiling windows framed by elaborate iron latticework. She'd gone to some effort to make it cozy out here in the living room. Soft furnishings and rugs, muted woodland colors and textures and the enormous u-shaped lounge that acted as the centerpiece.

She kept a vase full of fresh flowers in this room, always, because in spite of what she'd implied to Finn, she loved bringing the outdoors into a home. This week's flowers were Australian Waratahs, vivid red and framed against wide leaves of various shades of green. A cleverly directed downlight illuminated them further.

She liked this place. She'd bought it hadn't she? But this was the only room she'd made much of an impact on. The rest of it stayed stubbornly intimidating. "It needs more stuff in it," she said. Maybe that'd make it feel more hers.

"How long have you been here?"

"Six months."

"And before that?"

"New Jersey. We still have research and development facilities there. But management now happens here in Manhattan. As the company grows, there's bigger need to manage things like global market share and taking on other trading partners and they like to see a show of wealth.

Makes them more comfortable when the time comes to do business."

"You're not getting any less impressive," he said. "Are you still involved in the R&D?"

"I oversee, yes. But I don't get down and dirty in the labs much these days. When I started the company I never imagined that the management elements would become my priority." She set her half-finished meal aside and picked up her wine. "Live and learn."

"Is that what you want?"

"I want to build this company as fast as I can in these next three years. I want to work hard and smart. Play hard and fast. And then on my thirtieth birthday I'm going to reassess. Decide whether I need to take some time out to travel, see everything I want to see, experience everything I want to experience."

He shot her a puzzled glance. "Why at thirty?"

"Oh, I don't know," she offered awkwardly. "Pick a milestone." A woman's biological clock had things to say at thirty. Huntington's symptoms started to appear when affected people were in their thirties. Clumsiness, nervous tics, short term memory loss. "Where do you see yourself at thirty?"

"Performing still. I'm booked a couple of years in advance when it comes to concert halls and orchestras. When performance requests taper off, I'll still teach and compose. One thing my profession does is reward maturity."

"What if you're forced to stop through illness or injury?"

"That's end of the world talk."

"Really?" Take enough function away from a person and so went the will to live. She'd seen it up close and personal. Every time she visited her father she wanted to weep. "You mean life ending?"

"I wouldn't go that far." He shrugged. "Just. I wouldn't know how to begin to fill that hole in me. Could be I'm too singularly focused. Then again, for what I do I have to be."

She leaned back against the sofa and studied the play of light through the wine in her glass. "Don't get hurt or injured, I guess it's as good an ambition as any. Maybe you need to be more careful where you put your hands."

"I'm always careful in that regard. Wouldn't put them anywhere I wouldn't put my tongue, for example."

Words that slid in low and hot to pull in places beneath her skin. "You haven't had your cheesecake yet."

"Maybe later. Can people see in through those windows?"

"No."

He smiled and put his food on the table. He took her wine glass and put it on the table too, and then he lifted her up until she was sitting on the sofa and he was kneeling between her legs. He slid his hands beneath the skirt of her dress and urged her thighs wider apart.

"Again, so soon?" she murmured.

"Do you object?" His words whispered along her thighs.

"Not at all." She liked a man with initiative. "Mind your hands."

His lips curved on her skin. "Oh, I will."

✦

FINBAR SLID FROM sleep slowly, reluctantly, as was his wont. No waking instantly to full alertness, you could drive a bus to within an inch of him as he slept and he wouldn't wake up. You could play a tuba six inches from his nose and he'd merely stir. It had been proven. One of his old teachers had said that only in sleep could silence be found and Finn concurred. He needed silence just as much as he needed noise. Two sides of the same coin.

He stretched his back and finally rolled over, hoping to find Dawn still in bed but unsurprised when he didn't. That last time, the one with him coming halfway down Dawn's throat after ripping her to climax, had finished them both. She'd threatened to tie him down after that and swear to God his spent dick had twitched at the thought. She'd told him she had three hours left before she had to get up and go to work and she fully intended to spend them asleep.

Finn stretched, closed his eyes again, and listened for the sound of movement but heard nothing but his own breathing, not even the sound of the city outside. Double glazing on those showy windows. Triple glazing maybe. And he lifted his lashes and stared around at her bedroom in the daylight.

The walls were covered in wood paneling, the seamless Swedish kind. Put there to focus attention on the view from the floor to ceiling French windows or doors or some combination thereof that seemed to run the length of the apartment. There were no doors to her bedroom, just walls that ended well before that bank of glass. Some architect must have thought a lack of privacy in the bedroom a good thing.

Clearly they'd never grown up with siblings.

There was another space where a door should have been on the other side of Dawn's bedroom. Presumably it led through to some other room. Finn pushed the soft white bedding aside and eased to his feet. "Dawn?"

Not a sound, and that next room was set up as a study with bookshelves and a desk and more of that smooth Swedish wood on the walls. Not even a huge bunch of yellow-eyed daisies could make an impact on the room's minimalist aesthetics. For all of its wood, the room had no warmth other than what people walking into it brought with them.

Which gave him a thought.

He found his clothes in the living room, slung over the back of the sofa. He put his jeans on and got his violin out.

With the high ceilings and all the wood on the walls the acoustics would be good. *That* was how he could fill this place with warmth.

He stood in the middle of that wide open living space, closed his eyes and started with the third movement of the concerto he'd been playing yesterday, and it fit this space the way he knew it would. Letting the music dominate and soar, feeding it back to him off those smooth wooden walls.

He felt her rather than saw her. As he finished the third movement and swung back to the first, he opened his eyes and there she stood, leaning against the wall that shielded the bathroom from prying eyes, her hair a glossy fall and her skirt, jacket and top strictly corporate.

He immediately wanted to mess her up all over again. Play music for the woman whose bed he'd shared last night rather than this regal and untouchable solemn-eyed swan.

He stopped playing on the first discordant note he'd played by mistake in years, and lowered the violin to his side. "I thought you'd gone."

"No. I have meetings this morning. Had to do the hair."

"The hair looks good."

She aimed for a smile and fell significantly short. "I need to go. My cab's probably waiting."

He nodded. "They do that."

"Stay awhile if you want. Play. The door will lock behind you on your way out."

She had such beautiful eyes, but there were shadows in them today. Maybe it was tiredness. Maybe he'd put them there for some other reason. "Those tickets to a musical for your mother and aunt … you want me to organize them for you?"

"If it's not any trouble."

It'd take him one phone call. "What date?"

"Evening of the twenty-seventh?"

"Consider it done. Do I get a kiss?"

"For the tickets?"

"No. That sounds far too much like a clinical exchange of favors. You would kiss me because we spent the night together, and you're still here and because it's morning."

"Oh, I see." She didn't move.

"It's expected," he prompted.

"You have your hands full, and I need to go," she countered with a rueful smile. "If I kiss you again now, I might want to stay and that wouldn't be good."

A lot to think about in those few words. He sent her a shrug and let her get to the door before opening his mouth again. He'd needed that amount of time to figure out what he wanted to say next. He needed simple words. Ones that wouldn't scare her with his need for more.

"Dawn—"

She turned to look back over her shoulder at him and he'd never seen anything more beautiful.

"We gonna do this again?"

"Sure," she said as she opened the door and stepped through to the outside world.

And then the door closed with a muffled click behind her.

Chapter Four

FINN WAITED ALL of three days before calling her. Enough time to lose the scent of her. Not nearly enough time to dim the memory of the heaven he'd found in her arms. He met her for coffee on Wednesday afternoon. On Friday night he came to her place after rehearsal again and this time she didn't flee the next morning. Instead, she pulled bacon and eggs from the refrigerator and together they made breakfast before heading back to bed, whereupon she showed him the remote controlled projector screen that descended from the ceiling and the state-of-the-art projector hidden behind a wall panel.

That took care of Saturday afternoon.

He rang her on Monday afternoon in his rehearsal break simply because he wanted to hear the sound of her voice and because it made him happy.

And that gave him pause because that right there?

That didn't sound like just sex at all.

✦

TUESDAY AND WEDNESDAY were the longest two days of Dawn's life. She was twitchy at work, curt with her sales staff, scathing of her research department and generally a boss on the warpath.

All because a certain musician hadn't called.

On Thursday, a delivery came for her. Finn had made good on his promise of show tickets for her aunt and mother and had included a ticket for Dawn also. They'd arrived half an hour ago and were for tomorrow night's show. Dress circle seating.

The bouquet of Australian wildflowers that had arrived along with them had also been a thoughtful touch.

Dawn put them in a vase by the water cooler and silently dared anyone to comment.

Finally James, her chief research officer, cornered her in her office and with a pointed glance at the flowers asked her whether she was doing anything interesting this weekend.

"My mother's flying in from upstate this afternoon, and tomorrow we're going to see a show. Hence the need for flowers," she said.

"Is that why the card says, *The dead Finnish guy's a demanding bastard but recording finishes this afternoon. Want to do something?"* James asked, deadpan.

"There's a card?"

"Little square one about this big. It had fallen down

between the leaves. It's signed Finn." James nodded, clearly enjoying himself. "Marcel repositioned it for you, front and center."

"Good of him." Dawn drummed her fingers on the desk. "Can that be a firing offence?"

"I wouldn't recommend it."

No. Guess not.

"Lucky for you there was no phone number to call. Half your staff would have texted either the dead Finn or the live one to come and get you. Mainly as a way of getting their miserable hardass boss out of the office." James's face softened. "Go home, Dawn. You're pushing too hard. You dropped files all over the floor this morning, you're slow to make decisions and you're snapping at people who try to help. That's not you."

Not yet.

Dawn closed her eyes and ran a hand around her neck. "You're right. I'm going to get out of here. I can be home by the time my mother gets in. There can be food for them. I can call a hardworking musician and tell him to drop by sometime this weekend."

"Good plan."

"Are you making an okay sign behind your back?"

"Of course not. I was scratching an itch."

"There are worm tablets for that."

"Oh, *now* you start getting your smart on."

Dawn failed to stifle a smile. Hardworking, ambitious

and a key member of her executive team, if James had come in here to tell her she was riding her people too hard then she was. "All right, I'll be out of here by lunchtime. You and everyone else can have a two hour early mark."

"Early mark?"

"It's an Australian term. It means you get let out of somewhere earlier than you expected to be let out."

"Like parole."

"No." Well, maybe. Hopefully her employees didn't regard this place as a prison. "You're going to tell me that people aren't necessarily going to *want* to be gone from work two hours earlier than usual, aren't you?"

"Dorothy, you're not in Australia. Let them choose when they want the two hours off. That or add an extra two hours to their timesheets."

Dawn sighed hard, suddenly weary and irritable all over again. She'd been at the top of this company pyramid long enough to know all this. Although … that's what human resources departments were for. "I'll call HR."

"I'll do it for you," he said, and Dawn nodded.

"Early marks used to be so much simpler when I was a kid. The teacher would open the door, out we'd go and she wouldn't see us for fine red dust."

James glanced over her shoulder towards the window that framed a New York City skyline.

"So why'd you trade all that red dust for New York smog?"

"I didn't." She might have still been there if her parents hadn't decreed otherwise. She'd *wanted* to be there with them. "I was pushed."

✦

TWO HOURS LATER, Dawn set the bag of groceries and Finn's flowers on her kitchen bench and dug her phone from her satchel. She should thank Finn for the tickets and the flowers. Arrange to see him at some point.

He was probably still in his recording session.

She really shouldn't bother him.

She could send him a congratulations text though. And the *thank yous*. As a friend who occasionally had sex with him, she could do that.

"Keep it casual, Dawn," she muttered, and sent the text and put the phone down and then picked it up and sent another missive. "My mother and aunt arrive this afternoon. You'll have to celebrate without me."

A minute later her phone rang.

Finn.

"Thank you for the tickets and the flowers," she said by way of hello. "Thanks to you, everyone in the office now thinks I'm having a torrid affair."

"Dawn?" Only that thread of laughter in his voice kept her on the call. "Dawn Turner, is that you?"

"Don't make me hang up on you. Because I will."

"It *is* you," he said next.

"How's the recording going?"

"It's done. I'm happy, the sound guys are happy, the conductor's happy. I played until my brain bled. I think I broke the orchestra though."

"There's a lot of that going round."

Finn sighed. "Want to play hooky with me this afternoon?"

"No. I have a schedule to stick to. World domination of affordable gene sequencing techniques to plan. Mothers to feed. Busy busy."

"Ever get tired?"

"Yes. Usually I work through it."

"Where do you get your drive from?"

"That's not an easy question to answer." Not for her. Possibly not for anyone. "Where do you get yours?"

"I think maybe I was born with it."

"Me too."

"And at thirty you're just going to toss it all in?"

"I'm just factoring in some burnout time." And the possibility of an ugly gene sequence that spelled a slow and agonizing demise.

"You could factor in more rest time now. Avoid burnout altogether. What are you doing tomorrow night?"

"You got me a ticket for a musical, remember?"

"After that. Or during it. I know the Chicago score. I spent six months in the pit of that show. I could play for you. With you. Feed you."

"Can you cook?"

"I can cook Irish stew, French mussels in white wine, and barbecue baby back pork ribs to perfection. Everything else is debatable."

"That's quite a selection."

"Well, I travel," he murmured. "Okay, they're my favorites. I had to learn to make them if I wanted to eat them on a regular basis," he added, and made her laugh.

"I might be able to get out of seeing Chicago, but I'd still like to eat with my mom and aunt before hand. There's no need to feed me."

"Next time," he said.

There were a lot of next time's piling up when it came to Finn. "Send me your address. I'll be there. And, hey. Congratulations on conquering Sibelius. I wish you the company of good friends this evening and many drinks. And then elevator music."

Chapter Five

"SO THIS FINBAR Sullivan," Dawn's mother began at dinner in a tapas restaurant the following evening. "How long have you been seeing him?"

She'd been seeing him in her dreams since she was seventeen. "Not long. A few weeks." Okay, two weeks. "It's a casual arrangement. He's busy. I'm busy …"

"You should have invited him to dinner," said her aunt. "We're casual too."

"Maybe another time." Dawn rarely shared her life or her achievements with her mother or aunt. Maybe it was because they seemed so complete without her. A lot of it was because her mother had failed to share her own trials and tribulations with Dawn. Some of it was because by the time Dawn had found out about the Huntington's, her father's symptoms were well advanced and that interim time where Dawn could have been there for both of them was gone. Her mother had her sister for support now and again Dawn felt like the outsider in her own family never mind that her Aunt Meg was lovely.

They came to visit her every couple of months, and, when they did, Dawn made time for them and tried to make their stay a pleasant one.

But that was enough.

If she could occasionally do more, be more involved emotionally, well … everybody had their flaws.

"Are you sure you won't come to the theater with us?" Her mother looked hopeful, those gray eyes so like her own showing a rare vulnerability. "Seems a shame to waste such a good ticket."

"I haven't seen Finn for a while. I figured tonight would be the best time to catch up. I'll be back to pick you up after the show."

"I'm sure we can find our own way back to your place," said her aunt. "I don't think anyone's going to object if you decide to stay the night elsewhere? Are we?" she asked, turning to her sister.

"Of course not." Her mother's eyes warmed. "It's good to see you making time for someone."

"Like I said," Dawn countered warily. "It's just a casual thing."

They parted ways after the meal, her aunt and mother to the theater and Dawn to Finn's. He lived in Columbus Circle, which was a decent enough neighborhood and presumably not far from where important musical fixtures were. Nerves assaulted her as she stood at the doorway to

Finn's apartment building just west of the theater district. Decent neighborhood and handy to his favorite music venues, she guessed, but a part of her still wondered why he hadn't stayed in Brooklyn where the rest of his family lived.

Finn seemed close to his family, for the most part.

Unlike her.

Dawn felt unaccountably nervous as she buzzed his apartment and a doorman let her in.

"You're Dawn?" he asked with a cheerful smile, and when she nodded, he willed the elevator doors open and held them there while she entered. "Tenth floor, apartment 101."

Finn met her at the elevator looking impossibly sexy in a faded black tee and camel-colored cargo trousers. Bare feet again, and she raised an eyebrow and caught his boyish grin. "You have a doorman," she said.

"Lot of valuable instruments in this building. We have a doorman *and* a lot of security. Probably accounts for the lack of fancy living space. Priorities."

"We all have them," she said as she followed him to a well-constructed door with two types of lock on it. "My mother thanks you for the tickets, by the way. How much do I owe you?"

"I don't even know," he murmured. "I'll have to find out. Or we could just forget about it."

"Generous, but I'd like to repay you. I don't like being indebted." He opened the door and gestured her inside and she stepped into a tidy living area of medium size, with a kitchen off to one side. Good smells came from that kitchen and a bottle of red sat on the bench alongside a half full beer. "I know you've eaten, but I'm running late and I'm starving," he said. "I've been living on takeout and couldn't stomach any more of it."

"What are you making?"

"Irish stew. All your talk of mothers got me thinking about mine. I wanted to tell her about the recording I've just finished. I wanted to celebrate an achievement. I told her all about it while I was peeling potatoes. I'm scaring you, aren't I?"

"Only if she turns up." She liked hearing about the love he still felt for a mother long dead. He could doubtless teach her something about grief and how to live with it.

She cast around for conversation that didn't involve mothers, something to comment on. A music stand sat in the corner of the room next to a wall lined with battered four-drawer filing cabinets of all different types and colors.

He followed her gaze. "Picturesque, isn't it."

"What's in them?"

"Sheet music."

"Ah." She looked around for more signs of the music that dominated his life but found nothing. "No posters of your concerts?"

"Are you serious? My family would never let me live it down if I turned this place into an ode to me."

"There's a poster of one of your concerts hanging on a wall at Sully's." She'd seen it.

"And it's a good one," he said. "Faith and Pop are allowed to brag. I'm not. Beer, wine or something else?" he offered as she set her bag on the ground and perched on a kitchen stool to watch him stir his home made stew. He had crusty bread to go with it.

"I could stand to have a little bowl of your stew in the interests of celebration," she said. "And a beer to go with it."

He got her one from the fridge and she studied the pictures on the door of that fridge as he opened it and set it in front of her. He got her a glass next and poured for her and her gaze was torn between those talented hands of his performing a task so menial and wanting to stare at the pictures of the little boy she'd seen with Finn at Sully's. A child's crayon drawing of a dragon had also been given pride of place, stuck to the door with bright fridge magnets from around the world. A stranger to Finn's world might think he was a father, given the adornments on that fridge.

Again, she didn't quite know what to ask. Again, Finn followed her gaze and offered more information.

"That's Gil. Faith *did* tell you about Gil. Didn't she?"

Dawn nodded and looked at a picture of a young Finn and another young man in an orchestra setting with violins in hand. Both of them cracking up, mucking up, if the picture was anything to go by. "Is that Gil's father?"

"Yeah. Joey. Josef Hann. We studied together at Juilliard. Good violinist."

"How did he die?"

"Bone cancer. First it was a sore wrist, then a dropped shoulder. Typical aches and strains that string players get. And then they made a diagnosis. He was dead six months later."

"Sad."

"He was a good friend. A good man. Gil's a good kid."

"How often do you see him?"

"Once every couple of weeks, if I can. Doesn't always work out when I'm away on tour."

"That's quite a commitment."

"It's not a chore." She could feel his eyes on her, intent in spite of his relaxed stance. "What about you, Dawn? Do you want kids?"

She hesitated, torn. As a child growing up she'd always thought that one day she would have kids of her own, more than just one, and a husband to go with it. That was back before miscarriage had filled her to overflowing with feelings of inadequacy and loss. And then there was her gene pool. "I'm fifty-fifty when it comes to wanting kids. Sometimes I do, sometimes I don't," she offered quietly. "Not exactly good odds. I told you before – my attitudes towards having a family of my own are complicated."

"Because you were abandoned by yours?"

"There are other reasons." She shrugged. "Best I can do

is say that I'm undecided. There are other paths through life and I'm not against them." She took a deep breath. "What about you? Is having a family on your agenda?"

"It is eventually. A wife to love, kids to bug, a home to come home to. I want all that."

"It's a pretty picture." But there was a whole lot of fantasy wrapped up in it. "You going to have time for all that *and* a performance career?"

"I hope so."

"It's going to take a special kind of woman."

"It is." His smile grew crooked. "Is this the part where you tell me you're not that girl?"

"I thought I already had," she offered coolly. "Would you like to hear my stance on this relationship again?"

"No, I heard you the first time." There was a gleam in his eyes that she didn't quite trust. "You're here for a small bowl of stew, friendly conversation and the sex. Mutual physical release." His voice deepened as he stalked her and backed her against the bench, his arms coming either side of her to pin her there. "It's not as if I'm against this notion."

She'd look him in the eye in a minute. Right after she'd finished starting at his mouth.

"I only have about three hours to spare," she murmured.

Not that she wanted to rush him or anything, but he hadn't kissed her yet. An oversight he needed to rectify fast.

"I can be done with the conversation any time you like."

He smiled and brushed warm lips against hers. The kiss deepened, and he lifted her up and she wrapped her arms and legs around him and clung. She loved the easy strength in him. There was more than he let on. She loved the way he handled her body, the hungry possession as he ran one hand up her spine and the other curled around one buttock and thigh. And how his fingers managed to brush along her center along the way. "I love your hands."

"You should. They worship you."

"How fast can you eat your stew?"

"I'm thinking food can wait."

He took her to his bedroom, a plain room with a king sized bed in it and she heartily approved. He reacquainted himself with every inch of her and she did the same to him. With lips and hands she worshipped and fed. One kiss sliding into the next, robbing her of breath and the will to more closely examine what was happening between them.

This was happening. And she'd never had any defense against it.

With infinite patience and a whole lot of devilry, Finn didn't stop teasing until he had her spread naked before him, wanton and willing to do anything for one more piece of him.

"I hate you," she said as he built her towards a crescendo yet *again* and then held off on delivery.

"No you don't."

No she didn't. He entered her in one smooth thrust and she clenched around him, so close to gone, and he buried his face in the curve of her neck and breathed in deep as he stilled and backed her away from the edge. "This no strings sex we keep having," he murmured, and ran his lips along her ear, possibly to make absolutely sure she was listening. "The kind where you surrender your soul to me and I feed it straight back to you?" He started to move, slow and sure. "People can spend a lifetime looking for this."

He didn't let her talk. He ripped her to climax instead and rode her straight through it, grinding down hard and not letting her subside at all before shooting her higher.

Only when they lay spent some twenty minutes later, curled into each other on their sides, short of breath and slick with sweat and other happy liquids, did he speak again.

"We could build on this," he offered as he smoothed her hair away from her face with tender fingers and Dawn felt her heart sink at the unspoken plea for more.

She couldn't do it.

"Second date syndrome," she countered quietly as blissful lassitude warred with her need to be on the defensive. "What I want from you hasn't changed. Don't go there, Finn. Please."

"It's too late." He pinned her with that glorious green stare. "I'm already there."

"You don't know me." Reaction was starting to set in. From the incendiary sex. From the threat he posed to her wellbeing. From the dice he didn't even know he was rolling when it came to his own wellbeing. "You won't like what you find."

"You don't get to make that decision for me. You give me a chance." Dominance was alive and well in him and part of her thrilled to it even as the rest of her trembled. She should have guessed. A man didn't get to *be* at the top of his profession without bulldozing through barriers fashioned by others. "Tell me what you *think* I won't like about you," he continued. "Something beyond our different goals. Because goals can change with the right person in place and there is *nothing* that can't be made to work."

"You're wrong." Her laugh sounded more like a sob as she pushed at his chest until he gave her some space. She rolled onto her back, but all he did then was rise up onto his elbow and stare down at her, his hand splayed possessively over her waist. "I can't do this," she told him raggedly. "Please. Don't look at me like that. Don't you look."

"What is it that you think I see?"

Nothing good.

"Pretty girl," he murmured. "Smarter than most. Strong-minded. You also know passion and how to surrender to it. Fascinating."

She couldn't bear his tender gaze. That which had

thrilled her ten years ago was now ripping her to pieces. Finbar Sullivan had so much to give. He'd find someone to share his life with. Someone who was all of those things and more. Someone who could unconditionally give him all he asked for. She pressed her lips to his collarbone and he trembled beneath her kiss, before rolling onto his back on the bed and looking at something else instead. In this case, the back of his eyelids.

"A secret for a secret," she said. "Tell me something you're not proud of and I'll do the same. You first."

He stayed silent for a while and Dawn closed her eyes on a sigh or relief because she thought that was the end of this line of questioning.

And then he spoke.

"The family pub. Sully's," he said gruffly. "The home I grew up in. The home where my mother's memory is strongest. I'd get rid of it in a heartbeat if I thought it would free my sister to do what she wanted with her life. I swear to God, Dawn, I hate it more than I love it. I hate my father's stubborn attachment to the place and his inability to fucking *run* it alone."

"Why can't he run it?"

"His heart's no good. He's not physically capable of doing a day's work, and he won't have the operation that could fix him."

She could hear the frustration in Finn's words. His inability to accept his father's decisions.

"Illness changes people," she offered tentatively.

"He could at least *try* to get well." Finn lifted his arm and raked his hand through his hair. "I know I get frustrated when people don't perform to their abilities. I know I should respect my father's decisions, but I don't. He's taking advantage of Faith, and it burns me to see her squandering her talent in service to him. That was the deal, right? To tell you something about me that I'm not proud of."

That was the deal, yes, and she wasn't reneging. But his revelations had surprised her. "Faith's unhappy?"

"Yes. Maybe. I don't know." Frustration laced his voice. "I'm ambitious, always have been, and not just for me. For Faith as well. Chances are I need to dial it down and let her be."

Intimate thoughts from a man who'd taken her at her word and bared soul secrets.

And now it was her turn.

She took a deep breath and then another, trying to still the hammers in her heart. Trying to figure out where she was going with this.

Nowhere good.

He took her hand and slid his fingers in hers as if sensing her inner disquiet. He was so very attuned to her, this man. "Your turn," he rumbled.

Her turn.

"I got pregnant once, years ago," she began, and

stopped.

Because this rehashing of history he'd played a crucial part in … this was just cruel. "I wasn't looking for it. Didn't want to be."

His fingers tightened around hers and gently squeezed, as if encouraging her to continue. "What happened?"

"I miscarried around the six week mark."

"Did the father know? Were you a couple?" He let her hand go in favor of sliding it over her abdomen and up towards her rips and heart as if touch alone could heal her. Maybe it could.

"No. The father didn't know." She cleared her throat and shied away from an even bigger reveal. "It wasn't that kind of relationship."

"What kind of relationship was it?"

"Fleeting," she said.

She'd been alone. So very alone. No one to confide in, not even her friends.

"I know a little about miscarriage," he said gruffly. "Enough to know that it can leave a woman feeling broken."

Intuitive, this man, but Dawn's damage hadn't only been emotional. "I didn't seek medical treatment afterwards, when I should have. Complications arose and were dealt with. My odds of having children diminished." She felt his hand slide lower to skim across her abdomen, warm and gentle, almost reverent, and hot tears began to gather.

"I felt shattered by my body's betrayal, shamed by my own stupidity, and unbelievably relieved. I didn't have to change my goals to accommodate a child. Neither did anyone else. It was punishment and reprieve. Sacrifice and deliverance and I never breathed a word of it. Not to anyone."

"Dawn, whatever you're thinking, whatever guilt you carry for wanting one outcome over the other, it wasn't your fault." He was back up on his elbow again, his concern for her thick and smothering.

"Then why does it haunt me?" She slid from the bed and turned away to pick up her clothes, unsteady on her legs and shaking hard but determined to be away from him. Surely her body could get her to the bathroom without tripping over itself. "May I use your shower?" She didn't wait for his reply. The bathroom was through a door off the bedroom and she locked the door behind her. She leaned against the door, naked and exposed before finally sliding to the cold tile and burying her head in her hands.

What was she doing here? To herself and to Finn?

She'd thought being with him all those years ago was stupid but this … this tearing herself apart over him all over again was a thousand times worse. What was she doing here?

Nothing good. Finbar Sullivan was a good man.

He didn't deserve this.

✦

DAWN WASHED HER pain away in the shower, taking forever, scrubbing hard with her nails until her skin was red raw and ugly on the outside. Only then did she turn the water off and reach for a towel. Finn's towel, and she couldn't, simply couldn't wear his scent again, so she stood there and shivered and flicked water from her body with her hands until she was a little less wet and then put her clothes on. Her bag with makeup in it was in the other room so she wiped the last of the makeup from around her eyes and went bare. Nothing at all to hide her ugliness from this man.

It was past time he saw it.

She'd known Finn was special all those years ago. Her body had known and had wanted all that he had to give, right up until the moment her body had rejected it. It had been for the best. They'd been so young, so not ready for a child. And then Dawn had found out about her father's disease and her chances of having it, and her offspring's chance of having it, and then she *really* knew it had been for the best.

There would be no children for Dawn if she had Huntington's. This was her line in the sand. No children for Dawn. No husband to sit in a chair beside her hospital bed, grieving for the woman she'd once been. This had to end here. With the choices she made and the life she allowed herself.

Thinking that she could control her feelings for Finbar

Sullivan had been a mistake. She couldn't. Not now. Not then. Better all round if she pushed him away now and saved him a world of heartache.

He'd given her an opening and she'd taken it, setting him up for a revelation she knew would hurt him. Strip him of his trust in her and drive him away for good. All she had to do was go out there and go through with it.

Cruel Dawn, cool and untouchable. Men had called her that and she'd let them. Married to her work. Too ambitious to put anyone else's needs before her own. A cold bitch. All true. All her.

It was the cost of believing that she could skim even a little bit of companionship and warmth for herself.

Usually she could get away with playing the aloof intractable bitch, but the lovemaking she and Finn had shared made a lie of that. Hard to believe that she didn't care when with every caress she gave him everything. Anything. Except a future.

She could go out there and tell him this wasn't working the way she thought it would. That he had to either accept the limitations of a relationship with her or let her go. And if that didn't work …

Don't do it, Dawn. Don't go there. Don't be that cold, cruel bitch.

Only if she had to.

Only if he pushed.

She squared her shoulders and lifted her chin but she couldn't look at her reflection in the mirror. Nothing there but ugliness.

Finbar Sullivan was gifted, charming and sensational in bed. He'd have no trouble finding someone else who could give him all he needed.

He'd see.

She'd make him see.

Because chaining him to a future with her was unthinkable.

✦

SHE WASN'T STAYING for the food. Finn could see it in her eyes and in the nervousness of her movements as she approached the bench. Her face was bare of makeup, revealing translucent skin and a smattering of freckles that only made her more beautiful. She had shadows under her eyes and in them. He'd spooked her, pushed too hard for concessions she hadn't wanted to give.

She'd wanted to share confidences and they had. And hurt herself doing it.

He couldn't spare her the pain of miscarriage but he could make her feel loved now. Loved and accepted. Appreciated.

"Beer's a little warm," he said, searching her face for some sign of warmth, anything to give him a clue as to where he might go next. He'd never played this tune before. He needed guidance. "You want a fresh one?"

"No. Finn—"

He didn't like the sound of that so he cut her off with a hurried step towards her. It didn't help that she immediately stepped back. Not in sync with him at all. "I know I'm pushy," he said. "See something I want and I go for it. It's as big a flaw as it is a strength. I don't mean to frighten you."

"All you need is someone who can keep up with you." Carefully, she picked up her bag and took another step back. "That's not me. I think I should leave."

"Or you could stay." There would be no letting her go easy. He'd done that once before and she'd haunted him for years. "Dawn, please. We're good together, can't you feel it? We always were. Let me show you my world. You might like it."

"I do like it," she said. "I like you. But I can't be what you need. Goodbye, Finn."

He moved towards her. She was susceptible to his touch, and he'd play dirty if he had to. "Dawn—"

"No!" This time she put her hand up to ward him off. That and the panic in her eyes sending a chill up his spine. "I can't do this and I'm sorry for that. I knew it from the start but I let selfishness lead. I keep secrets. Damaging ones. And you don't want to face them. Hell, *I don't want to face them*. I've done my damnedest not to. You have to let me go."

"Dawn, *please*. Don't riddle me. Say what you mean."

"I *am* but you're not listening." She picked up her

handbag, headed for the door and then pinned him with a bleak gray gaze. "I'm a solitary person. I don't *want* more than just sex. Do you really want me to nail this coffin shut with more ugly words or will you believe me?"

"You're not indifferent to me."

"I know. I never have been."

"Then *be* with me."

"I *can't*." She was yelling at him now, almost crying. Guess soundproof apartments were good for more than just playing music in. She all but ran for the door, and he watched as she fumbled and cursed in her endeavor to open it.

"Dawn—"

"You don't know me," she said, and tilted her head and let her shoulders droop. "There's nothing but ugliness here. That baby I lost—" she looked at him and there was a world of goodbye in her eyes. "It was yours."

✦

FINN OPENED HIS mouth. Surely some kind of response was called for, but he couldn't speak. She'd announced it in such a cool little voice. Life-shattering news given in a brusque postscript. A footnote.

It was as if she'd cut out his tongue, cut off his legs and left him bleeding. The sound he finally made wasn't one he'd ever made before. A desolate cry of incomprehension at life's cruelty. At her cruelty to him and to herself–

Christ it must have been hard for her. More than hard.

She'd been seventeen and all alone. She could have called on him for support, called on *someone* for help, but she hadn't.

Where had her friends been in all of this? His sister and Dawn's other friends. Mercy and Zel? She could have told them? Why hadn't she?

It was all starting to make a crazy kind of sense. She couldn't tell them because Faith was his sister. Telling them meant telling him. As for her parents or the aunt that she'd lived with, maybe she'd known she'd get no support from them.

She'd worn the consequences alone.

She was *still* alone.

Because she wanted to be.

Chapter Six

DAWN WAITED OUTSIDE the Ambassador Theater for her mother and aunt to emerge, and when they did she waved them over, threaded an arm through each of their elbows and took them to a restaurant for late night sweets and coffee with a kick in it. Conversation came easily to her mother and Meg – they'd always been sisters and as far back as Dawn could remember, they'd always been friends and confidants.

Family bonds, strong and true.

Dawn's own family bond with them had been lost at twelve years old when her mother had sent Dawn to Meg with no real explanation beyond the need for Dawn to get a better education. Aunt Meg hadn't been totally on board with this plan but not for the reasons Dawn had thought.

All those heated phone conversations between the sisters – all those times Dawn had overheard Meg trying to convince Dawn's mother to take Dawn back – they hadn't been about Dawn being a colossal disappointment at all.

Vivian Turner had wanted to protect her daughter from the ugliness of her father's failing body and mind.

Meg Dawson had vehemently disagreed with that approach.

Nothing to do with Dawn being ugly, unwanted and odd.

Dawn liked her aunt a lot. The rift with her mother, on the other hand, had never fully mended and Dawn didn't know if it ever would. She'd been so utterly lost when she'd first come to New York as a child. A skinny outback girl more used to bare feet and brown snakes than convents and the social politics of American teenagers. Football and proms. Juniors, seniors and clothes. Dawn's clothes had been sun-faded and threadbare when Dawn had arrived all those years ago. Not suitable at all. A childless Aunt Meg had taken her clothes shopping immediately and between them they'd chosen what they liked and got it utterly wrong.

"Do you remember that hippie coat?" she asked her aunt, coming in on the tail end of her mother's enthusiastic appraisal of costumes. "The blue corduroy with the … I don't know … was it Aztec trim?"

"I loved that coat," said Meg.

"So did I." Dawn turned to include her mother. "No one else did. The kids at school thought I was so weird. I swear, half the reason I went to St. J's was for the uniform. I hated that uniform but *everyone* had to wear it. Much better than inflicting my debatable fashion sense on a regular school system."

This kicked off a spirited conversation about the merits of various school systems and Dawn was content to sit back and listen and occasionally, when asked, give her opinion.

Only when Dawn signaled for the check half an hour later did Vivian Turner return her attention to her daughter.

"Dawn, you're very quiet. Did you catch up with Finn?"

"Yes. We caught up."

Her mother and her aunt shared a glance, and there it was again. A closeness Dawn didn't know how to be part of.

It always had been far easier for Dawn to keep secrets than to share them.

"I know I haven't always been there for you," her mother began quietly. "But if you ever want to talk …"

"We talk." They were talking now and Dawn desperately wanted to stop. "C'mon. I'll ask the cab driver to take us past Times Square. All the pretty, pretty lights."

"No, Dawn," her mother replied with a strained smile. "You look tired, and contrary to popular belief, I do know when my daughter is hurting. Let's just get you home."

✦

SLEEP DIDN'T COME easily to Dawn that night. Horror at

what she'd done to Finn warred with sorrow at her self-inflicted distance from her family. She tossed and turned, flung her covers off and ten minutes later wrapped them around her again. Her bedroom windows had blackout shutters and when she couldn't sleep she'd make them go down, drenching the room in darkness the better to encourage her body and her brain to let go of wakefulness.

Tonight those blackout shutters did nothing but make her feel even more trapped inside her skin.

And more awake than ever.

Three am found her in the kitchen, opening cupboard doors by the cook-top light, in search of the super strong headache tablets she rarely had cause to take. Tonight though, or what was left of it, maybe they'd help her sleep. She thought she was being quiet, but she mustn't have been quiet enough, because the next thing she knew, her mother was padding into the kitchen, yawning as she fastened a silky blue dressing gown around her waist.

"I'm sorry, did I wake you?" asked Dawn.

"Wasn't asleep." Her mother surveyed her through faded gray eyes that were the same color as Dawn's. "Nothing to do with your apartment, which is beautiful, or the bed, which is comfortable. I heard you poking around so I got up. Maternal instinct. I was worried about you."

Dawn shrugged and finally found the tablets. "Headache."

Her mother made that humming sound. The one that

Dawn imagined mothers the world over had perfected. The one that meant they had more to say but weren't quite sure how to go about it.

And then her mother sighed and looked away towards the floor to ceiling windows framed by exterior latticework. "It's like a cage in here," she said. "A beautiful, elegant refuge that no one can breach." And then she smiled again and turned back. "I could sure use a slice of that cheesecake. You?"

"Me too."

So Dawn brought the box over to the bench and got a knife from the drawer and two plates and fussed about trying to find dessert forks, or sporks, or whatever they were called.

"It wasn't really a date tonight," Dawn said finally.

Look at her, confiding in her mother. Dawn didn't know whether to celebrate or be afraid.

"What was it?" The gentle encouragement in her mother's eyes made her feel even smaller than she already did.

"More of a disaster."

"Oh."

Dawn rubbed at her face, wondering if she looked as beaten as she felt. "Finn's a great guy. Everything a woman could ever want or need. All he has to do is look at me and I feel … beautiful."

Her mother smiled. "I know that feeling."

"I've been trying to keep things strictly casual between

us, but they're not. He wants a future and I can't give him one. I just—can't. So I turned him away for good. I deliberately hurt him."

"I know that feeling too. I did it to you."

Dawn shook her head, fighting back tears. "I don't want to talk about that." She focused on turning the cold water tap on and reached for the glass, she couldn't see on account of all the unshed tears. She got it to the sink before she lost her grip on it. It broke, the way fine glassware was inclined to do when dropped. Dawn swore.

"I'm sorry," she said next, hands shaking as she tried to pick up the pieces. No! Turn the tap off first, that's what she should do. "It's nothing. It slipped."

And then her mother was beside her, reaching out to turn the tap off and gather up the bits of glass.

"I could have done that," Dawn protested faintly. But she tucked her hands beneath her armpits, too afraid to try again and fail.

It was her mother who found another glass, a cut glass crystal one this time, textured to the touch rather than smooth as the other one had been. She filled it up with water from the tap and set it in front of Dawn.

"I used to do this for your father," her mother said, eyes heavy with disquiet. "Have you taken the test?"

"I'm not thirty yet." Dawn tried for levity. "And, well … I'm not sure I'm going to need the test."

"You shouldn't have symptoms yet. If you have it.

Symptoms don't appear until later in life." Her mother's voice was calm, very calm.

"Symptoms don't usually appear until later, no. I know the literature and the progression of the disease as well as you."

"Oh, Dawn." Her mother turned her back to the sink and leaned against it, her arms tightly folded across her waist. Holding on hard because letting go meant acknowledging the obvious.

"I've been forgetting stuff at work. Little things."

"Maybe you're overworked."

Dawn toed at the tile beneath her foot. "I'm getting clumsier."

"Overworked and overtired."

"That's what my distribution manager says. I'm pretty sure," Dawn whispered. "I wouldn't have done what I did to Finn if I wasn't pretty sure." Tears started to spill over. "I only ever wanted a little bit of him, you know? Something to remember and make me feel good. Just for a little while."

"Oh, Dawn." Her mother's tears had started too as she gathered Dawn into her arms and held her close.

"I'm pretty sure," Dawn choked out on a sob.

"I know you're scared. I'm scared too. I'm so sorry your father and I brought this down on you. I'd give anything to take it away, but I can't." Her mother pulled back enough to press her forehead to Dawn's. "I know you don't want to take that test yet, baby. But the not knowing is coloring your choices. You're living as if you already have the disease and you're hurting yourself and the people around you with the not knowing. Fifty-fifty, Dawn. Take the test. It's time."

"I know."

"What's going on?" It probably shouldn't have come as a surprise that her aunt was the next to speak and that at some point she too must have made her way to the kitchen. Wonderful woman, her aunt. Stoic in the face of suffering. Dawn wanted to be her when she grew up.

"Dawn's going to test for Huntington's," her mother said with one last squeeze before letting go and directing Dawn towards one of the kitchen stools.

"Okay," said her aunt. "Good."

"She thinks she's got it."

Her aunt stayed stoic. "Not so good."

"She blew off her young man last night because of it. And she has a headache."

"Well, hell." Her aunt planted her butt on a breakfast stool. "We're going to need more cheesecake."

Her mother pulled back to pick up the headache tablets and hand them to Dawn along with the water. "When are you thinking of getting it done? Can you do it in your labs?"

She could, but she wouldn't. If she was going to do this, she was going to do it the right way, through the right channels. She didn't want people in her labs knowing before she knew. Before she'd lined up damage control measures when it came to the impact this could have on her company. "I'll get a referral to a specialist. Become someone's patient. I know who I want."

"Your father's specialist?"

Nothing wrong with her father's specialist, except for the fact that he was based in the Adirondacks. "A specialist in Manhattan. I know him through medical conferences and research papers and such. We've collaborated before. He's good, he's close by and he'll do it right." Dawn wiped at her eyes and pushed her uneaten cheesecake in her aunt's direction. "Fifty-fifty, right?" Those were her odds and she'd clung to them all her adult life. Trading knowledge for uncertainty because that way she could hold onto hope.

Maybe she *was* just tired and clumsy and forgetful. Stress could do that to a person.

There was still a chance.

You never know until you know.

Chapter Seven

DAWN DIDN'T KNOW how she managed to walk into Sully's on Thursday evening one week later for her monthly get together with Faith, Zel and Mercy, but she did. She'd considered sending her apologies by text and just not showing up, but she owed them a little more than that. She was planning to cut ties with them before too long, yes, but this time she'd at least do it face to face.

There was no sign of Finn as she made her way towards the end booth where the others waited, and for that she was truly grateful. Composure could only stretch so far and hers was already stretched thin. Once her mind had been made up when it came to getting tested, she'd been able to make an appointment with Aaron Chen. Aaron had waived some of the pre-counselling requirements of the testing procedure on account of her extensive knowledge of the genetic diseases and the ethical questions surrounding genetic testing, and he'd been able to fit her in to get the blood test done immediately, but there had been no fast-tracking the wait for results, and there would be no waiving of the after counselling requirements once those results came in. Aaron had made that very clear.

All the theoretical knowledge in the world mattered little when shit got personal.

“Ladies,” she said when she reached the booth. “You started without me.”

“We thought you weren’t coming,” said Faith, signaling the barman for a drink for Dawn.

“I got held up at work and truth be told the thought of bailing did cross my mind. But I’m here now and boy do I need a drink.”

“CEOs,” teased Mercy. “Always the same.”

“I’ll have you know I’m unique,” said Dawn. “Just look at my face. On second thoughts, don’t.” She knew she looked tired and drawn. That’s because she was.

“I have a remedy for those bags under your eyes,” said Zel. “Sleep. What have you been doing? Running the country?”

“No, I’ve been honing my company’s forward research plans and bringing venture capitalists on board.”

Zel’s eyes narrowed. “You’re letting people buy into your company now?”

“I’ve never wholly owned the company. I used other people’s money from the start. Right now we’re expanding. Rapidly. It’s time.”

Otherwise known as getting all her ducks in a row before she stepped back from day to day management altogether.

"You should have said," said Zel. "I could have approached my brother and The Madison Foundation on your behalf."

"Is your relationship with your brother even functional?" Mercy asked, and Zel suddenly found her mojito fascinating.

"Well, no. My relationship with Seb is as broken as ever. But he's a good businessman."

"Can I quiz you about the business of running a medical research company at some point?" Mercy asked Dawn. "The Master of Business student in me wants to know more."

Mercy was from a family of vintners whose very good wines held significant global market share. She'd come to New York to get a Master's degree, and maybe, just maybe, get away from her parents' loving reach. "How's the study going?"

"Well, I'm not yet ready to hunt down venture capitalists for my next brilliant idea, put it that way."

"You don't need to," said Dawn with a grin. "You're already expanding at a pace your family is comfortable with."

"My father's not that comfortable with it," Mercy said. "He wants to market our next rosé in the premium price range. I want it to be an award winning mid-range wine.

Maybe I should *threaten* venture capitalism."

It was Dawn's first real smile in a week. "Perfect."

"He'll make you come home," warned Zel. "He's done it before."

"Not this time." Mercy lifted her chin. "I've earned this."

"Oh, shite," muttered Faith.

"I think we're boring her," said Mercy.

"No, just intimidating me beyond belief." Faith's attention was focused somewhere over Dawn's right shoulder. "Finn's playing here tonight, which I thought would be a good thing because it usually is. And then he rocked up two hours ago breathing fire and brimstone and making everyone want to throttle him. He's in a mood."

Zel straightened. "What kind of mood? A playful mood?"

"More of a *God help anyone who gets in his way* mood."

"He's a passionate man," said Mercy. "I approve."

"He's a pain in the arse," muttered Faith. "And I'm worried about him."

"Can you talk to him?" asked Mercy.

"I don't need to." Faith reached for her half-empty brew. "The minute he picks up his violin and puts the bow to it, his music will tell me everything I need to know about what's wrong with him. It's his gift."

"His *gift*?" Mercy queried. "Sounds more like the curse of a caring, intuitive sister."

Dawn let their words wash over her without comment as she adjusted to the thought that Finn wasn't elsewhere this evening. He was right here. And she was so screwed.

"Didn't Finn ask you out a few weeks back?" Faith suddenly asked her.

"He did, yes," she offered with a smile that bordered on cool, never mind the turmoil within. "Nothing came of it."

The fact that Finn was here and she was here was bad. This was his place of safety, not hers. And Faith was looking at her as if she knew things she had no business knowing.

"He asked me something weird about you the other day," said Faith, still watching her closely. "He asked me if you'd ever been sick at school. Only time I could remember was on altar wine night."

"Well," Dawn said faintly. "It was really bad wine. And we did drink rather a lot of it."

A violin sounded in Sully's bar, low and mournful. Tuning took place but Dawn couldn't see it. She wasn't facing the stage tonight and no way was she about to turn around.

If she looked, she'd fall in thrall all over again. There was something about musicians, the way they wove a spell over a crowd. She *knew* what he could call forth with that violin. "I should go," she muttered, wondering if there was a back way out that she could sneak through.

"You just got here." Now Zel was looking at her oddly

as well.

And then Finn's voice came across the microphone, rough and warm as he greeted the crowd and told those who didn't already know that he'd grown up here and that every now and then he headed back here to touch base with his family and with his roots. He told them that an old violin teacher of his was here in the crowd tonight and that he hoped he didn't disappoint him.

"I've been composing," he said next. "Because every now and again I decide I'm Beethoven. And I hope you don't mind but tonight I need a test audience and you're it. It's around seven minutes long and it's not the kind of music I usually play here. If you let me get through it all, I'll stand you all a drink. It's called *Sorrow.*"

"It's for all the things that never were," he added quietly, after a moment's hesitation.

"Oh, Jesus," whimpered Faith, and Dawn agreed.

Why didn't he just walk up and rip out her heart and be done with it?

From the first note it was clear that this music was personal. Grief flowed and love wove around it, thready but unbreakable. Anger rose and wept. Accusation. Indignation. And underlying all of it a sorrow that went soul deep. Two minutes in and not a word was being spoken. Dawn sat as silent as the rest of the audience, head bowed and her eyes fixed on the wooden table in front of her.

Three minutes in and silent tears were streaming down

Dawn's cheeks and there was nothing for it but to let them flow. Mercy's hand crept into hers and squeezed, but Dawn was trembling with the effort to stay contained and barely felt it.

Haunting loneliness crept into the music and stayed there.

She'd tried to explain how much losing the baby had haunted her. He'd listened and said little. What could he have said? He hadn't felt it.

Not then.

This here, this was personal. It was as if he'd crawled inside her skin and lived in it. Every thought and feeling she'd ever had, this was Finn, exposing it, playing it, with a depth of understanding that she couldn't comprehend.

He knew what it had been like for her.

He knew.

Seven minutes after he started, Finn lowered his violin to a room full of hushed silence. Not one cough or clinking glass.

Dawn turned in her seat, she had to see him, just once before she left, never mind the tears that still flowed. She had to see what he'd done to himself in order to play what he'd just played, but his face was downcast, a study of shadows lit only by the outside light from a nearby window. He sat on his stool, fiddling with the strings near the bridge of his violin.

As the silence continued.

And then somebody, Faith's father, JP, moved. "Sweet *Jaysus*, Finn. Care to cheer us *up* now?"

Finn glanced up at his father, eyes wet but his features composed and said, "Sure."

He lifted the violin to his chin again.

"Wait," said an old man sitting at a table for two over by the window. "Let it sit a while." And he started clapping.

Others joined him. *Everyone* joined him, including Dawn. And pretty soon there were catcalls.

Finn summoned a grin from somewhere. How did he *do that* after having just bled out in front of a crowd? "Gimme a minute," he said and stepped from the stage and handed his violin to the old man who'd told him to wait.

Then he headed towards her.

Dawn stood as he approached, her trembling hand still firmly clasped in Mercy's. She'd pay for the damage. A new hand, maybe.

He stopped in front of her and studied her face, before reaching out with both hands to cup her cheeks and wipe his thumbs over the tearstains beneath her eyes.

"I would have been there for you if I'd known," he said, and then kissed her gently on the mouth. "I would have understood. You didn't have to be alone."

And then he left her again and went back to the old man who held his violin, and then got back up on that stage again and closed his eyes and started playing fast and loose with an Irish jig. Cheerful music, and if his soul wasn't in it, well maybe he masked it for many with his technical brilliance.

It was time to go. Past time for her night with the girls to be over, but her legs weren't working too well. Five minutes, then.

Dawn reached for her beer but decided against raising it to her lips. Instead she wiped at the condensation on the glass, drawing fairground stripes on it and let the silence stand.

This was the end. The end of everything. It was time to say goodbye to these wonderful women.

"Dawn?" Faith asked quietly. "What was that?"

"Sorrow, I guess."

Felt like it.

"Why?"

Was there any harm in telling? She'd already told Finn. Perhaps the truth would help them let her go. "Finn and I got together once. Early on. At your brother's twenty-first. It was kind of beautiful."

Faith sat back against the wall of the booth and eyed Dawn narrowly. "So?"

Dawn took a deep breath. "I paid for it afterwards. That night, when we were drinking the altar wine?" She tried a shrug on for size but it slid from her shoulders and landed somewhere at her feet. "I was miscarrying."

Silence met her statement. The same kind of silence

that Finn's music had met.

"Finn *knew*?" asked Faith finally, her voice dangerously quiet.

"No. Not then. I told him the other day."

Faith's brows drew together in a frown and her eyes flashed fire. "For heaven's sake, Dawn, why? Why tell him now and not then?"

Good question.

"Anything *else* you haven't told us?" muttered Zel, looking shell shocked, but otherwise neutral. A little bit like Switzerland.

So much more she hadn't told them, yes. "My father has Huntington's disease. I don't know if you know what that is, but it's ugly. He lives but he has no speech left and barely any movement. From dropping a glass to what he is now in fifteen years. I only found out about it a couple of years after I left St. J's. It's genetic."

"Meaning?" said Zel.

"I have a fifty percent chance of inheriting it. I think I might have it. I have some of the symptoms."

"Is trembling one of them?" asked Mercy gently and Dawn choked back a sob.

"That's just trembling."

"Oh, Dawn."

Mercy reached out to touch her wrist, silent comfort and she wanted it, she did. She just didn't think she deserved it. "I took a test. I'll know for sure soon." She stood abruptly. “I’m sorry. I shouldn’t have come here. This is Finn’s home, not mine.”

“How soon?” Urgency laced Mercy’s voice as she reached out once again and clasped Dawn gently around the wrist. “Dawn. When do you find out?”

“Tomorrow. At two o’clock.”

“We could stay with you afterwards. Slumber party,” Mercy offered instantly and Zel nodded. Even Faith nodded, but Dawn shook her head.

“No. My mother’s here. So’s my aunt. They’ll keep me company.”

“What about afterwards?” Mercy was nothing if not persistent.

Dawn smiled and tried to find the strength to make a final, decisive break, but she couldn’t. Mercy’s mercy was her undoing. “Some other time perhaps. Afterwards, I think I’m going to go see my dad.”

Chapter Eight

FRIDAY MORNING DAWNED gray and gloomy for Finn. He'd spent the night on his brother Ty's houseboat in Brooklyn, rambling drunkenly for the most part about gray-eyed women and lost souls. Miscarriage had come into it. Ty had listened and said little and at some point must have poured him into the forward bunk, thrown a blanket over him and hopefully got some sleep before having to get up and go to work.

Ty was an attorney for the Legal Aid society. A goddamn knight in battered armor, using words of law instead of a sword. Finn loved his upright, law-abiding brother so much, and never more than when he saw the box of aspirin sitting next to a glass of water on the kitchen bench.

Big brothers were awesome.

Finn took three tablets, washed them down with water and had the fastest shower ever before heading back to the pub. His father and Faith would be opening up soon. He could ask Faith if she really had locked his violin up in the safe last night in order to stop him playing yet another mournful Irish dirge.

God, he hoped so.

"Well, son," said his pop as soon as he saw him, and clapped his hand down hard on the curve where Finn's shoulder met his neck for good measure. "I may not have a customer left after last night, but I enjoyed it. Your sister wants to talk to you."

"I'll bet. Does she know where my violin is? Do you?"

His father smirked. "She's in the taproom."

Great. Just great. The cave of doom.

"You *screwed* my *friend*," said Faith, swapping out good reason for bad language at the same time she tapped a new beer barrel. "Ten years ago, and you never said a word!"

Finn sighed. Maybe he was due this, but he'd had good reason at the time. Or so he'd thought.

"If Dawn had wanted you to know, I figure she'd have told you," he muttered.

"And she *did*." Faith's voice had risen. "Last night after your *spectacularly* self-indulgent performance reduced her to tears.

Ouch. Low blow.

Although maybe, just possibly, she had a point.

He'd had a point to make too, and he'd made it the best way he knew how. No words could encompass what he'd felt after Dawn had told him about the child that never was. There were no words.

It had to be music.

"Did she say anything afterwards?" he asked. "Why did she go?"

"You mean it isn't *fucking obvious*? She's in love with you, Finn."

His temper and Faith's were never a good match. Usually they took turns.

Carefully, deliberately, he took a step back. "Dawn say that to you?"

Faith suddenly found the beer barrel fascinating. "Not in so many words, but I know her. And I know you. You're both miserable. I did some reading up on Huntington's disease and it's awful. I can see that. I can see how you might want to protect yourself from that, but"

"What?" Finn stared at the top of his sister's head as she fiddled with the keg. "Protect me from *what*?"

"Dawn's Huntington's. That she thinks she has."

Faith finally deigned to stop screwing about with the beer barrel and look at him. Whatever she saw made her suddenly turn pale. "You don't know."

"*I have not one single goddamn clue what you're talking about*," he roared. "How much clearer do you want me to get?"

✦

"OKAY," SHE SAID faintly. "Okay. So, ah, Dawn's father has this disease called Huntington's."

"And Dawn has it too?"

"She thinks so."

Certain things began clicking into place. Dawn's relationship restrictions. The way she chased her research ambitions as if there was no tomorrow. The way she gave him everything during lovemaking and then got up and stepped back. Nothing special. Don't look at me for too long.

You won't like what you find, she'd said.

"She finds out today." His sister's eyes grew apologetic. "I spent the morning worrying for her and cursing my selfish, fair-weather brother but I should have known. I *know* you. I know you both. God. She didn't tell you."

No need to keep reminding him. "Did she say where she finds out? Will she find out at work?"

"I don't know." Faith shook her head and corkscrew curls went bobbing. "All I know is that she said she finds out at two o'clock."

It was well past eleven am now.

He reached for his phone.

Two minutes later he all but threw it across the taproom.

"She's not answering," Faith said gently. "Zel, Mercy, me. We've all tried to call. She's not at work. We tried there too."

"Have you tried her at home?"

His sister looked desolate. "I don't even know where

she lives."

He did. And maybe, just maybe, she'd be there.

He needed to get to her. To make her see, once and for all, that she didn't have to walk though life alone. What else did he need in order to get through to her? Patience? Understanding? And almighty dose of calm? Did Dawn need another friend there? "Coming?"

Faith's eyes filled with tears, even as she shook her head. "Pretty sure she's not going to want two panicking Sullivans at her side. One's probably enough. Go."

"You'll call me if you hear from her? Or if you find out where she is?"

Faith nodded. "Mercy's busy phoning every gene mapping medical specialist in Manhattan. I mean, how many can there be, right? Go. Keep me posted too."

He started towards the door and stopped abruptly. He backtracked and spared a kiss for his sister's forehead. "I love you. I'm sorry I swore at you."

"Go."

Chapter Nine

FINN MADE IT to Soho in record time and jammed his finger to Dawn's intercom with enough force to make him wince. When he heard a voice say hello he closed his eyes in pure relief.

"It's Finn. Let me in."

"It's Finn," the voice said. Not Dawn, then, and the connection went silent but the door buzzed open and he figured that for good enough. When he knocked on Dawn's actual apartment door one elevator ride and six floors later, he managed to do so with a little less urgency and a whole lot more politeness because somewhere in the whirl of his brain he remembered the presence of mothers and figured that what with all that was going down, Dawn's mother might be somewhere around.

The door opened and a woman stood there. An older woman with eyes the same color as Dawn's. "Mrs. Turner?" he said, feeling all of seventeen years old again. "I'm Finbar Sullivan." At least he'd had enough sense to introduce himself. "Is Dawn around?"

"She's not here right now." There was another woman behind the first one. More gray eyes, these ones tinged with blue. Which one was her mother and which one the aunt?

"Would you like to come in?" the second woman said.

"No, I—no. I just need to find her."

The door opened wider. The first woman's fine features took on an implacable set. "Come in, Finbar."

He went in.

"This is my sister, Meg Dawson," she said, gesturing towards the other woman. "I'm Vivian, Dawn's mother. As you surmised."

Yes, yes. Points for him. "Do you know where she is?"

"Yes." He could see where Dawn got her cool assurance from. "Coffee?"

"No, I—"

"Vivi, stop torturing him."

Yes. He was all for that plan. "I only just found out about the Huntington's and the test," he said. "I need to see her. Now. Before she finds out."

"Young man." Dawn's mother was implacable. "My daughter let you go for a reason. If she has this disease she's in for a rough time, and so are the people who love her. Take it from someone who knows. Being with someone who has Huntington's is not for the fainthearted."

That was the second time this morning that someone had questioned his feelings for Dawn.

"I am *not* faint of heart." He had fortitude and determination enough for both of them. "I've been reading on the way here in the cab. She's still got time. *We've* still got time."

"To do what?" Dawn's mother asked quietly.

"To make life beautiful and meaningful and full of memories we can grow old with. It's not too late for Dawn and me. She's only twenty-seven. We've got time."

Dawn's mother seemed to crumple, just a little bit.

"Vivian," her sister said softly, coming closer to stand by Dawn's mother and gently touch her on the arm. "Do you really want Dawn to do to him what you did to her? Pushed her away in the mistaken thought that she'd be happier away from it all? Because I'm telling you from the sidelines, that didn't work out so well. Not for anyone. Give him the address."

"There's a referral letter on the desk in Dawn's study. The address is at the top of it," Vivian said quietly. "Will you get it for me please, Meg?"

Meg retreated in the direction of Dawn's bedroom. Finn watched until he could no longer see her and then ran a hand through his hair and wondered whether it had seen a comb this morning. He didn't think so. Desperate, hungover and untidy. Not a good look to bring to an introductory meeting with Dawn's mother.

He took a deep and steadying breath, turned his attention back towards the woman who was currently studying him like a bug under a microscope, and he waited for some new hammer to fall.

It was that kind of morning.

"Dawn hasn't told me much about you. How you met. What you do," Vivian Turner began.

"We met ten years ago through my sister. I'm a musician." He gave her the abbreviated version.

"Are you a good musician?"

"I like to think so." Although after last night … "I'm not short of work. Or money, if that's what you're thinking. I have a good reputation."

"If you stick by my Dawn and she has Huntington's, your career's going to suffer. Your priorities will change. Are you ready for that?"

"Not yet," he said stubbornly. "But I will be."

She smiled a little at that.

"For fifteen years I lived the dream. The man I loved at my side, both of us teaching and making a difference to children's lives. It was fulfilling work and they were bright blue days packed with laughter and a daughter with sunshine in her smile. I was so blessed."

Finn waited and said nothing. Prayed for Dawn's aunt to hurry up.

"And then my husband got sick, and we sent Dawn away hoping to spare her and instead we turned her into a woman who trusts no one for fear of being sent away or left behind. Abandoned, by those she loves. These days, Dawn makes sure to leave first. She hurt you for a reason, Finbar. She gave you a way out."

Finn felt his lips tighten.

"You don't know what you might be in for. *She* knows. Better than you do. If I were *your* mother I'd tell you to run."

"My mother's dead," he offered flatly. "You see I *do* know something about love and loss. And that's not the advice she would have given."

Kathleen Sullivan had known better than anyone that when Finn's mind was made up, it was made up.

"My daughter's going to try and push you away. She pushes everyone away."

"I know that, Mrs. Turner."

"Don't let her."

He was never not going to be helpless against grey-eyed women with eyes that saw straight through to the heart of things. "I won't."

Dawn's aunt returned and he took the piece of paper she handed to him with a gruff, "Thank you."

"You should leave now if you want to catch her at the doctor's office. If you miss her, we'll tell her you called."

"Thank you," he said again.

It was way past time to leave.

It wasn't until he was back outside the apartment block that he stopped memorizing the address long enough to turn the paper over.

In small, neat handwriting Dawn's aunt had written: *We like you already, Mr. Finbar Sullivan, otherwise you wouldn't have got through the door. My niece cares deeply for you. Good luck.*

✦

DAWN SAT IN the waiting room at the clinic on the grounds of Columbia University and tried not to stare at the clock. Over the past week she'd answered surveys and had a physical examination, gone through her family medical history and taken more than one psych test. She hadn't had any brain imaging tests yet but that was only because they'd skipped straight to predictive genetic testing.

There were perks to being the head of a leading research company focused on genetic testing. Aaron – Doctor Aaron Chen – had waived a lot of the pre-counseling given that Dawn was already well-versed when it came to ethical, economic and emotional intricacies surrounding such testing. He'd fast tracked the DNA test.

She took a deep breath and stopped watching the clock in favor of counting how many tulips were in the fishbowl vase on the receptionist's desk instead.

Twenty.

She drummed her fingers on her leg, caught the receptionist's sympathetic smile and smacked one hand down over her wayward fingers to make them stop.

Her mother had wanted to come to the appointment

but Dawn had refused. She was hanging onto her control by the merest of threads and if the news was bad she would need time to collect herself. A counselling session had been pre-booked. She would move from one specialist's room to the next.

Fifty-fifty, Dawn. Breathe.

The door to the clinic opened and a man walked in, bringing with him an air of controlled energy that had every head in the room swiveling towards him.

Finn.

He sat down beside her and slid her a glance. Hard to believe that green eyes could burn so hot, but they did.

He was everything she'd ever wanted, and didn't think she could afford to have.

"Why are you here?" she asked quietly, well aware of the others in the room and the almost invariable listening in.

"Same reason you're here. To see what our future holds."

"*My* future, not yours," she corrected. "Walk away, Finn. You're not part of my world."

"Do you realize," he said almost conversationally. "That you're doing to me almost exactly what your mother did to you?"

The receptionist looked up, eyes narrowed. And then she glanced back and forth between him and Dawn and softened, just a little bit as she stood and came out from behind the desk.

"I can offer you Doctor Grant's room if you need somewhere to talk." She nodded firmly, her gaze fixed on Dawn. "Ms. Turner? A little privacy for your conversation?"

Guess she'd navigated these kinds of situations before.

Reluctantly, Dawn stood. "Thank you."

Dawn followed the receptionist to a nearby door and Finn followed Dawn.

"I'll come and get you when the doctor is ready to see you," she murmured, and shut the door behind her.

He wouldn't have caused a scene, but he was nonetheless grateful for the use of the room, even if Dawn perched her delectable butt on the edge of the desk and refused to look at him. Instead she stared out the window, at the carpet, at the clock on the wall. Anywhere but at him.

But she was giving him a hearing, and he was determined to make the most of it.

He took a deep breath and began to speak.

"I care for you, Dawn. Very much. And you care for me. If you have this disease you've got what … ten years before symptoms appear?"

"Maybe less," she said faintly.

"Spend them with me. We'll do your bucket list and mine. Live life to its fullest. Loving. Exploring. Experiencing everything. You and me."

He almost made sense. Dawn sat on her hands to stop them reaching for him and tried to be the sensible one here. The one who knew what they were in for if she had this disease. “And then what?” she said. “You walk away unscathed? You’ll have spent the best years of your life on me. No kids. No growing old alongside a healthy, functional partner.”

“No one can promise that anyway.” Finally, she saw the crack in him. It was there in his eyes, full acknowledgement of the burden her illness would bring. “Cost to bear.”

“Walk away.” She couldn’t bear it if he stayed and she had the disease.

“I hear your chance of having it is fifty-fifty. I’ll take those odds. I’ll take you in sickness and in health.”

“No. If I’m in sickness I *will* not have you.”

He squared his shoulders. “What’s on your bucket list? The Northern Lights are on mine. Then the ice sculpture festival in northern China. Dog sledding in the Arctic –that one’s been there since I was a kid. I want to take my father to Ireland and go on a whisky trail and roll him home. I want to learn bagpipes in Edinburgh. Your presence at that one’s optional given the nature of bagpipes. You’re welcome.”

“You’re crazy.”

“I want to take you to the Musikverein in Vienna. It’s a concert hall, a very beautiful one, and when you play in it, the sound swoops and soars and fills every bit of it. I can see us there. This year or next.” His voice cracked. “Come with me, Dawn.”

She bit her lip and took to staring at the clock again rather than at the man sitting next to her weaving a future out of hope and feathers.

"They've asked me to write a concerto in three parts for violin," he continued undeterred. "First movement's about love. You've heard the second. Think I'm going to call the third one hope. You haven't seen me when I'm composing yet. *Apparently* I can be difficult. Faith brought me a plastic tiara once, flashing lights and everything. I was in the middle of scoring a film and she had some creative suggestions as to where I could put it. According to her they don't always have to go on your head."

"Your family," she murmured with a shake of her head.

"Is my strength. I've got this, Dawn. You think I don't know love and loss? I do. I know the cost. The rest of my family knows it too and they'll be there for us. You don't have to do this alone. Let me walk with you, Dawn. No matter what."

He held out his hand for her to take. It was a strong hand. Square palm, long fingers and neat nails.

"I love you," he said.

The clincher.

She took his hand as the clock on the wall signaled the hour. "There's a fifty-fifty chance I love you too."

"Have you ever danced at the edge of the ocean in the moonlight?"

"No."

“Would you like to?”

A memory flashed unbidden. “I know this place in Australia. This little tucked away beach below a lighthouse.”

He squeezed her hand and she squeezed back.

“I had to come,” he said.

“I’m glad you’re here.”

And then a knock on the door sounded and Dawn said, “Come in.”

The clinic receptionist opened the door. “Ms. Turner? Doctor will see you now.”

“Want me to come in?” asked Finn.

“No, I—I want—” If the news was not good she was going to need a moment to break and remake herself with no one looking on. If she broke—

The look in his eyes told her that she wouldn’t be the only one.

Was she really going to do this? Walk through life at this man’s side, holding nothing back, no matter what? “Yes. Please. Come with me.”

It was kinda sweet, how quickly he dragged her towards the door. “Do you still have the tiara?” she asked.

“Yes.”

“I bet I can out princess you. Wait ’til you see me breaking down genetic code.”

“You’re on.”

“The only thing that can tempt me away from my work when I get obsessed is cheesecake.”

"Noted."

"And blindingly good sex."

She glanced his way and found him … smug.

With good reason.

Aaron's office was at the end of a bland white corridor and the door stood open. She stepped inside the room and Finn followed. Aaron looked from her to Finn and summoned a professional smile as he stood up and came around to lean against the edge of his desk. "Dawn. And…?"

"Finn, this is Doctor Aaron Chen colleague, friend and, as of a couple of weeks ago, my physician. Aaron, this is Finbar Sullivan, my, ah …"

"Beloved," Finn said firmly.

"You didn't have one of those on your forms," Aaron said dryly.

"He's a new addition – as of your waiting room."

"Violinist, right?" Aaron held out his hand.

"That too." Finn shook it.

"Well, I hope you can keep up with her." Aaron turned and picked up a thumb drive from his desk and handed it to her "I know you'll want to look at the results yourself." His smile turned into a grin that stretched from ear to ear. "Don't drop it. Apparently you're naturally clumsy and forgetful. The results are negative."

Time stopped. She couldn't breathe. Colors dimmed and space contracted until there was only one thing in it.

Finn.

Looking as poleaxed and unable to process events as she was.

He looked like he needed a hug.

"Oh, sweet Jesus, *yes*!" he said as he arms closed around her and he buried his face in her neck. "Where's that beach?"

"So, about counseling," Aaron said. "Finn, you'll need some too."

"Don't need counseling. I just need a moment."

"Share the joy, my friend." Aaron was clearly enjoying himself. "You hear the verdict, you get the counseling."

"Do I have to like him?" Finn murmured. "Will he be coming to dinner?"

"Probably."

"I'll do the counseling."

"Good man, princess," Dawn whispered against his chest.

"I wish I'd never told you that."

"I was impressed." Dawn couldn't keep her smile down. The cocoon that was just her and Finn widened. "I need to ring my mother."

"And your friends."

"You do Faith. I'll do the rest."

"And I would love to do dinner," said Aaron. "Get out of here. Nice to meet you, Finn. May I call you Finn?"

"Yes." He and Finn shook hands again. Dawn hugged

Aaron; she could talk about her blurring of boundaries in counselling, she figured. And then she hightailed it out of that sterile interior space and into the open, with the sun on her face and blue sky over head.

On the steps of the building she stopped and took a deep breath. "I don't even know what to do next. I don't know this world. All I know for sure is that you're here with me and the possibilities are so beautiful."

"Are you crying?"

"No," she lied, and flung her arms around him and buried her face in his neck to hide the fact. "I love you. I love you and I'm holding you to every word you said in there."

"You're on," he rumbled gruffly, and she could feel the reverberations of his chest against hers and the rapid beating of his heart. "And there's somewhere I'd like to take you right now, a place we can go to celebrate the good news. Your family and friends. Mine too. They all need to be there."

"Where?"

"Sully's."

Chapter Ten

AN HOUR AND a half later, Finbar pushed open the door to the pub he'd called home and ushered Dawn inside. The warmth of the place greeted him instantly, the familiar scents and sounds of his youth bathing him in the comfort of old memories. For a man who professed to have a love-hate relationship with the place, he'd sure as hell headed straight for it when the time came to celebrate good news.

The pub wasn't busy at this time of the afternoon. A few regulars graced various tables and booths, but the lunch crowd had gone and the evening crowd had yet to arrive. Three hours, maybe a little more, since he'd last been here but the difference between how he'd felt then and how he felt now was amazing.

He looked to the long bar and smiled at who he saw there. Faith and his father were doing the tending, and Ronan was there too for some reason, happily at rest between Mercy and Zel. Dawn's mother was there. Dawn's encouraging aunt.

"Gang's all here," he murmured as Dawn slid her hand inside his.

"You're enjoying this."

"I am."

"I'll have you know that I got at least half those people offside with me last night. Maybe all of them. Deliberately."

"They love you."

"I love them too."

Faith saw them first and her smile split her face as she started cheering and hefted a bottle of champagne and let the cork fly. A row of champagne glasses sat atop the gleaming old bar and in a showy display his sister ran liquid into the lot of them without ever breaking the flow. That brought on another round of cheers, although maybe it was just that they'd spotted Dawn. Faith then reached down and brought another two champagne glasses full of ice and lime and mint and something fizzy and set one in front of Zel and one in front of Dawn's mom.

Drinks clearly had been sorted but before they could get to them, Mercy and Zel had to hug Dawn, and then Ronan had to hug her too and introduce himself while he was doing it, much to Finn's narrow-eyed amusement. Dawn's aunt had to hug her. And then it was just Dawn standing in front of her mom.

"Hey, Mom." Dawn's voice held only the slightest wobble. "No more fifty-fifty. I don't have it."

Her mother nodded but didn't seem to be able to speak.

"Did you—did someone tell Dad?" Dawn asked next.

Dawn's mother nodded again, and then her eyes filled with tears as she gave a heaving sob that she seemed to have been saving up for years. "Oh, Dawn, he cried. I cried. I haven't stopped crying." Finn glanced at his father who nodded in confirmation. "It's such a burden gone. I am so, so glad."

And then Dawn was in her mother's arms and crying too.

Finn's father brought forth a box of tissues from behind the bar and gallantly offered them around, and Finn was never more grateful to the old man when the next thing he did was raise a frosted glass of Guinness and press a glass of champagne into Dawn's hand.

"A toast," his father said and made sure everyone else had a glass of something to go with it. He held his beer out at arm's length and Finn, Faith and Ronan stretched so that their glasses almost touched his. They knew this toasting circle of old. It was a Sullivan tradition.

"C'mon," Faith urged Mercy and Zel. "The glasses have to almost touch, that's the rule and no spilling. Then when the toast is said, we clink."

"I love being Irish by association," said Zel.

"You're not alone, lassie." His father had put on his thickest Irish brogue. "Sláinte Mhaith."

Sláinte Mhaith.

A chorus in reply and the clinking of glasses for percussion.

To good health.

“So has everybody met each other?” asked Dawn and got a round of yesses in reply. “Mom, Meg, this is Finn.”

“We’ve met,” said Meg. “Of course, if you want to help us out a little more here, you might tell us the status of your relationship.”

“Oh.” Dawn blushed beautifully. “Of course. He’s my, ah …”

Finn smiled at her and nodded encouragingly.

Dawn cleared her throat and started again. “He’s my beloved.”

Damn right he was.

“Oh, word of the *day*,” said Mercy admiringly. “Bee-lov-ed. Love it.”

“Hey, Finn.” Zel grinned at him. “JP’s been telling us all about you as a kid. Tales of great valor and bad haircuts. Pictures and everything.”

“I’ve told them nothing about your tiara,” Faith offered solemnly. “And I never will. Come here so I can kiss you. You too, Dawn.”

Faith did a damn fine job of hugging them, the bar in between notwithstanding.

His father did the same. “I’ve been singing your praises to Vivian and Meg at full volume. Thought you might need a little help in that direction." Pop grinned. "You intending to play for us again this evening? Something cheerful?"

He could.

Call it duty or respect for his family but Finn had never once refused to play in this bar when asked to. Tonight though, he hesitated. "There's a song in my heart and in my head, but I don't have the notes for it yet," he said, trying his best to explain where he was at with the music. For the first time in forever he wanted to focus his attention elsewhere. "I don't want to perform for a crowd tonight. I will in the future, you know that, Pop. But tonight I just want to ask Dawn to dance."

Mercy sighed. So did Dawn's Aunt Meg.

"That does it," said Faith. "I'm calling Case and I'll try and get hold of Ty. I am officially declaring tonight a Sullivan *event*."

✦

THREE HOURS LATER, Dawn sat with her friends in the last booth at Sully's, a booth that now had another table butting neatly against it, and half a dozen chairs scattered around it. A jug of virgin mojitos and a jug of water sat on the two tables amidst the debris of plates, cutlery, napkins and condiments that went with a pub supper.

At some point the two tables had been laden with mini burgers and skinny fries, steak and Guinness pies, garden salad, Caesar salad, baby back pork ribs, and to top it all off, an entire baked cheesecake with a wild berry topping.

The main meals had been eaten and so had half the cheesecake. No one appeared to be in any hurry to leave. Her mother and aunt looked as flushed and happy as Dawn had ever seen them. JP, Faith's father, sat with them, and Faith, in the interests of singing Finn's praises to Dawn's family, had brought out the 'Finbar-Sullivan-poster-collection'. The first one she unrolled was a glossy picture of Finn playing on the steps of some famous concert hall in Europe.

"Berlin," said Zel when she saw it. "Classy."

The next one was of Finn and three others in a room, and he was younger then.

"Juilliard Quartet," said Faith with the snap of her fingers. "I remember that one. This is Josef. Gil's dad."

Out the posters rolled, and with them Finn's bemusement. He hadn't been expecting this, Dawn could tell.

He wasn't used to it.

Faith taped them all to the wall, and then JP carefully pulled out his wallet and withdrew a photo of his beloved Kathleen and taped it smack bang in the middle of all of them.

Because, *"Kathleen, she'd want to see this for herself."*

Finn's other brother, Casey, had arrived, along with a raggedy array of musician friends. Ty hadn't been sighted yet – getting hold of him when he was in court was akin to winning the lottery, Faith told them.

He was missing out, was all Dawn thought. On family. On this night bursting with joy. And maybe most of the joy was hers but sharing had never come easier.

Dawn loved and was loved, and her future stretched out like a glorious, glittering road. No telling what it held, but not Huntington's.

Not Huntington's.

Finn's father had been taking photos and sending them through to one of the nurses at the nursing home where her father was. How he'd gotten hold of the nurse's number was anyone's guess, but Dawn figured it involved the Blarney Stone.

Apparently the nurse was showing them to Dawn's father as they came in.

A father who could no longer talk but he could still recognize loved ones and there was no one he loved more than his wife and daughter.

Every time JP sent the photo through, Dawn's mother laughed and cried and hugged Dawn some more.

"This is crazy," said Dawn as she extricated herself from the latest round of hugs. Casey had wanted to hug her too, and had, until Finn had chased him and Ronan to the stage and followed in their wake.

"If he plays, we're all going to cry again," said Mercy. "Stop that man!"

But Finn didn't take the stage with his brothers. Instead, he approached the nearest table, and moments later the people sitting at it were standing and dragging the table back a foot or so. He repeated the process with a different table and then another, and then a smiling Ronan stepped up to the microphone.

"So welcome to Sully's and if you don't already know us, I'm Ronan Sullivan and this is my brother, Case. Our other brother, who's making you shift the furniture, that's Finbar. You might have heard of him. He plays the violin." Ronan began tuning his guitar and Casey did likewise with his banjo. "Our father, JP, is up the back and so's our sister, Faith. They run the place. We've one other brother who can't get here right now, and we're going to kick his arse for that later. His name's Ty, just in case you see him first."

"Hey, Mercy. Remember Ty?" murmured Zel. "I do. All the way from my punishment chair to Mother Superior's office."

And then Ronan began speaking again.

"We're going to play a little tune for you that Finn's requested. I tried to talk him out of it because we haven't played this one since we were teenagers. I told him I couldn't remember the words and therefore couldn't play it. Truth is I know them by heart and so will many of you. Little banjo riff to start off with. Little song about a young lad who sees a girl on a village green when she's sweet sixteen. And falls in love with her." Ronan glanced at his brother who nodded and stopped tuning. “This one’s for Finn and Dawn and we wish them nothing but love.”

The first notes of an old, old ballad drifted on the air as Finn walked towards her.

“Oh, wow,” said Mercy. “JP, where are the tissues? I’m going to need them.”

“Use a napkin,” Faith murmured, with a smile that lit her from the inside. “We’ve run out of tissues.”

And then Dawn only had eyes for Finn as he stopped in front of her chair and held out his hand. Love stamped his face and his mossy, forest green gaze was just for her.

“I have déjà vu,” said Mercy. “Didn’t this happen ten years ago too?”

“Speak for yourself,” said Zel. “I wasn’t here. How could I have *missed* this?”

“Will you dance with me, Dawn?” Finn asked quietly and she nodded and took his hand and he led her to the tiny open space he’d cleared between tables and the stage.

He turned when they got there and she stepped seamlessly into his arms as if they’d done this before, a thousand times or more.

In her dreams they had.

“Not exactly the beach in the moonlight,” he murmured.

No, it wasn’t. “This is perfect.”

Ronan sang of love and Finn echoed him. “I love you, Dawn.”

"I love you too."

"Will you be with me? Live with me, walk through life at my side, no matter what?"

"I will." Never had she been more certain. "I'll dance with you anywhere."

The End

Tempting the Knight

A Fairy Tales of New York Romance

Heidi Rice

Dedication

To Kelly, Amy and Lucy, the other musketeers! Let's do this again…

How about Fairy Tales of London next? Maybe? Anyone?

Dear Reader,

When Amy Andrews originally suggested doing hot new versions of classic fairy tales, I said… WTH? Seriously? That sounds like a crap idea, I can't stand fairy tale princesses, they're all such wimps and so annoyingly sweet and good. Then Amy said, these are 'oblique' versions, with non-wimpy heroines, who idiot. Well, she didn't say idiot, but she should have… Because how wrong was I?

Once we started brainstorming, and Kelly Hunter and Lucy King got involved too, I discovered Zelda, my bad girl super-model Rapunzel who is anything but a wimp (or sweet or good, frankly). And Ty Sullivan, dedicated legal aid attorney and Zel's very reluctant knight in battered denim who busts her out of her ivory tower one hot, naughty Labor Day weekend in Brooklyn.

I hope you love these two as much as I did, and get a chance to read the other terrific books in the Fairy Tales of New York series. We had far too much fun writing them, so it seems only fair you guys should have as much fun reading them. And if anyone ever tells you fairytale princesses are wimps ever again, send them our way and we'll sort them out.

Cheers Heidi x

Prologue

Ten years ago, St. John the Apostle's Academy, Upstate New York.

NEVER GET DRUNK on altar wine, because the hangover will probably kill you.

Zelda Madison gritted her teeth to accommodate the thundering pain radiating out from her temples and met the emerald glare of the man sitting opposite her.

Tyrone 'High and Mighty' Sullivan had been staring at her as if she was a bug under his shoe ever since Dawn had been ushered into the Mother Superior's Office five minutes ago. Her friend Faith's eldest brother obviously had something against Zelda. She had no idea what, as she had never met the guy before today.

Squinting her eyes to reduce the blaze of sunlight coming through the stained glass window of Christ on the Cross that bore down on them from the vaulted hallway, Zel attempted to glare back at him.

The glare wasn't one of her best. Probably because her

retinas felt as if they'd been lasered off, and there was a huge bottomless chasm opening up in her belly at the thought of what might be waiting for her once the Mother Superior had finished giving Dawn the gestapo treatment.

She broke her glare-off with Sullivan and stared at her sensible shoes. He could bugger off. Right now, his disapproval was the least of her worries.

Getting stoned on unconsecrated communion wine hadn't been the smartest thing the four of them had ever done. But it had felt good at the time. Hiding in their dorm room with her three best friends—Faith, Dawn and Mercy—the giggly buzz of the alcohol had raced through her bloodstream, blurring all the jagged edges and making her feel euphoric. Until Sister Ignatius had marched in, thrown a complete hissy fit, and ruined everything.

The buzz was long gone now, but at least the killer hangover that she'd woken up to this morning had stopped her from having to contemplate the possible consequences of their actions. Until now.

She glanced at Sebastian, her older brother and guardian, who sat stoically beside her in his creased travel clothes and had arrived an hour ago. He looked remote and broody and indifferent, the way he always did.

While Faith's brother had given his sister a hug and told her 'not to worry, we'll figure this out,' Seb had shot Zelda his what-the-hell-have-you-done-this-time look, and then blanked her. He sat next to her now, as they waited their turn with Mercy and her parents and Faith and Mr. High and Mighty to get a roasting from the Mother Superior, still ignoring her. His booted foot tapped on the polished wood floor, the patient thud, thud, thud echoing in Zel's skull like a death knell in time with the loud ticks of the grandfather clock.

With his hair shorn off in a brutal buzz cut, his skin darkly tanned from his latest tour in the French Foreign Legion, the blank expression on his face neither angry nor consoling, Seb seemed like even more of a stranger than the last time she'd seen him. Four months ago, when he'd dropped her at St. J's after she and Mercy had spent the Christmas break at the Madison townhouse in Manhattan. Before Seb had headed off to his latest posting with the Legion. Or rather, before he'd run away from her. Again.

"It was only a few glasses," Zel whispered, attempting to get him to at least acknowledge her existence. "Iggy totally overreacted," she added, using the nickname she and her friends had coined for their least favorite sister.

Seb turned and blinked, as if surprised to see her there. Then shrugged. "Whatever, Zelda."

She slumped back against the uncomfortable bench seat, her panic increasing. He was wearing that weary scowl again, the one he'd worn when he'd sent her off to boarding school three years ago, despite all her pleas and protests and angry tears, and the two times she'd been expelled since and she'd been sent off somewhere new.

But this time was different she wanted to yell at him. This time she didn't want to leave. And she didn't want to return to the Madison Mausoleum. There was nothing left for her in their huge family home on Manhattan's Upper East Side anymore, the shadowy hallways and empty rooms as moody and miserable as her brother, and she'd finally figured it out.

She glanced across at Mercy, whose cheeks glowed pink under her olive toned skin before her friend's gaze darted away. Mercy's mother whispered something in hissed Spanish while her father sat on her other side, stony faced.

I wish Mum and Dad were here to be mad at me.

Zelda swallowed down the choking feeling in her throat. The cramping pain in her stomach a cruel echo of the agony she'd been in three years ago.

It can't be happening again. I can't lose my friends now, too.

The four of them couldn't get chucked out of St. J's. She couldn't bear it. Faith, Dawn, and Mercedes were her only friends. They were all she had now. The other school misfits. Ever since she'd arrived at St. J's a year ago and been assigned to their dorm room, she'd bonded with them. Maybe not at first, because she'd been so hurt and angry and still determined to cause as much trouble as possible so Seb would notice her and let her come home. But gradually she'd come around, and figured out that all the things that made her friends strange to everyone else, made them fascinating and fun and perfect to her.

Mercedes' thick Argentinian accent, which they had all dedicated themselves to helping her lose. Her stalwart loyalty and passionate temperament, so unlike the demure expression she wore now for her parents' benefit. Faith's quiet grief, and dogged determination, the incredible pictures she drew and the funny stories, which Zelda would beg her to tell them all late at night, about growing up over her family's Irish pub in Brooklyn. Dawn, the scholarship girl, who the other girls teased because she was tall and gawky and who Sister Bridget had said they should all respect with a sneery tone in her voice that really meant the opposite. But who Zelda and Mercy and Faith knew was really super smart and super witty. All those things made them the closest thing Zel had now to family. Zel, the bad girl, who spoke with a British accent the rest of the school accused her of faking because she'd been born in New York, who'd been expelled from two boarding schools in the UK already and who had only got to go back to her family's townhouse in Manhattan for Christmas with Mercy in tow after begging her brother for months.

Of course, this wasn't the first time she'd lost herself in that special buzz that only alcohol could offer. That had been the afternoon of her parents' funeral. Age thirteen. When she'd discovered the drinks cabinet at her aunt's house in London and gotten hammered while Seb, only recently returned from the hospital, had been locked in his bedroom upstairs, brooding and ignoring her.

That had been a bad hangover, but not as catastrophic as this one. Who knew that two hundred year old brandy was a lot less hard on the head than the wine the sisters at St J's used for communion. Then again, Mercy—whose family were celebrated vintners in Argentina—had warned them, declaring it was not a good vintage before they'd all chugged their first glass.

Zelda had had her sixteenth birthday two weeks ago, but she suddenly felt a million years old as the door to the Mother Superior's office opened, and Dawn appeared, her shoulders bowed, her face a sickly shade of grey and her eyes shiny with unshed tears. Dawn must have a killer hangover, too, because she looked really crappy. Then again, Zelda had a vague recollection of her looking pale and shaky last night, after locking herself in the bathroom, even before they'd started drinking.

"Go to your dorm and collect your belongings," Sister Ignatius announced.

Dawn's being expelled? No, no, no.

Panic hammered at the pain in Zel's temples. But as Dawn nodded, the nun added. "When you come back from your suspension, you will bunk with the year fours. To show you the meaning of humility and sobriety."

Relief gushed through Zel. Dawn was okay. Suspension wasn't the worst that could happen. If they didn't expel Dawn, they couldn't expel the rest of them, because they'd all made a pact not to tell who had stolen the wine. And Zel knew none of her friends would rat, no matter what the

Mother Superior threatened them with.

Screw her.

Because they'd made a pact, they were one for all, and all for one, just like the Musketeers.

Dawn sent Zel a weary smile, that seemed to want to say everything would be all right but wasn't too sure. Zel smiled back, even though it made her head hurt.

Zel heard Mercy's mother whisper something else across the hall, but she didn't look round as Sister Ignatius approached her and Seb.

"Mr. Madison, thank you for coming. The Mother Superior will see you both now."

Seb nodded as the Sister headed back towards the office at the end of the hall. His once warm, brown eyes were empty though when he turned to her. Black holes of nothingness in his darkly tanned face. As empty as they'd been three years ago, when he'd been eighteen and broken, in body and soul, and she'd sat by his hospital bedside and bawled like a baby, praying that her brother would be okay—only to discover the brother she'd once known was never coming back when he finally regained consciousness.

The thin scar that cut into Seb's lip twitched as he stood up. "Let's get this over with."

She stood, brushed her uniform kilt with trembling hands, and prayed it wouldn't be the last time she wore it. Her belly bottomed out as Seb strode off ahead of her, the heavy boots thumping against the polished wood like the toll of the doomsday clock. She caught Faith's eye. Faith smiled, but like Dawn, her smile looked worried. And forced.

Then Zel made the mistake of making eye contact with Faith's hard-ass brother again, who was still glaring at her as if he were Superman trying to drill through lead.

The hot pool of anger that had been bubbling under her breastbone ever since she'd discovered she would never see her parents again erupted without warning, and the burning desire to wipe that pissy look off his handsome face consumed her.

Who was he to judge her? Just because he was older and bigger and a guy and had done a few years of law school, and probably had every girl in Brooklyn, swooning over those wide shoulders and that dark messy hair, which curled around his ears and made him look kind of hot.

He didn't know shit about her, or her life.

She lifted her chin and stuck her tongue out at him, swaying her hips for all she was worth.

He went rigid, those forbidding brows drawing down in anger.

Up yours, arsehole. Like I care what you think of me.

The emerald glare went nuclear as he gripped his knee, the knuckles whitening as the grey fabric of his suit pants wadded up under his fist and he exercised every last ounce of his self-control to keep from leaping up and doing... Something.

Heat blasted across her backside, the phantom slap he couldn't deliver thrilling her as she sent him her best screw-you grin and headed after Seb. But she could feel Tyrone Sullivan's glare blazing down her spine all the way to her bottom, as she sashayed down the darkened corridor towards the door marked Principal's Office. The tips of her breasts and the hot spot between her legs throbbed deliciously with a thrilling combination of defiance and excitement, the heady rush of adrenaline as intoxicating as the wine the day before.

Mr. High and Mighty might be an arsehole, but at least he'd noticed her.

But then she stepped into Mother Superior's office, the cloying aroma of lavender polish and incense and old leather wrapping around her like a shroud, and the buzz died. The dim lighting made the place look like a tomb. The small elderly woman rose from behind her desk like a black crow, compounding the horror movie effect. Nausea galloped up Zel's throat, and the pounding pain behind her eyes threatened to split her skull in two.

Just lie through your teeth and everything will be okay. They can't hurt you if you don't care.

✦

IT TOOK LESS than five minutes for her to discover that lying didn't help. And that they could hurt her. Especially her brother. And she couldn't do a thing to stop them, because she was just as powerless and pathetic now as she'd been at thirteen.

And she was still dumb enough to care.

Chapter One

Ten years later, Brooklyn.

TYRONE SULLIVAN CRACKED open an eyelid as the jaunty jingle of Irish pan pipes and fiddles blasted him out of a dream starring Mila Kunis and a quart of Rocky Road ice cream. Darkness and the gentle sway of the Brooklyn Bay registered alongside the throbbing in his groin, before the fiddles and pipes returned.

What the hell was his brothers' band doing playing on his house barge in the middle of the freaking night?

The fiddle and pipes stared up again. And memory flashed, flushing out the last images of Mila dripping ice cream.

Son of a bitch, his youngest brother Finn had loaded the band's signature tune onto his iPhone as the ringtone yesterday when he'd gone 'round to Finn's new place to share a beer after work.

Ty bolted upright. And pain exploded across his left eyebrow at the exact same moment he remembered he'd zoned out on the house barge's cramped front bunk while reviewing his latest case—a single mom battling an eviction notice in Bensonhurst—instead of making it to the bed in the back.

He groped for the phone, his boner deflating as all thoughts of Mila vanished in a puff of agony.

"This better be good," he growled into the phone as he rubbed his now throbbing brow and swung his bare feet to the floor.

"Is this Tyrone Sullivan? Faith's brother? The attorney?" The woman's voice sounded clipped and tense.

"Sure, who is this?" The cut-glass accent seemed to originate from the Upper East Side by way of Buckingham Palace, so whoever the woman was, she sure as hell wasn't a potential client. And why the heck was she calling at, he checked the phone's clock—two o'clock in the goddamn morning?

'It's Zel.'

Huh? 'I don't know anyone called Zel.'

She cleared her throat. "Sorry, Zelda Madison, I'm a friend of your sister Faith's. We met once at St. John the Apostle Academy. You probably don't remember me, but I…"

"I remember you." He cut off the hurried explanation as shock was edged out by temper, and the weird pulse of heat in his crotch—which had to be a layover from Mila and the Rocky Road.

Even if he could have forgotten how this woman had nearly got Faith expelled from the boarding school his old man had saved every penny to pay for, he could hardly have missed how her antics had been plastered over the tabloids, not to mention every scandal sheet and glossy magazine in the country, ever since her misspent youth. Not that he read that shit himself. But the woman was legendary, or rather notorious, for her bad choices and her even worse behavior.

An American ambassador's daughter who'd had every privilege known to man—and woman—and every natural gift God could have given her. And she'd thumbed her nose at it all to indulge in an endless cycle of hedonistic parties, public lover's spats, drunken antics, and reckless misdemeanors.

The press, of course, loved her, with her outspoken personality, and that killer face and figure, especially when she'd managed to make an even bigger fortune out of her notoriety, falling into a high profile career as a model six years back, and becoming the face of some fancy shampoo that sold for a fortune in Bergdorf's but probably didn't smell any better than the two-dollar brand his mom had used. He despised people like Zelda, but he would have been able to ignore all that—her and her class weren't exactly on his radar—but for the fact he knew Faith had carried on being pals with her. Enough to have her deign to come to Sully's occasionally—and it stuck in his craw. Like

Faith needed to compare her life—spent doing good honest work while running his family's pub in Bay Ridge—with the all-expenses paid, high-class funfair of controlled substances, globetrotting decadence, and million-dollar shopping sprees that was Zelda Madison's useless existence.

But none of that explained why the woman was ringing him at two a.m. with that quiver of urgency in her voice.

"Excellent, I'm glad you remember me," she replied. "That saves me having to waste time making introductions." The cut-glass accent spiked his temper more.

He happened to know she'd been born in Manhattan—on the Upper East Side to be exact, in that massive Gothic townhouse where the Madisons had lived for generations. And while that may as well have separated her from the people he'd dedicated his career to represent by several million dollars of disposable income, the last time he'd looked, East Fifty-Second Street was still part of America, so why the Sam Hell did she talk with the crisp, holier-than-thou voice of a British royal?

"Doesn't it just." he muttered, knowing he was sounding surly but not really caring. It was the middle of the freaking night, he had a lump growing on his forehead the size of a baseball, and a bad case of sexual frustration thanks to the perfectly good erotic fantasy she'd just interrupted. Not to mention a single mom and four kids who were depending on his advocacy skills being razor-sharp for the court hearing he had tomorrow at nine. "So how about you cut to the chase."

"Um, well the thing is, I'm in a bind. A bind I'd sincerely appreciate your help with."

She had to be kidding. "Look, lady, if you've torn a fingernail or something, call Faith, you're confusing me with someone who gives a …"

"I'm not phoning Faith, because she's not an attorney. You are." Zelda interrupted, the hint of steel in the cut-glass surprising him. "Now will you shut up for two seconds and let me explain. I don't want to waste anymore of the desk sergeant's precious time. I've only got one phone call and you're it."

The desk sergeant? One phone call? What the fuck?

He straightened, his natural instinct to preserve liberty and protect a client, even one as unworthy as her, kicking in despite his better judgment.

"Okay, let's have it, Zelda. Where the hell are you? And what the hell have you done this time?"

He scrubbed his fingers through his hair as he listened to her explanation—which had more holes in it than a slice of swiss—while a chill shot down his spine. Damn it, did the woman have no regard at all for her personal safety? Then he scribbled down the address of the station house she'd been taken to by a couple of beat cops who had a lot more sense than she did.

The woman didn't need an attorney—she'd only been given a citation—she needed a damn keeper. And for tonight it looked like her keeper was going to have to be him. He tugged on his clothes in the dark, recalling her sticking her tongue out at him ten years ago, with the dancing light of challenge and defiance in her eyes. His palm twitched as he grabbed his wallet and car keys.

She'd needed a damn good spanking back then. Apparently that hadn't changed if the dumb stunt she'd pulled tonight was anything to go by.

It wasn't until he was stumbling up the marina's gangplank in the dark, though, en route to an assignment he was already regretting, that it occurred to him to wonder how the hell Zelda Madison had gotten his cell number.

Faith was a dead woman next time he saw her.

Chapter Two

"HEY, MS. MADISON, looks like your knight arrived, you wanna grab your stuff? Let's get you the hell out of here."

Zelda sent the burly middle-aged sergeant a blinding smile that she knew could knock out any man at three hundred paces—because she'd perfected it for photographers, advertising executives, and even the odd sugar daddy, over the last ten years.

"Thank you, Officer Kelly," she said, beyond grateful for his relaxed and amused response earlier in the evening to what could have been a very sticky situation indeed. "I appreciate everything you and your partner have done tonight."

Holding her head high, she did her best Paris Fashion Week walk as she followed him out of the empty interview room she'd been left in for the last hour, to contemplate what an idiot she was after Kelly had let her call someone to pick her up.

A someone who had sounded on the phone like he was a lot less relaxed and amused than Officer Kelly about the prospect of riding to her rescue.

Of all the people to have to rely upon, Tyrone Sullivan aka Mr. High and Mighty, would not have been her first choice. But given the circumstances, she hadn't had a lot of other options when Faith had given Zel her brother's cell number and insisted she give him a call.

"All part of the job." Officer Kelly smiled back at her showing a gold tooth. "We're here to protect and serve."

"Even stupid people?"

"Sure." He chuckled. "Them most of all."

The mild censure in his tone was the very least she deserved.

She hiked up the train of her evening gown as the walk of shame took her through the station house. The sound of a ringing phone, the tap of computer keys, and a parade of bold stares from the small number of officers on night duty followed her every step of the way making her humiliation complete.

"I'll leave you here." Officer Kelly stopped as they arrived at the door leading to the front desk at the station entrance. "Just don't do anything that reckless again, okay? Or at least not on my watch."

"You have my word." She crossed her heart with her little finger. "Pinkie swear."

"Good girl." He sent her a paternal smile, tipped his

hat, and left.

Pushing open the door, she noticed the tall lean man standing by the admitting sergeant's desk with his back to her.

The combo of worn T-shirt and jeans marked him out as a civilian, although the hipshot stance as he leant on the desk and chatted to the admitting sergeant made it clear he was more than comfortable in this environment. His unruly hair gleamed black under the fluorescent light, much darker than the chestnut curls of his sister Faith.

Tyrone 'High and Mighty' Sullivan, her knight in battered denim.

The unwanted pulse of awareness hit Zel in the solar plexus.

As her knight shifted to sign a sheet of paper handed over by the sergeant, she noted the magnificent width of his shoulders. Now in his early thirties, he'd gotten a lot more solid than the last time she'd seen him, scowling at her as she waited her turn to get eviscerated by the Mother Superior on her fateful, final day at St. J's.

Sucking in a calming breath, she strode towards him.

Her heels echoed on the concrete floor as she approached the desk and her knight whisked round. Bold, vividly green eyes alighted on her face. The spark of irritation was only marginally more annoying than the judgmental once over he gave her, his gaze snagging for a second on the jeweled bodice of her Versace gown.

"Hello Mr. Sullivan, thank you so much for coming," she said, keeping her expression blank. There was no point wasting her enslavement smile on a man who was making such a concerted effort to fire daggers of disgust at her.

"I've paid the fine," he said, neatly cutting off any more unnecessary pleasantries—the knife-edge in the tone sharp enough to slice through bone.

"You didn't have to do that," she said, trying her very best not to resent the high-handed attitude. "I just needed someone to…"

"You don't need a lawyer. It was only a citation," he said. "And anyway, I couldn't act for you, even if I wanted to."

"Why not?" she asked, hating the tiny quiver of vulnerability in response to his pissy attitude.

She prided herself on being strong in any given situation. But she'd just spent the last two hours sitting in a police station contemplating how much she'd relied on others in the last six years to organize her life.

Appearances to the contrary, she hadn't actually planned to get picked up at midnight on Manhattan Beach for disorderly conduct. Okay, going for a swim by moonlight to celebrate her decision to finally jack in her modeling career hadn't been her smartest decision of late. In fact, it had definitely been one of the dumbest. But the beach had been deserted, the hurricane-damaged residences that backed onto it apparently empty. And the feeling of freedom, of liberation, of excitement had overwhelmed her at the thought of how far she'd come. That she no longer needed to be at the beck and call of an army of publicists and stylists and agents and personal assistants to keep her life in order. She'd wanted to mark the moment—and the water had beckoned, cool and inviting in the muggy night, and edged by the magical twinkle of city lights on the opposite shore and the canopy of stars that shone through the smog.

And frankly, how could she possibly have known that one of those apparently dark, empty properties actually housed a couple of old biddies who spent their nights scanning the vicinity with telescopes on the lookout for runaway supermodels swimming in their underwear?

Sullivan's disdainful look became pitying, spiking her temper. "I work for the Legal Aid Society. I doubt your income would qualify." He slung a hand in his pocket, still sending her those you-are-such-a-waste-of-my-time vibes. "Plus there's a clear conflict of interest."

"Which is?" she asked, drawing herself up to her full height. At five-foot-eight, she rarely had to look up to speak to guys, especially when she added on the three inches supplied by the heels of her Laboutins. Ty Sullivan, though, still had a good two inches on her. And he was using every millimeter of his height advantage to look down his nose at her.

The bastard.

"I know you." He leant forward, invading her personal

space enough to overlay the scent of cheap disinfectant, vomit and perspiration that permeated the precinct house with the whiff of laundry detergent. "Personally."

"Yes, but it's fairly clear you can't stand me. So, where's the conflict?"

"It still qualifies," he said, not denying the accusation. But then what was the point, when those emerald bright eyes were firing rotary blades at her now, instead of just daggers.

He turned back to the desk sergeant. "I'll take Ms. Madison off your hands, Officer Benton. Give my thanks to Kelly and Mendoza too, for bringing her in so she didn't get mugged or worse." He sent her a cautionary look, as if she were a disobedient three-year-old. And she hadn't already thanked both officers personally. "Does she need to sign anything before we head out?" he added.

"Here you go, Ms. Madison." The sympathy in the sergeant's friendly, brown eyes made his hangdog face look comfortingly homely as he passed a form across the desk. "You be careful from now on, no more swimming at night. It's not safe. Or smart."

Zelda sent him her best 'aren't you a sweetheart smile' but before she could open her mouth to promise she would behave herself from now on, Ty Sullivan got there ahead of her. "She won't. I guarantee it."

Without another word, he gripped her upper arm and proceeded to haul her off the premises like a harassed parent corralling a wayward child.

Struggling to keep up with his long strides in her heels, the lamé gown wrapping round her legs like an anaconda, they were all the way down the steps of the station house before she managed to get over the shock of being manhandled enough to yank her arm out of his grip.

"Will you let me go. I can walk out on my own, you bloody baboon."

He shot her the self-righteous glare she recognized from ten years ago. The brittle contempt might have wounded a more fragile woman. Luckily Zelda Madison was not fragile.

"That's rich, princess. I just shelled out two hundred of my hard-earned dollars to pay your fine and get you out of the hole you managed to dig yourself into tonight."

She didn't miss the insinuation that her cash wasn't hard-earned. She took two deep breaths, crossing her arms over her chest, which heaved with exertion and indignation, in an attempt to quell the lava flooding her veins.

Eight hours ago she would have agreed with him—in a purely existential sense. Modeling might be physically demanding and emotionally grueling at times, but it was not going to change the world for the better. But after the night she'd had, and the amount of humble pie she'd had to swallow already, she was not in the mood to be patronized.

Still, she bit down on the urge to slap back. She'd woken him at two in the morning and he'd come. She would be contrite and magnanimous now if it killed her. "Which I greatly appreciate. And which I will pay you back as soon as I can get to a cash point."

"A cash point?" The icy disdain in his tone hit critical mass. "You mean an ATM. What's with the fake British accent? Real American not good enough for you?" he said, in the thick Brooklyn accent which seemed to have gotten even thicker for her benefit. "'Cause I happen to know you were born in Manhattan."

And had spent nearly all of her childhood in London while her father was a diplomat and then the American ambassador. Not to mention several years in a Swiss Finishing School and then the last eight living mostly in Paris, Barcelona, and Milan while not on assignment. And even though she had been born in New York, her mother had been British and Zelda held both British and American passports.

She also spoke five languages fluently. Two more well enough to get by in. But unfortunately none of them had the surly Brooklyn twang that would make her a 'real American' in Tyrone Sullivan's judgmental eyes. Sullivan's accusation reminded her of the year at St. J's when all the other girls except her friends had delighted in mocking her 'snooty accent'. But she didn't intend to bother enlightening Sullivan now by explaining why she spoke the way she did. Because she'd learned at the age of sixteen, while sitting in the Mother Superior's office, being accused of things she hadn't done with her brother's hollow indifference making her stomach hurt, that if people insisted on assuming the worst of her, it was useless trying to defend herself.

She tapped her Laboutin on the sidewalk. "Fine, I will pay you back when I get to an ATM." She glanced around. "Now if you could direct me to the nearest taxi rank or subway station, I'll get out of your hair."

"The subway isn't running after midnight all this week, they're working on the line. And you're not catching a cab in that get up." His gaze seared down to her cleavage again with enough self-righteous superiority to seriously piss her off. "Where's your car? I'll take you to it, assuming you're not too hammered to drive," he added, sounding even more exasperated.

"I don't have a car. I don't drive," she replied, ignoring the snipe about her sobriety. Let him believe what he wanted to believe, he wouldn't be the first.

The sky was still defiantly dark behind the convenience store on the other side of the station parking lot, so she was probably several hours from dawn yet, and as her phone was dead and there was very little traffic, catching a cab was probably out. "When does the subway open?"

"If you're not catching a cab in that costume, you're not catching the subway either," he said as if he were the boss of her. "How the hell come you don't drive? What are you, the Queen of England?"

"No, I suspect the Queen probably drives," she managed, clinging to magnanimous by her fingertips.

She'd stopped driving after hitting a tree in Fontainbleau forest five years ago, in her brand new Jaguar convertible, while over-celebrating her twenty-first birthday with ten too many Kir Royales at La Coupole. The subsequent shots of her in a bloodstained T-shirt with the words 'Crazy Bitch' sequined across her bust had scored a full-page spread in Paris Match and been syndicated round the globe. She hadn't gotten behind the wheel of a car since. Obviously Mr. High and Mighty didn't read the tabloids though, so she didn't intend to enlighten him.

"Just out of curiosity, who put you in charge of my welfare?" The last thing she needed after taking five years to get free of her minders was another one. Especially one as pissy and rude as this one.

"You did." He shot back. "When you decided to haul me out of bed to deal with your latest drunken stunt."

"I wasn't drunk."

She hadn't touched a drop for five years—not that she cared whether he believed her or not.

He narrowed his eyes, not looking convinced. "Uh-huh? So what were you doing skinny dipping on Manhattan Beach at midnight?"

"I wasn't skinny dipping, I had underwear on."

"According to the desk sergeant your underwear consisted of three pinpoint triangles of red lace that became transparent when wet. In my book that counts as skinny dipping. You're lucky you didn't get raped."

She flinched. "The beach was deserted. There wasn't a soul about and I hadn't planned to come out of the water to find two patrol cops standing guard over my clothing."

"Doesn't sound like you plan a whole hell of a lot now, does it? Just, FYI, next time you're in a fix call one of your lackeys or, better yet, one of your brother's pricey legal team. I bet they've got a ton more experience dealing with your bullshit."

If she'd known she was going to get this much grief she would have. Despite the fact her brother would have given her that indifferent look that made her stomach hurt, and the presence of anyone from Goulding and Hatchard, the East Side lawyers Seb used for the Madison Foundation's business, at the Sheepshead Bay precinct house at three in the morning would have put her in grave danger of having the press alerted. Then again, arguing at top volume with a pill like Ty Sullivan right outside the station house probably wasn't helping to keep this debacle under wraps either.

"True, but you were closer and I thought you'd be a lot less conspicuous," she replied, keeping her voice as nonconfrontational as possible.

From everything Faith had ever told Zelda about her big brother Ty—and what she'd witnessed all those years ago in St. J's foyer—he was the stick-up-your-butt, hopelessly self-righteous, I-know-best type. And his current snotty reaction wasn't disabusing her of that fact. Plus she'd had more than enough run-ins with her own brother to know it was next to impossible to win an argument with a person who assumed they were always right simply because they sported a pair of testicles.

The only difference with Ty was that he seemed to be engaging his emotions in this debate, if the huffing and puffing was anything to go by. Unlike Seb, who never lost the controlled, detached, closed-off look that was his fallback position whenever they had a disagreement. Up until this particular moment, she would have believed she preferred the emotionally-engaged reaction… But at three a.m. while stranded in Brooklyn, with her hair looking like a bird had been nesting in it for days, and the two thousand dollar Versace gown she had been loaned for her red carpet appearance at the Foundation's charity gala in Manhattan last night, sporting unidentifiable stains on the hem courtesy of whatever was on the floor of the station house? Not so much.

She'd never been vain about her appearance. She knew her modeling career was a result of good bone structure, lucky metabolism, and her above-average height, all things she'd had nothing whatsoever to do with acquiring. Plus when she spent two hours in styling and then three hours posing for the camera, just to get a couple of signature shots, she knew how much of her success as a supermodel was down to her and how much down to the expert eye of the photographer or the talents of the makeup artist and hair stylist. But even so, Ty Sullivan's superior glare was starting to make her much more aware than usual that she did not look her best.

Figuring out how she was going to explain tonight's disaster to her sponsor at AA and then her brother was taking up enough of her diminishing brain power, after being awake for the last twenty-four hours. How she was going to avoid the handful of paparazzi who would probably be staking out the Mausoleum by now after hearing of her nonappearance at the charity gala was taking up even more. So she simply did not have the headspace to worry about what Ty Sullivan did or did not think of her.

"Conspicuous?" He barked. "Conspicuous how?"

"Conspicuous as in I don't want the tabloids getting ahold of this story if that's okay with you. I get enough grief from them as it is." And was liable to get a lot more when they discovered she'd decided not to sign her latest three million dollar contract with Fantasy, the hair care company who had employed her as the face of their signature shampoo brand for six years. The poor, little rich bitch tag had been one she'd worked hard to play down in the last five years; this stunt would not help that.

Ty looked momentarily taken aback by her explanation before his glare intensified. "You know what your problem is, princess?" he said, the grinding disgust in the tone suggesting that whatever her problem was, it wasn't one that was going to register on his 'problems that deserve my sympathy' list.

"No, but I'm sure you're going to enlighten me," she growled back. "Being as you're such a prince."

His eyes flashed with green fire and she remembered she was supposed to be doing contrite, not confrontational… A moment too late.

"You need to get the hell out of your ivory tower. If you lived with four kids under six in the Marlboro Projects and were fighting an eviction notice, like the client I'm representing in …" He pulled out his phone and checked the time. "Six hours. You'd have a real problem to deal with. Instead of whether you were gonna get splashed over the centerfold of the New York Post for some dumb stunt entirely of your own making."

Contrite came surprisingly easily at the mention of his client. The last of her temper fizzling out as she noted the lines around his mouth. The firm sensual lips pursed in a flat line of displeasure. He was right. He had a real job, with real consequences. And she was the one who had screwed up. While Faith had been the one to suggest calling him at this ungodly hour when she'd been on her way to the station house before her mobile had died on her, it would have been fairer and more honest to simply ring Seb and take the heat.

"Unfortunately, it doesn't matter where my ivory tower

is located," she said, resigned. "I'd still get stalked by the press."

"Don't kid yourself, if you were hanging out on my house barge, no way would you get caught by the press. But that's never gonna happen, because we're not big on ivory towers in Brooklyn."

The comment was delivered with such contempt; Zel's reflex action was instant and unstoppable. She might have been sober for five years, but her wild streak would never be completely tamed. Hence the decision to go for a midnight swim on Manhattan Beach to celebrate the sheer joy of finally escaping from the hollow, pointless world she had despised for so long. Or the impulse to call Ty Sullivan's bluff now.

"That's where you're wrong. I'd love to hang out on your house barge. Invitation accepted."

"Huh?"

He looked so surprised, his dark brows shooting up to his hairline, that she couldn't resist a wry smile.

Funny how everyone always assumed she'd led such a charmed life. When in reality, so much of it had been marred by the sudden loss of both her parents at the age of thirteen—and the subsequent disintegration of her once close relationship with her brother. Money was useful, and it would be disingenuous of her not to admit that having such a lucrative job had helped to paper over a lot of the cracks. But smiling for the cameras while she felt hollow inside, and never being able to stop long enough in one place to enjoy more than a few soulless shags in yet another anonymous hotel room, took its toll on a person's psyche, too… Not in the way grinding poverty did. So maybe she didn't deserve Ty Sullivan's sympathy. But she wasn't the shallow thoughtless egotist he had obviously pegged her as. Or at least she was trying hard not to be.

All she needed to do now was prove it. "Let's get going before the press finds us here."

"Hold up a minute…"

"It will be easier all 'round if I stay at your barge tonight. It will solve you having to worry about how I'm going to get back to Manhattan at this hour," she added, deciding to do the decent thing and help him out… as well as herself. Knowing his overdeveloped sense of responsibility, he would insist on driving her home and that would only make her conscience kick up even more of a fuss. Plus staying the night at his barge—under that surly wave of self-righteousness and disapproval—would be her penance for being such a monumental ninny and getting herself into this fix in the first place. "And don't forget you've got a wake-up call in five hours." She looped her arm through his, ignoring the pleasant flutter of reaction in her abdomen when his muscular forearm flexed under her fingertips—which was simply her normal biological response to a good-looking man. "You need your sleep, and I've taken up more than enough of your time." She directed him towards the car park, her conscience kicking up another notch when he relaxed and allowed himself to be led. "I don't want you fluffing your lines tomorrow," she continued. "Your client with four kids under six might get evicted from her Marlboro Project and then I'd have that as well as your sleep deprivation on my conscience."

Lifting the car keys he had looped over his thumb, she flicked the unlock button, and the tail lights on a shiny black SUV flickered across the lot.

When they got to the car, he stopped dead, those deep emerald eyes glassy with fatigue but strangely intense as they roamed over her face. "You sure about this? The barge isn't up to your usual standards." For the first time he sounded unsure, and more confused than pissed off, so she ignored the implied dig—and the misconception.

He had no idea how low her standards had sunk, before she'd gotten into the program. Back when she was sofa-surfing the fleshpots of Continental Europe and doing her utmost to lose herself in a haze of booze and other controlled substances, a house barge in Brooklyn would have been the height of luxury. Plus she'd always been surprisingly frugal and low maintenance, despite her often luxurious surroundings. Because she'd been born with a serious case of wanderlust, and she'd learned at an early age that material comfort could often mask an emotional wasteland.

That wanderlust had led her astray in her teens, when it had stopped being about enjoying new experiences and instead become a plea for attention or a uniquely self-destructive way of dealing with all the things in her life she couldn't control.

"Don't worry about me," she said, pulling open the heavy door of his SUV. "You won't even know I'm there."

"Yeah, right," he grumbled, giving her another steely-eyed once-over, which set off unfortunate sizzles of reaction all over her skin.

Seriously, what a shame the man was such a monumental grump, because he could bottle sexy with that glare.

"But if you'd rather not, I really don't have a problem waiting for the subway to open if you drop me there," she added, giving them both a final get-out clause.

She'd certainly been in worse places than Sheepshead Bay at the crack of dawn.

"Forget that. Faith would murder me." He climbed into the driver's seat and waited for her to get in on the passenger side. A maneuver that was less easy than it looked given that Versace hadn't factored SUV travel into the design of the gown.

Once she was finally settled, he turned on the ignition.

"But just so we're clear," he said. "You get the couch."

"Not a problem," she said graciously as he reversed out of the lot. "Take me to your house barge, Sir Galahad," she added, unable to resist teasing him, when he glared back at her across the console.

"Why do I get the feeling I'm gonna live to regret this," he grunted, before driving off into the night.

Chapter Three

TY JERKED OUT of a groggy dream, to the piercing beep of his iPhone alarm ringing in his ear. Hauling himself up, he scrubbed exhausted hands down his face. Jay-sus wept, as his pop would have said, his body ached as if he'd been hit by a truck last night.

Sunlight streamed into the snug cabin past the crack in the shutters and gleamed off the flat-screen TV anchored to the wardrobe at the end of the bed. He needed caffeine, preferably tongue-scorchingly hot and lots of it. Whipping back the sheet, he stared at his shorts. Weird, why had he kept those on? When he always slept in the raw in the summertime. The pulsing in his groin wasn't all that surprising though, given the freaky dream he'd been in the middle of involving Faith's fancy friend, Zelda Madison, emerging from the water on Manhattan Beach, buck naked. Freaky, psychedelic, and kind of disturbing, because it had been so vivid it had given him an epic boner.

Throwing on a T-shirt, he waited for the thing to deflate, before he tugged back the screen door. He strode into the boat's main living area, making a beeline for the coffeemaker, only to smack into an invisible wall when his gaze landed on the barge's couch.

Lying face down under a haphazardly slung sheet—one slender arm and one long, toned leg thrown over the side of the bunk and the graceful line of her naked back visible right down to the slope of her ass—was the star of his psychedelic dream. Looking real solid for a figment of his imagination.

"What the hell?" He whispered through chapped lips. Blood rushed into his groin and his head at exact the same moment, making his body sway into the tidal swing of the boat.

The apparition stirred, one slim shoulder shifting but then snuggling back into the bunk. Thank the Lord, the last thing he needed now was for his surprise guest to flip over and give him a full-frontal shot of her naked rack.

The unedited version of last night's trip to the Sixty-First precinct house flooded full-throttle into his foggy brain, clearing out the cobwebs faster than his mom on the warpath, back when he was a kid and watching a Yankees game with Pop and his brothers had left their living room looking like a bomb site.

While his temper spiked, the burning pulse in his crotch refused to die.

His dream was a reality and she looked dead to the

world. Probably because, just as he'd figured, she'd been wasted last night.

Of course, she'd seemed sober, but then he guessed party girls learned early how to hold their liquor. She must have been on one hell of a bender to have ended up swimming on Manhattan Beach, not to mention agreeing to come back and sleep on a house barge.

How tall was she? Too tall for the dimensions of the bunk it seemed. Her neck cricked at a funny angle under the pile of sunshine hair that had made her a fortune. Her signature feature puffed over her face in a cloud of blond fuzz, the long tangled tresses trailing over her slender shoulder and spilling over the side of the bunk in a golden waterfall. Like some fairytale princess from a storybook. The one with the hair in a tower with the weird name. He titled his head to one side, noticing her tattoo. A ring of black thorns circled her bicep.

The fantasy became dark and edgy and discordant.

Not a lot of fairytale princesses got caught skinny dipping in Brooklyn Bay.

And her hair didn't look anywhere near as well groomed as it did in the giant billboard ad that had looked down over Times Square last Christmas. But it did still look soft and tactile, reminding him of the summery scent that had invaded his SUV while they drove home together in the moonlight. That had to be some shampoo, able to keep her hair smelling that good even after getting dunked in the Bay and spending a night at the station house.

He shook the sentimental thought lose, while resolutely ignoring the dumb reaction in his crotch as he filled the kettle and headed for the shower cubicle in the barge's compact bathroom.

Twenty minutes later he was dressed in a crisp shirt and tie, and a dark blue Calvin Klein suit. He slicked his damp hair back as he gulped down his first shot of caffeine for the day and concentrated on stopping his dick from getting delusional.

His houseguest was still comatose on the bunk, the pile of hair and the pearly soft skin lustrous in the morning light. She was going to have one hell of a sore head when she finally came to. Although he would have gotten some satisfaction out of telling her 'I told you so', he figured it was probably for the best he wouldn't be here to see it. Quite apart from his dick's dumb reaction, something about that radiant, ethereal beauty, which could stun a man into speechlessness even in the middle of the night in the Sixty-First Precinct House, when they were sporting a fairly bad case of 'who the hell signed me up for this gig', really unsettled him. He hated to be predictable, and he had always despised women as high maintenance and high class and generally useless as Zelda Madison. It was lowering to realize that despite his crusading belief in defending the civil rights of the poor and huddled masses, that he should be as susceptible as the next guy to the woman's pampered, patrician beauty.

He jotted down a note and attached it to the table next to the couch, then dug through the week old pizza boxes and takeout cartons and the piles of court reports to find his case files for today and stuff them in his briefcase. One of these days he needed to find time to shovel out this dump. His mom would have killed him if she could see it now. To Kathleen Sullivan, a speck of dust had been considered a mortal sin.

He quashed the prickle of guilt and grief that always accompanied thoughts of his mother. After all, it hadn't been his idea to invite Zelda Madison, supermodel and high-society party animal, back for a visit.

He stole another glance at the woman in question before his breakfast Pop Tart popped out of the toaster. Grabbing the sweet treat to go along with his briefcase, he headed out the glass door onto the boat's deck, ready for another day of fighting for truth, justice, and the American way. And forced himself not to look back.

He'd be glad when the woman was gone. Out of his hair. He was going to have a hard enough time focusing in court today after she'd robbed him of a decent night's sleep.

She might be stunning to look at, but her reckless, irresponsible behavior made her a danger to herself and a liability to everyone else.

Fighting off the fogging feeling of fatigue, and dismissing the dying heat in his crotch, he took the gangplank two rungs at a time, busy justifying the lingering pulse of attraction while he keyed in the code to exit the marina's security gate. With his workload, he hadn't gotten laid in over eight months, and if he didn't count that weekend hookup after the office's Christmas party, with Shelly the court reporter which hadn't ended well, it was more like a year. He had enough responsibilities crammed into his busy schedule, to his clients and his family, without inviting any of Zelda Madison's unnecessary drama into his life.

Even so, he couldn't quite throw off the ripple of disappointment as he headed across the marina's parking lot towards the crosstown bus—at the thought that when he returned this evening, his uninvited houseguest would be long gone.

You can call a cab from the convenience store across the lot. If you want to return the two hundred dollars, don't get the money out of the ATM in the store, it isn't safe, just mail a check or hand it to Faith next time you're in the pub. The code to exit the marina is 1562.

TS

Zelda squinted at the neat, black script on the Post-it note stuck to the table next to the bed, inches from her nose. Clearly Ty Sullivan had not wanted to risk her missing his little missive… Or the hefty hint that he expected her to be well and truly gone by the time he returned. Or the even heftier hint that he thought her completely incapable of making even the most basic arrangements without a string of condescending instructions from him.

Holding the sheet up to her breasts, she slid her feet off the narrow bunk which also doubled as a couch. And sniffed the delicious scent of fresh caffeine in the air. Spotting the coffee pot nestled in the corner of the small kitchenette behind an empty carton of Pop Tarts, she circumnavigated the law books stacked 'round the table to get to it. Finding no clean mugs in the cabinet, she washed out one of the dirty mugs soaking in the sink, then nuked the black coffee in the microwave after deducing that the crumbs, which coated the inside of the machine, were fairly harmless. With the sheet draped around her, she cradled the coffee in her hands and propped her butt on the countertop to survey the compact living area of the barge in the daylight.

The space wasn't huge, but it would have looked a lot more spacious if it weren't for the mountains of crap everywhere. An explosion of paperwork covered all the available flat surfaces while dirty dishes doused with cold soapy water were piled high in the sink. As if someone had been on the verge of actually washing up only to be interrupted by a zombie apocalypse.

The wet room that doubled as a bathroom was small

and muggy and smelled disconcertingly of Ty's cologne and pine-forest scented shampoo—which she borrowed to wash her hair. The bedroom at the back of the barge—which had an unmade double bed taking up most of the space—looked like even more of a bombsite than the living area. Clothes draped an easy chair and lay in mounds on the small amount of available floor space, having been dumped everywhere but the basket in the corner—which remained defiantly empty. Either Ty Sullivan was a terrible shot, or he had simply not bothered to put anything away. Ever.

She raided his wardrobe for something to replace her stained Versace gown. Amid the stacks of clean shirts and underwear in their laundry paper, she finally located a secret cache of newly purchased white Fruit of the Loom shirts still in their plastic wrapping. The large V-neck cotton tee hung down to mid-thigh and made a rather snazzy mini-dress once she had belted it with one of his silk ties.

After digging for twenty minutes, she failed to find a hair dryer or anything resembling a hair brush, so she had to settle for attacking the tangles in her damp hair with the tiny comb she'd found in the bathroom—because the man obviously had a religious objection to conditioner. Cursing the unruly and uncooperative bird's nest of blond tangles, she glared at her reflection in the bathroom mirror.

Her hair had become a symbol of everything she had

come to hate about her life and her modeling career. When she was first sober it had been important to her to keep her job. Because she had needed at least some semblance of stability and continuity, and she had wanted to prove she could still function in the environment in which she had once floundered so spectacularly.

Confident in her sobriety now, she didn't need to validate herself and her decisions anymore. She had earned more than enough money in the past five years to give herself time and space to find a new career that would finally fulfill the burning need inside her to do something useful with her life.

Selling hair care products didn't quite cover that.

But she wished now she hadn't been quite so rash and euphoric last night after speaking to her agent for the last time.

The decision not to step out of the limo when it had arrived at the red carpet event—and she'd seen the barrage of flashbulbs firing at the actress who had stepped onto the carpet ahead of her—had felt justified at the time. Now it felt reckless and immature. She'd made a commitment to attend the event that she should have followed through on. The decision to tell the limo driver to keep on going and take the expressway out of Manhattan and into Brooklyn was considerably more idiotic, because it would be construed in the press as another sign of her wild behavior. And be accompanied by the usual heated speculation about whether she was back to her wicked ways.

Well, she wasn't. But she had no desire to face the furor just yet.

If she could stay in Brooklyn, incognito on Ty Sullivan's house barge, where no one would find her, over the Labor Day Weekend, the headlines would have time to die down. She would have to do a press conference once the news got out that she'd ditched Fantasy shampoo's generous new contract offer. But their PR people were still chasing her agent—and no way would Bob tell them she had let him go, because she was the only big client he had. So she had a few weeks grace before the story hit the headlines.

She dumped the comb into Ty's minimalist grooming supplies, conceding defeat as it resolutely refused to make any inroads into the thatch of tangles. Another good reason why deciding to take that midnight swim had not been her brightest idea to date.

She knotted her hair like a hunk of rope and headed into the living space to find her purse.

Ty was going to be less than pleased to find her still here when he got back. His note had been fairly clear on that score. So she'd have to try a lot harder to schmooze him than she had last night. Surely the man could not be as schmooze proof as he appeared. She glanced around the messy house barge. Maybe there was a way she could get into his good books while he was out fighting the good fight for the people of the Marlboro Projects.

He thought she was a princess, a high-maintenance lush who couldn't and wouldn't do for herself. What better way to prove him wrong than to give the barge the spring clean it so desperately needed? Especially as she planned to live here too for a few days and ever since she'd been sober she'd become a bit manic about keeping her living space meticulously clean.

From the stack of pizza boxes and takeout cartons stacked on top of his kitchen bin, which she shoveled into a black plastic bag, he also didn't eat much other than junk food. She'd go to the market, there had to be one around here. She happened to be an excellent cook, because she'd taken classes while finding other things to do instead of partying all night. And if there was a way to schmooze the unschmoozeable Mr. Ty Sullivan maybe it was through his stomach.

Leaving the barge, she dumped her first sack of rubbish into the dumpsters by the security gate and headed out of the marina.

First things first. Her phone was dead. She needed to get it charged so she could call her AA sponsor. Walking out on her modeling career was a decision she'd already discussed in depth with Amelie, but she needed to tell her about last night's escapades. Her sobriety always had to be her first concern and she wanted to be sure that the midnight swim wasn't in any way a sign of her losing control.

It hadn't felt that way at the time—it had felt like a statement of purpose and empowerment, of joy and freedom from the things that had shackled her for too long. But still, she'd be happier once she had Amelie's input.

Then she needed to track down her nearest meeting. If she was going to be in Brooklyn for a few days, she needed to find one nearby. And then she would get to the market. She could leave off calling Seb until she returned to the Masoleum. If he was true to his usual form, he'd be unlikely to even notice that she'd gone missing.

But after leaving the marina and crossing the parking lot onto Knapp St., she spotted the red and white spiral of a barbershop on the opposite corner of the junction. She crossed over to the shop and surveyed the massive beehive on her head making her reflection in the window look like Quasimodo.

She strolled into the shop. A chubby man sat in one of the chairs, his face swaddled in a hot towel as the barber cleaned an old-fashioned straight-blade razor.

"Good morning, *kochanie*, are you lost?" The thin white-haired barber smiled at her, as he wrapped the razor carefully in a cloth.

"Not if you do haircuts here." She smiled back when his paternal gaze took in the mess on her head.

"I do only men's haircuts. Maybe you try the ladies stylist in Cherry Hill?"

"No need." She climbed into the chair next to his customer who was peering at her from the depths of the hot towel with as much curiosity now as the barber. “No styling necessary. Just chop it all off.”

His bushy grey eyebrows launched up to his receding hairline. “Are you sure?” He untied her hair and ran his fingers through the knotted strands as best he could, arranging it across her shoulders and letting it fall down her back.

The heavy weight felt cloying, not unlike the last few years of her career as a supermodel. Cloying and vain and vacuous.

“It is very beautiful,” he murmured, stroking the hair between his fingers as if testing the texture.

No it isn’t. It’s a burden.

A burden she no longer needed. Or wanted. Her hair was the last of the remnants from her old life. She wanted it gone now she was finally ready to make a new start. Not just as a sober person. But as a person who had purpose beyond the pursuit of vanity and fame and money. This was part of the old her. A part she hadn’t been able to lose straightaway, but one she was more than ready to lose now.

Plus she couldn’t think of a better way to stop herself getting recognized than to lose the one thing that had become such an important part of her brand.

“I’m positive.” She smiled at his reflection, already feeling lighter inside. “Hack away.”

Chapter Four

TY GRAPPLED ONE-HANDED with the knot on his tie as he closed the marina's security gate. The sun scoured the worn uneven boards as he made his way down the rickety gangplank to the boat dock. Sweat slicked his brow as he tugged off the tie and shoved it into the pocket of the suit jacket slung over his arm. His stride corrected itself naturally to the rocking as he walked past the haphazard row of barges moored to the dock, the soft thunks as they jostled together matching the gentle thud of his footsteps. This was what he loved about living on the barge. The peaceful oasis in the middle of Brooklyn. But right now he was ready to crash headlong into bed.

Damn, this had been the longest day ever. He'd barely been able to keep his eyes open during his last case. Luckily, the plea on behalf of a group of small businesses facing the foreclosure of their loft in Red Hook had been straightforward, because he'd done his homework. But he needed to sleep for ten hours straight now.

He sent up a small prayer of thanks for the long weekend. He needed the break.

He waved at Mr. Genero as he passed the retired traffic cop's barge. The old guy was sipping a beer on his deck with his fishing line over the bow like he did regular as clockwork every Friday evening at six o'clock—even though to the best of Ty's knowledge he'd never caught a thing.

"Hey, Mr. G. Getting a jump on the Labor Day weekend? Maybe you'll get lucky and catch something this evening?"

"That's the general idea, sonny." The guy lifted his can of Bud in a familiar salute, and Ty cracked a smile in return. He was thirty-two, a qualified attorney with three years' experience working for the Legal Aid Society, and the oldest of five grown children, but he'd always be sonny to Mr. G.

"Although, even if I catch a fifty-pound tuna, I'm not gonna get as lucky as you this evening." Mr. G's genial smile took on a saucy tilt. "Caught yourself one hell of a looker this time out. If I was forty years younger I'd fight you for that sweet girl myself."

A looker? Sweet girl? Who the hell?

And then it dawned on him. The heat which had been lying dormant most of the day seared his insides at the vision of just who had been sleeping naked in his barge when he'd left that morning.

Obviously the old guy had spotted Zelda leaving. The

pulse of heat was quickly tempered by the tug of regret. Which he ignored. The last thing he needed or wanted was some high maintenance princess messing with his weekend of R and R.

"If you were forty years younger, you'd beat me to her for sure," he shouted back, enjoying the old guy's chuckle if not the annoying heat in his crotch which refused to die.

Perhaps he should see about getting some real sex over the next couple of days. Because all the fantasy sex he was having wasn't exactly taking the edge off. But even as the thought occurred to him, he remembered Shelly giving him a roasting for forgetting to call and knew he couldn't hit on her again. He'd tried real hard not to mislead Shelly, and told her straight out he wasn't looking for anything too heavy. But when he slept with a woman, he owed her respect. His mom had drummed that into him and his brothers as a kid. So calling Shelly again felt wrong.

He only had room for one passion in his life at the moment. And that was the law and what he could do with it to help the most vulnerable members of his society. Getting laid would have to wait until he had enough downtime in his schedule to date properly and start the search for his Miss Right, a woman who would have the same background and priorities and ambitions and unshakeable work ethic as he did.

He gave a weary sigh—but given his current workload, he'd be unlikely to find enough downtime in his schedule to hit on Miss Right until his fiftieth birthday. No wonder he'd gotten a little sidetracked by Zelda and her spectacular rack.

He swung open the low gate on the house barge's front deck and stopped, disconcerted by the sight of the two deck chairs he'd had stashed in the back, now out and proud and furnished with plump pillows. Where had those girly cushion covers come from? And what had happened to the mound of beer cans he'd been saving to take to the recycling? Or the used battery that doubled as a footrest?

Then he turned to the barge's sliding glass doors, and the sunshine glinting off the glass nearly blinded him. He did a double take, to make sure he hadn't walked onto the wrong barge. But no, this was his boat, the sign with his name and the slip number to the right of the door confirmed that.

He frowned. Why the heck was the brass nameplate gleaming like a brand new penny, too?

He scrapped his hair back from his brow. And wrenched open the door which wheeled across so fast it cracked against the wall. Hang on, why didn't it stick anymore?

Okay, what the hell was going on here? Had he been visited by the Neat & Tidy Fairy?

Before he could answer that puzzling question, he got sidetracked by the bright, airy, well-ordered living space and the scent of furniture polish which nearly asphyxiated him.

What the ever-loving fuck has happened to my stuff?

The desk which usually overflowed with case reports and law tomes was cleared of all debris, the polished laminate matching the manic sparkle of the stainless steel appliances in the small kitchenette. The checkerboard pattern on the tiled floor gave him another start, winking at him like the centerpiece for a floor polish commercial. He blinked, confused, until he realized the reason the pattern looked unfamiliar was because he hadn't seen it in months.

The scent of fresh herbs and citrus fruits accompanied the clean smell of air-freshener and polish, drew his gaze to the array of cold cuts and fancy salads laid out enticingly on the low table by the bunk Zelda had been occupying that morning. Damn, his whole place looked like it had been dressed for the cover of *House Beautiful* magazine.

Had he entered an alternative reality? Dropped through a wormhole in time like Doctor Who?

A rich, smoky, soulful voice singing a recent R and B track at half-speed floated through the uber-clean and un-dusty air from the far end of the barge. Then the woman he'd been trying real hard to erase from his consciousness stepped into the living space from the bedroom.

She halted in the doorway, her arms full of neatly fold-ed bed linen, and the slow seductive rendition cut off abruptly.

Holy shit.

Zelda Madison was still here.

Or at least he thought it was Zelda Madison. How could it be an apparition– with the heat loosening the muscles in his abdomen at an alarming rate? But even though she had Zelda's height and elegance, those striking midnight blue eyes and mile long legs, the short white sundress she wore barely covering her butt looked a lot like one of his new Fruit of the Looms, instead of the fancy designer couture from last night.

And she was bald as a baby.

'Hello, you're home a bit earlier than I expected.' The crisp upper-crust accent sliced through the fog of shock and sent a surge of temper through his tired limbs to combine with the unwanted shot of heat.

"Where's all my stuff?" His gaze lifted to her hair, which he realized now wasn't completely gone but sat in short, sassy waves cropped close to her head, framing that remarkable face and turning her cheekbones into a work of art. "And what the fuck happened to your hair?"

✦

ZELDA TOUCHED HER fingertips to the short curls, reminding herself, and not for the first time that day, that her hair was now as short as a boy's. Or rather one of Jakub Pawel's regular customers. The first sight of her new hair cut had shocked her a little, so it was probably no surprise that Mr. Grumpy was staring at her as if she'd grown an extra head.

But even so, did he have to look quite so ruggedly

handsome in his creased shirt and suit trousers with that fierce scowl on his face?

Apparently Ty Sullivan's demeanor hadn't improved a bit from last night. If anything it had gotten worse. And all her efforts at schmoozing him by spending the better part of six hours sifting through, clearing out and/or filing away his precious stuff had not had the desired effect.

She took a deep breath to contain the urge to tell him where he could sling his crappy attitude. She needed him on her side if she was going to get him to agree to let her camp out here for the next three days.

She let her hand drop from her hair. Refusing to be intimidated by the glare of disapproval as she placed the sheets in the cupboard by the bathroom door. One thing she was not going to be was defensive. "I had it cut by Mr. Pawel at the barber's shop on Knapp St. I think he did an excellent job."

Ty dumped his briefcase on one of the chairs next to the small table at the end of the space and then slung his jacket across the back. She curbed the urge to tell him to put his briefcase away and hang the jacket up in the bedroom wardrobe—where it belonged, next to the rest of his newly dry-cleaned suits. She would not allow his slovenly habits to turn her into a neat freak… Or at least not until she'd schmoozed him into a weekend invitation.

"It looks…" His gaze roamed over her hair, and a wash of heat hit her cheeks, which was bizarre for two reasons.

She never blushed. And she had absolutely no interest whatsoever in what Ty Sullivan thought of her new hairdo.

"Cute," he said with more surprise than enthusiasm. "But how do you plan to earn your living now? Who's gonna shell out millions of bucks for an ad campaign for shampoo featuring a model with no hair?"

The critical comment sliced under her ribs like a knife. She let the quick stab of temper mask the idiotic hurt. What did she care what this self-righteous do-gooder thought of her career?

"Are you always such a charmer when you return from work in the evenings?"

No wonder he didn't have a girlfriend, or a significant other. What woman would want to spend time living in this dump with a grump like him? Not that she'd looked through his wardrobe for any signs of female cohabitants, particularly. She just happened to have gleaned that information in passing while gathering up his junk and doing his laundry.

"You want charming don't get me up at two a.m. in the morning." He glanced round the barge. "And don't mess with my stuff without my permission."

"If by your stuff you mean the decades-old takeout box from Mr. Po's Chinese Restaurant or the very interesting substance I found bonded to the underside of your sink, I'd have to wonder what exactly is so precious about it."

"By my stuff, I mean the court reports and case files,

which I need at my fingertips. Where the hell are they?"

"Oh, you mean the paperwork that was doubling as a mountain range of crap the size of the Andes?" She flicked a regal hand towards the filing cabinet tucked under his desk which had been empty until she'd gotten to work. "They're filed in alphabetical order. You ought to be able to figure out how to find them," she continued, unable to resist the droll stare. "Assuming you know how to alphabetize." She slapped her hands together. "Now, why don't you wash up so we can have some supper. I found the fabulous Russian Market on Cherry Hill and made us some dinner that didn't come out of a box."

"Did I ask you to make me supper?" he countered.

The surly statement, delivered with the gruff murmur of righteous indignation was too much for a saint. And Zelda Madison had never been a saint.

The ungrateful son of a bitch. She'd worked her butt off today to clean up this crap heap, sort his laundry, file his precious paperwork, and even prepare a nutritious and delicious meal. And this was all the thanks she got?

She glanced at the plate of potato salad, nestled among the array of cordon bleu entrees she'd spent over an hour slaving over in his newly scrubbed kitchen. "I see. Are you telling me you're the only man in America who doesn't like potato salad?"

"That's not the damn point and you know it?"

"Fine." She scooped up a generous handful of potatoes,

homemade mayonnaise, capers, and pimentos. "If you don't want to eat it, how about you try wearing it." And let it fly.

It smacked into his forehead with a gluey plop and imbedded itself into his hair.

He cursed as he dug the cement-like mixture off his brow before it could drip down his face. "What the fuck is wrong with you?"

The laugh popped out without warning. He looked so furious, with his dark hair sticking up in an indignant tuft like a single devil's horn. "Oh, I don't know," she managed to get out 'round a slightly hysterical giggle. "Maybe it's that I've spent the whole day trying to make this place nice for you and you've got about as much gratitude as a spoilt two-year-old."

"Yeah?" The furious glare narrowed, going squinty round the edges, but then to her astonishment his sensual lips hitched up on one side in a challenging grin that made his misty green eyes sparkle with mischief. The sight took her breath away.

Good lord, Ty Sullivan was even more of a lady-killer when he bothered to smile.

Unfortunately she was too busy admiring the lopsided half-smile to clock the sly tilt to his lips, until one of her Caribbean crab patties splatted against her breastbone and dropped into her cleavage.

He sucked the crab paste off his thumb, the crooked

smile now a fully blown smirk. "Damn, this tastes pretty good." His grinning gaze wandered pointedly down to her boobs. "Looks great on you, too. You should wear it more often."

"You bloody, buggering bastard."

"Now, now, Miss Priss," he said, raising his hands as she armed herself by dipping a Ukranian dumpling in cream cheese. "You don't want to go messing up all your hard work," he added, chuckling at her aggrieved expression.

"Like you care." She hurled the dumpling, aiming for the spot on the center of his forehead again.

Unfortunately he ducked this time, and caught it in his fist. Then lobbed it straight back at her. She dodged to the side but cream cheese skidded off her eyebrow—proving he had a much better throwing arm than his empty laundry basket suggested.

It was a declaration of all-out war.

Suddenly patties and pastries were bulleting across the room, salami slices hurtling like discuses. Cream cheese and homemade guacamole exploded against the kitchen counter accompanied by the gasps and shouts and grunts of battle. She got in a couple of direct hits, but he was sneaky and fast and a much better shot. She redoubled her efforts until the ammunition ran out. He made his move while she was stooping to scoop some tabouleh off the floor. Charging her, he trapped her throwing arm, wrapping strong arms around her body. They crashed onto the bunk together in a hail of herbs and spices, his hoot of triumph echoing around the barge with the peals of her laughter.

Manacling her wrists above her head, he settled on top of her. "Gotcha, you hellcat."

Tears had formed in his eyes; he'd been laughing so hard, giving the misty green added sparkle.

"Look what you've done to my minidress," she cried, trying for outrage, but failing miserably thanks to the breathless giggles bubbling out of lips coated with… She swiped her tongue across her bottom lip … Mmm, Hungarian hummus.

His gaze locked on her mouth, the husky chuckles cutting off. The searing appraisal trailed down to her cleavage napalming everything in its path. Her breasts heaved, swollen and heavy, pinned down by the hard contours of his chest.

"Uh-huh?" he murmured. "Funny how your minidress looks mighty familiar."

She squirmed, but he had her caught fast. Not just by the weight of his body, but the mesmerizing intensity on that harsh handsome face. The dimple in his cheek looked particularly incongruous for a guy who, until ten minutes ago, she would have sworn walked around with a stick permanently shoved up his butt.

The ragged pants of their breathing added spice to the scent of freshly chopped coriander hanging in the air.

Her nipples puckered into rigid peaks, the lack of a bra suddenly very obvious with the thin cotton of his T-shirt soaked in papaya juice.

"I can't think why?" she countered, the weight in her abdomen sinking low. She widened her legs, her thighs straddling his hips so the satisfying bulge forming in his trousers could settle against her aching clit.

"Yeah? I'm thinking I should ask for my Fruit of the Loom back." The comment was gruff and surprising. Who knew Ty Sullivan had a naughty streak?

She rocked her hips, suddenly desperate to feel that heavy length inside her.

She hadn't had sex in months. Not since a one-night fling with the photographer on her last photo shoot in Rome—which had turned sour when he'd offered her a line of cocaine to complement her afterglow.

"You want it back," she dared. "You're going to have to take it back."

"Don't think I won't."

"All I hear is talk," she challenged, loving the flare of his nostrils.

Holding her wrists in one hand, he kept his eyes locked on hers as he lifted the hem of the T-shirt. His hand swept up to cup one naked breast. She arched her back, loving the feel of his callused palm as the nipple swelled and hardened.

"Damn, but you're beautiful," he said, on an anguished

sigh.

She'd been called beautiful before, but never with that rough combination of desire and stunned disbelief. The evidence that he didn't want to be attracted to her, was like a red rag to a bull.

She tugged her hands from his grip and sank her fingers into his food encrusted hair to draw his mouth down to hers. She licked and nipped against the seam of his lips, until he opened for her. Thrusting her tongue inside, she directed the kiss, until his tongue tangled with hers and a dance of dominance and surrender began. The battle for supremacy became wild and reckless until they broke apart, the pants of their breathing deafening despite the rumbling hum of the conditioning unit.

Suddenly they were wrestling their clothes off. He hauled her up, dragged the stained, sodden T-shirt over her head. She scrambled to unzip his suit pants. Buttons popped as she wrenched his shirt apart to glide her hands down the tensed muscles of his abs and into his boxers. She pushed the waistband down, relishing his strangled groan as she wrapped her fingers round the thrusting erection.

God, but he was beautiful, too, so thick and long and hard, the circumsized head slick and ready with pre-come.

Somewhere a million miles away, a voice whispered 'this is Faith's uptight brother and you can't stand him'. But the voice was drowned out by the pounding ache in her pussy as he wrenched off her panties, then plunged his fingers into the hot wet folds and found her clit. She bucked and the heat coiled, tighter and tighter as he stroked and circled the hard nub with alarming proficiency. Cradling the back of her head, he yanked her up to lick a nipple, before sucking the peak to the roof of his mouth. Sensation, so sharp it was almost painful, arrowed down as his fingers continued to play, his thumb teasing the perfect spot.

She sobbed, choking on pleasure, as the coil burst free at last, radiating through her battered body in a devastating cascade.

"Jesus, I want you so much." His voice sounded hoarse, muffled by the buzzing in her head as he grasped her hips, and angled her pelvis, ready to plunge.

"Wait. Condoms? You need a condom." She slapped open palms against his chest, shaking fingers skidding off the oiled contours, as she pushed him back, her common sense bursting through the daze of afterglow.

"Shit. Yeah. Right." He levered himself up and, holding his trousers, his shirt tails flying, shot into the bathroom.

She heard more cursing, the crash of something hitting the cubicle floor, then he returned. He should have looked ridiculous with his shirt hanging open, his fly down, his trousers hitched up with one arm, the washboard lean abdominal muscles glistening with oil, his collarbone peppered with bulgar wheat, and his hair gelled with cream cheese… If he didn't look so fricking hot. And smell so totally delicious. Better than any three-course cordon bleu meal…

Or at least better than the one he was currently wearing.

"Here, let me." She took the foil package from his greasy fingers, ripped it open with her teeth and then rolled it on the massive erection.

Goodness, the man was seriously built in more ways than one.

He kicked off his trousers and boxers, then grasping her hips, settled between her thighs.

She stretched her arms up, flattening her palms against the top of the bunk, desperate to feel the punishing thrust that would bury his huge cock to the hilt and stop her from thinking about what the hell she was doing, banging Faith's uptight brother.

But as she braced for it, he stilled, the head of the erection nudging her entrance.

"You sure about this?" he asked, searching her face.

"Of course I am." She cried, ready to beg or threaten or, better yet, batter him if he stopped now.

But he only nodded and then thrust hard.

She gasped, shocked by the depth of his penetration, her sex struggling to adjust to the immense fullness.

"Damn, are you okay? Did I hurt you? You're so tight."

He sounded as shocked as she felt. But the concern on

his face was unsettling.

She let go of the bunk head to grab hold of tight muscular buns. “It feels marvelous. Now don’t you dare stop or I may have to castrate you.”

He gave a strained laugh and the moment of tenderness was gone. Thank goodness.

He pulled out, surged back, going even deeper, then established a devastating rhythm. The pressure built again slowly, surely, her sex clenching ’round the thick intrusion as his cock rocked against the perfect spot. Sweat slicked their bodies, dripping off him, his heavy testicles slapping against her bottom as his hips pistoned. The rhythm became faster, harder, more frantic.

She let go of his butt to find her clit, and stroke herself, desperate to come again ’round that thick girth before he climaxed. He sped up, his gaze locked on hers, in a furious race to the finish line.

“That’s it,” he said. “Make yourself come for me.”

She cried out, the sound echoing against the thin walls of the barge as sensation burst up from her core at his command. He grunted, then yelled, as he followed her over moments later, and collapsed on top of her.

Chapter Five

SHIT, SHIT, AND *double shit.*

Ty dropped his forehead against Zelda's shoulder, inhaled the light subtle flavor of her perfume—bergamot and citrus—over the scent of OJ, cilantro, and sweat-soaked sex, as his heartbeat punched his collarbone.

He slipped out of her, his body aching from the turbo-charged ejaculation, but kept his face buried in her neck as the last of the afterglow faded to be replaced by aftershock. The short strands of her hair tickled his nostrils as he struggled to bite back the groan of dismay.

Jesus H Christ. Had he actually just banged his little sister's fancy friend from here to next week? Not to mention slung food around his place like a five-year-old on a sugar rush?

He hadn't laughed so hard since he was a kid and his brother, Ronan, had managed to wedge his head in an empty whiskey barrel. There had been hell to pay when his mom had found them and all five of them had ended up going to bed with no supper and stinging butts, even his little sister, Faith. But he'd taken the brunt of the punishment, because he was the oldest and his mother expected him to be responsible and not let his brother stick his head in a whisky barrel on a bet.

Thoughts of his mother had the mortification slamming into him full force. He got up and grabbed his pants off the floor, tugging them on as a hefty dose of shame helped smother the last of the endorphin rush.

He'd lost control and banged a woman he barely knew. A woman who, until about fifteen minutes ago, he would have sworn he didn't even like.

He hadn't felt this guilty since he was twelve and he'd been caught by his pop paying Mary Jane Calhoun five dollars to look at her breasts behind the bandstand at the Fourth of July picnic.

Standing stiffly, he whipped off the condom before fastening his pants and heading to the bathroom, being careful not to look back at the object of his desire still lounging full length on the bunk.

He washed his hands and face, scrubbed a washcloth over his chest and picked the last of the pimentos out of his hair.

What the hell had he just done? Ever since the afternoon his mom had made him apologize to Mary Jane, he'd always tried to behave like a gentleman with women. But he'd just behaved like an animal with Zelda. Not to mention like a judgmental asshole.

He'd dedicated his career to helping the most vulnerable members of his society, and because of that, he'd thought he was a better person than Zelda could ever be. He'd decreed Zelda was wild and reckless and shallow, that her problems were down to the bad choices she'd made in her charmed life. And because of that, he'd persuaded himself she didn't rate his respect.

But he could see now his assumptions about her weren't the whole truth. In fact, he was beginning to wonder now if they were even half of the truth. How many supermodels spent the day shoveling out someone else's shit? Or looked just as stunning in a guy's T-shirt as they did in a designer gown? Or were totally cool about letting a Brooklyn barber lose on the signature, golden locks that had made them a fortune?

And if Zelda Madison wasn't vain or useless or a snob, how many other ways had he misjudged her?

He stared at himself in the bathroom mirror, forced to finally acknowledge the worst of it. He'd judged and criticized Zelda for her willful behavior—right back to that day ten years ago when his palm had itched to give her a spanking he'd decided she richly deserved—because the truth was her wild behavior had turned him on.

He returned to the living room intending to survey the damage. And apologize to Zelda, not just for jumping her but for being such a damn hypocrite.

Contrary to his expectations though, Zelda still lay on the bunk, naked and relaxed and watching him—and not looking at all shocked by his dickish behavior. What she looked was satisfied.

With one slim arm stretched above her head and the neatly trimmed curls covering her sex, proving she was a natural blond, she was a golden Salome, her slender body unashamedly displayed like a smorgasbord of carnal delights.

Despite his guilt, his cock perked right up again.

He tried to get it to behave. But the insolent look in Zelda's heavy-lidded eyes, bold and uninhibited, only made him recall how good it had felt to have her muscles milking him dry as she came.

"So, counselor,' she said. "Is it normal for you to be so talkative after sex?"

The wry comment, delivered in that snooty British accent had a smile cracking the rigid line of his lips.

"I'm sorry I messed up all your hard work," he said.

It must have taken her the better part of the day to get the place as spotless as she had, and he'd behaved like a total dick about that, too. Probably because he'd been so pissed about the shot of delighted lust that had seared him when she stepped out of his bedroom wearing nothing but that butt-hugging T-shirt.

"Are you? I'm not the least bit sorry," she replied, her gaze dipping to his waist.

The unlikely blush crawled across his collarbone like a Virginia Creeper.

He looked away. Out onto the dock. Hell, he hadn't even bothered to close the drapes. Mr. G could have walked past on his way to the trash receptacle and caught them banging each other senseless on the couch.

He walked over to close the drapes, then turned back to Zelda, her naked body now spotlighted by the sunlight shining through the side windows.

"I should also apologize for jumping you like that," he added. "I don't usually treat women with so little respect." The apology felt pretty hollow, seeing as he wasn't sure he regretted what he'd done. So, basically, he was guilty not just of balling a woman he barely knew but also guilty of lying about whether he felt sorry about it or not. If he ever got to Father O'Riley's confessional again in this lifetime, he'd have to say a few thousand extra Hail Marys.

"I'm not sorry about that either," she declared. "I enjoyed it immensely." She cocked her head to one side, studying him. "How fascinating, you're blushing."

The heat scalded the back of his neck, horrifying him a little more.

"Is that Catholic guilt?" she said. "I always wondered what it looked like when they tried to drum it into me at St. J's?" A wicked smile hovered, telling him she was having a heck of a lot of fun at his expense. "But really, you don't need to feel guilty. I don't. When it comes to respect, I'm all for respecting the restorative qualities of good, hard sweaty sex. Clearly we both needed a good shag. And as God in his infinite wisdom made you so shaggable, I considered it my divine duty to jump you at the first opportunity."

Had she jumped him? He was pretty sure he'd jumped her. But now he wasn't so sure.

"And as for showing respect for me as a woman," she continued. "I think you and your phenomenal cock both excelled yourself."

Damn but the woman was as badass as she was beautiful. A laugh choked out at the outrageous statement, as his admiration for her increased. "Good to know."

"Isn't it though," she said, the cheeky grin on her face easing his guilty conscience considerably as she got up from the bunk.

"You want to grab the first shower?" He gestured to the bathroom, not quite able to take his eyes off her, even though he knew he should if he wanted to exert some semblance of control over the new erection pressing against the front of his pants. "I can clear this mess up and then dig out another …" He coughed judiciously… "Minidress for you?"

"Sounds like a plan."

His gaze got momentarily fixated on those cherry ripe nipples bouncing enticingly as she strolled towards him. He jerked his gaze back to her face trying not to behave like a teenage boy who'd just scored his first copy of *Playboy*. Or paid for his first chance to see what the opposite sex had on their chests.

Unlike what he could remember of Mary Jane, Zelda wasn't all that well-endowed, her breasts small and firm in keeping with that long slender frame. But he knew more than a couple of journalists had written sonnets to that rack when she'd posed topless for some arty Vanity Fair cover a few years back.

The thought of her fame, and her wild reputation, went some way to dousing the fire igniting his pants. But not much. He could hardly claim to be the poster boy for mature and sensible behavior after the last twenty minutes.

"I'll get dressed again on one condition?" Drawing level with him, she cradled his jaw.

Her thumbnail scraped through the whiskers on his chin. The five o'clock shadow prickled, sending shivers of awareness zinging down his spine. And straight into his nuts.

"Which is?" He cocked an eyebrow. Not really sure he wanted her clothed, but knowing he'd never get anything done if he didn't agree to her terms.

"You promise to let me rustle up a replacement supper. You look washed out and I consider that my fault."

He rested his hand on her waist, forcing himself not to let it slide down and cup one of her delicious butt cheeks. "I'm a big boy. One bout of hot sweaty sex isn't going to kill me." *I hope.*

"Actually I was talking about last night and that two o'clock wake up call," she said, pricking his conscience again—because he knew for sure he didn't deserve her sympathy after his dickish behavior then too.

"I certainly hope you're not exhausted from the sex," she added. "Because I may demand another round, once you're sufficiently recuperated to appreciate it."

He chuckled, the audaciousness of the comment as saucy as the defiance in her eyes. Jesus but the woman was a ball buster. Why did that only make her more irresistible? "Don't tempt me. My resistance is pretty low at the moment."

"Even better," she said. "Because I have a favor to ask you."

"Okay," he said, intrigued.

Was it wrong to hope her favor might involve another round of hot sweaty sex? Probably. Definitely. "You better go grab that shower first." He gave her naked rump a playful slap, any last lingering strains of Catholic guilt now officially toast. "So I can get to work on this mess."

"Don't push your luck, Galahad." She shot him an outraged look, delighting him even more. "Or I might have to lop it off." She threw the remark over her shoulder as she sashayed into the bathroom and slammed the door.

And God help him, he laughed.

✦

"SO, FIRE AWAY."

Zelda looked up from her plate to find Ty watching her in that focused, intense way that made her feel like a witness about to be cross-examined. She'd been catching him doing it all evening—while he cleared up the mess and she made a new selection of dishes from the supplies she'd stocked in the fridge—and she still wasn't sure what to make of it. Or him.

And that was starting to bother her, because she usually found men transparent and easy to read, especially after she'd slept with them.

Tyrone Sullivan, though, had surprised her.

She'd expected the heat, but not the forthright apology afterwards. Because when had any man ever been concerned about showing her the proper respect, especially when it came to hot sex? What surprised her most of all though, was the approval in his eyes now, because it didn't seem to be only about the hot sex.

"Fire away about what?" she asked, at a disadvantage. Again.

His wide shoulders in the plain, white T-shirt made the chair creak as he tilted it back. He lifted the bottle of Sam Adams he'd retrieved from the fridge. "What's your favor?" he prompted.

Oh yes, that.

Her gaze tracked to his mouth, as he touched the neck of the bottle to his lips and took a long draught. It had been a while since she'd felt the tiny trickle of saliva in the back of her throat, a signal of the yearning to take a sip of the cold, yeasty brew—but it passed quickly. The prickle of anxiety, at the thought that he might say no to her request, wasn't quite so easily controlled.

No need to get her knickers in a knot. She had other options—just maybe not any as intriguing as the thought of spending a few days on Ty Sullivan's house barge. The unfortunate thought that she was now more interested in discovering a bit more about the unknowable and un-schmoozable Mr. Sullivan—and his ripped body—than she was in avoiding the press didn't do much for her anxiety levels.

"I was wondering if you'd be interested in letting me camp out here for a few days?"

He tipped the chair forward, the front legs smacking the floor.

She held up her hand. "And before you get entirely the wrong end of the stick. This request has nothing whatsoever to do with our impromptu bonk. That was spontaneous and unplanned and is unlikely to be repeated." She had to admit she wasn't entirely convinced by that last bit, but she wanted him to realize that sex wasn't an issue. Well, not for her anyway.

"How long do you want to stay?" he asked, his voice even, if a little strained.

Okay, so that wasn't an instant no.

"I don't know, probably just the holiday weekend. Until the news that I skipped out on that charity gig last night is forgotten. I've spoken to Seb's housekeeper and there's several paparazzi camped out at the Mausoleum," she said, using the term she'd used for her family's twenty-five room townhouse on the Upper East Side. "But really, I'm not that big a deal, they'll probably lose interest in a day or two and I can go back to the house. Me being irresponsible is an old story."

Speculation about her private life followed a familiar theme and surely couldn't sustain more than one or two tabloid headlines. She'd never apprised the press of her sobriety, so any and all willful behavior had been written into the whole Zelda Is Off the Rails Again scenario. She considered that collateral damage, and was prepared to weather the odd misinformed headline rather than put her sobriety under constant scrutiny. But if they got hold of her citation for disorderly conduct on Manhattan Beach at midnight, she'd find herself in the midst of a media circus which was more hassle than she needed at the moment. Especially with her brother, who'd been his usual austere, autocratic, and distant self ever since she'd arrived in New York several months ago.

Her stomach muscles twisted at the thought of Seb's reaction to her latest faux pas. He could be a total beast about it if he was getting door-stepped by the paparazzi, so laying low in Brooklyn until the storm blew over made sense.

The only problem was, now she'd made wild passionate love to Ty Sullivan on his couch, she'd complicated what should have been a simple request.

Shame she hadn't considered that while wrapping feverish fingers round his phenomenally gifted cock.

"What charity gig?" Ty asked.

"I was scheduled to appear at the Madison Foundation benefit on Thursday night at the Guggenheim for …" She paused, struggling to recall what the two-thousand-dollar a plate gala supper the foundation had organized had actually been in aid of. "Some very worthy cause."

"So worthy you can't remember it?" The question didn't sound particularly judgmental, but it didn't sound particularly complimentary either.

"I don't pick the causes, the foundation's management team does."

"Obviously it's a cause close to your heart," he said. Was he teasing her? Because the quizzical expression on his face was hard to read.

"It doesn't have to be close to my heart for me to contribute to it," she said, hating herself for the defensiveness.

"I guess not," he said.

"I'm not asking for your opinion on my integrity." She plopped her fork down on the table, hating the fact that he was right—she hadn't given a lot of thought to how the charity she couldn't remember might be affected by her disappearing act. "What I'm asking for is a place to stay for a couple of days," she continued, deciding she would make a hefty donation to the charity—whatever it was—when she got back to Manhattan. "If the answer's no, just say so—you can save the lecture, I've heard it before."

Which made it all the more unsettling that his opinion of her could still sting. A little.

"Yes."

"Excuse me?"

"I said, yes, you can hang here until the press loses interest."

"Really?" she said, then immediately wanted to kick herself for sounding so pleased.

Play it cool, Zel.

"You're sure you want to risk it?" she added. "My lack of integrity might be infectious?"

His mouth tugged up on one side, giving her another glimpse of that boyish grin which had blindsided her earlier. Its effect was still potent.

"My integrity's pretty robust. But …" The grin disappeared. "There's not a lot of space on this barge and…" His gaze flicked to the couch. "Given what already happened, we should probably get a couple of things straight."

She smiled, his sober expression ridiculously endearing. No doubt about it, Ty Sullivan was even cuter when he was being noble.

"What things?" she asked.

But she figured she already knew. Faith's big brother was the model citizen, knight-in-shining-designer-suit type, who'd probably never done anything irresponsible before in his entire life. And he was clearly still a little shocked by their no-holds-barred sex-capade on the couch.

"Just so there's no confusion about…" He paused, looking uncomfortable. "About why you're hanging here. It makes sense for us to keep the sleeping arrangements the same as last night." He cleared his throat.

It took her a moment to realize what he was getting at. And while she could have gotten mad that he would assume she would want to share his bed, she somehow knew that hadn't been his intention at all. Ty Sullivan was hopelessly gallant. And he just wanted to make sure she didn't feel awkward. Or compromised.

That he should be prepared to protect her honor felt oddly humbling, especially as she knew she didn't actually have any honor to protect.

"Absolutely. I'm glad we cleared that up," she said trying hard not to smile at his discomfort.

Maybe he was also worried that she might misconstrue their impromptu bonk as the start of something more?

No doubt a guy who looked like he did, who was as smart, sincere, and upstanding as he was, had a solvent career, a very nice house barge plus those magic fingers and such a gifted cock, had to fend off eligible women all the time. What he didn't know was that she had no desire to catch any guy. And she would never be eligible, not in any permanent sense. Because she'd never been naïve enough to believe in Happy Ever Afters—and fighting her demons would always be a full time job.

"Okay, good." He lifted her hand off the table and rubbed his thumb across the back. "So I guess that means we should lay off the hot sex? So we don't confuse stuff."

He sounded unsure, which she took as a very good sign.

"If you say so." She tugged her hand out of his, deciding now might not be the best time to tell him she'd never found anything confusing about hot sex.

"I need to crash." He stood, the weariness in his stance very apparent. "Leave the dishes, I'll handle them tomorrow."

"Crash away." She stood to stack their dirty dishes. "And I'll handle the dishes. While I never offer hot sex for room and board, I can offer excellent services as a chief cook and bottle washer."

"Cool, thanks." He paused. "I'm gonna take the bed in back. I'd offer to let you have it." He glanced at the bunk and screwed up his face in a comical look of distaste. "But the couch is kind of snug when you're six-two. And I'm not that much of a gentleman."

"No problem. I'm grateful for the couch. And it fits me fine."

"Great, well, thanks for supper." He let his gaze roam over the living area which was back to its pristine state after their food war. "And for cleaning up the place. I should have said that before."

"You're welcome."

"And for…" He shook his head, his mouth doing that half-smile again that had her insides heating. "Forget it; I'm not thanking you for that."

"There's no need. It was my pleasure."

His gaze drifted to her lips and she felt the energy and awareness pulse between them.

"Cool," he said again. "I'll see you in the morning. If I wake up before noon."

"Sleep as long as you like. I'll probably head to the mall. I need some new clothes for the duration." She lifted her arms. "I can't spend the whole weekend in your T-shirts."

"I guess not," he said, but she detected the definite hint of regret.

As he closed the bedroom door, it occurred to her he'd lied.

He was very much a gentleman.

Gallant enough to make her almost wish she could be a damsel in distress. Instead of the Evil Queen, who was already contemplating how much fun she could have tarnishing Ty Sullivan's armor.

Because, frankly, what else were Labor Day weekends for? But to unwind and de-stress… And get as much hot sex as you could. When no strings need be attached?

Chapter Six

TY EMERGED FROM the bedroom at a quarter after noon, to the sight of his new houseguest happily laying out sandwich fillings on the kitchen counter, her hips bumping and grinding in time to the low hum of an old soul classic on the radio.

He scrubbed his hands through his hair and over the rough scrape of the scruff on his chin. He felt like a bear just out of hibernation. And probably looked worse.

She must have gotten to the mall and back while he'd been comatose.

In a pair of Converse pumps, sunshine yellow three-quarter length pants and a bright blue T, she looked young, fresh, and cute. Add to that the sassy cap of hair and her clear skin devoid of makeup and she was rocking "sexy tomboy" this morning. The woman, he was beginning to realize, was something of a chameleon with a look to suit every occasion. On the last day of summer, young and super cute worked.

The dull ache in his crotch, which had accompanied a stream of erotic dreams during the night, agreed.

The aroma of fresh coffee had his stomach rumbling. He needed his first slug of the day, like now. He leaned past her to lift the coffee pot off the hot plate and her head jerked up.

Turning down the radio, she smiled. "Hi, I hope I didn't wake you?"

"You didn't." He got a whiff of her scent—sultry sin overlaid with summer flowers. "I needed to get my ass out of bed before I became part of the damn thing." He poured himself a mug, took a long gulp of the hot liquid, and sighed. "That's an awesome cup of coffee."

"Thank you. I consider coffee making an essential and much maligned art. I got them to grind the beans fresh at the gourmet market." Wiping her hands on a dishtowel, which looked new, she surveyed the sandwich makings. "I'm afraid you missed breakfast, but I was just going to make a picnic and head to Manhattan Beach."

"Returning to the scene of the crime, huh?"

"Something like that." The smile tipped up. "But I'd be more than happy to make you a sandwich before I go. If you tell me what you'd like?" She swept her hand over the array of fillings she had out on the counter—ham, bologna, Monterey Jack, tuna, mayo—she seemed to have covered all the bases and then some.

"You planning on eating all that?" he asked. "I thought

models had to starve themselves?" Although her thin frame managed to look slender not scrawny, he knew for a fact he could span that tiny waist with one hand.

"I like food and I like variety. And starving yourself is so passé. Which is one of the reasons why I jacked in my modeling job."

He straightened from the counter. "Since when?"

"Since Thursday night just before I skipped out on the Foundation's charity do. Hence my celebratory swim on Manhattan Beach. Which I now plan to repeat in broad daylight and hopefully without the 'disorderly conduct' bit."

So that explained the hair then. He wanted to question her some more. But she had a challenging look on her face, as if daring him to try. He guessed it wasn't any of his business. But he was still super curious. Why would anyone jack in a multi-million dollar job, which only required them to stand around and look good? Not something that took a great deal of effort for her, he'd guess. Up close her skin was almost translucent, those dark, blue eyes wide and slanted at the edges giving her an exotic, unusual beauty. In person, she was even more stunning than in her billboard ads.

"You want some company?" he said on impulse.

He didn't have any specific plans for the Labor Day weekend. He knew Faith would be expecting him at the pub that afternoon for the family's annual Labor Day barbeque. But he'd happily give that a miss.

He generally avoided visits to Sullivan's—the neighborhood pub in Bay Ridge his family had owned for two generations—if he could. He certainly didn't love the place the way his pop and Faith and his three younger brothers did. He'd worked his butt off to get a scholarship to Columbia Law and make a career for himself at the Legal Aid Society, fighting for the rights of the poor and downtrodden, because he came from a solidly blue-collar, Irish American background that he was proud of. But he'd always found Sully's a depressing place to be.

The bitter scent of Irish stout that clung to the dark wooden booths, the tinny sound of the traditional reels and jigs his old man played on a loop whenever his brothers weren't around to provide live music, even listening to the regulars shoot the breeze with Faith about 'the old country' while she wiped down the bar, brought back memories of his mother, and the back-breaking hours she'd worked when he was a kid to keep the place going.

Hours that had taken their toll but which his pop never acknowledged and his siblings didn't seem to remember. But he remembered, far too well.

"Haven't you got plans for today?" Zelda asked, neatly cutting into his grim thoughts.

"Nothing I can't break," he said, dumping the last of the cooling coffee in the sink. He'd text Faith, tell her something had come up. Although he didn't plan to tell her Zelda was staying with him. He kind of hoped she didn't already know. Something else to quiz Zelda about. Had Faith given her his cell number? Weird he wasn't as pissed with his little sister about that as he had been the night before last. "Give me ten to shower and change."

He headed off to the bathroom, pleased to have an excuse to ditch his family and hang out with Zelda, somewhere public, where they wouldn't get into any more trouble.

Zelda Madison had a wild, reckless streak that was bold and beautiful and exciting, which was why shampoo companies would pay a fortune to make her the face of their brand. But she was a guilty pleasure a guy like him couldn't afford. He had a plan for his life. A plan he'd put in motion in middle school. A plan which involved hard work, dedication, determination and no distractions—such as surprise booty calls with runaway supermodels. Plus he'd promised himself he'd be a gentleman from now on. So he needed to keep his hands off her for the next couple of days. Only problem was, his resolve this morning didn't feel a whole lot stronger than it had yesterday evening, because even in her tomboy pants and T-shirt she still looked good enough to eat—or at the very least lick all over.

A picnic on the beach would be the perfect place to enjoy her company, without risking having his libido torpedo his good intentions again. It was a bright sunny day, the temperature in the high eighties, and it was the start of the Labor Day weekend. Manhattan Beach would be packed. Even a bad girl like Zelda couldn't tempt him into too much trouble when they were both under the watchful eye of hundreds of Russian Orthodox Jewish mamas.

"Wait a minute," she called after him. He swung 'round. "You didn't tell me what sandwich filling you want?"

"Whatever you've got's good. I'm starving."

Starving for what though, he wasn't going to think about.

Better make that a cold shower.

✦

"WOW, IT'S A lot busier than the last time I was here." Zelda shielded her eyes from the glare of the mid-afternoon sun and tried to ignore the flex and bunch of Ty Sullivan's shoulder muscles under the royal blue polo shirt he wore with ragged denim cut offs. The man looked even better in his beachwear than he did in a creased two piece designer suit. He'd slicked his thick dark hair back from his high brow, and hadn't bothered to shave off the day-old stubble. She noticed the dark, swarthy skin that seemed to have tanned even more in the ten minutes since they'd walked through the park from the road where they'd finally found a free space to park his SUV. Faith had once told her Ty was one of the black Irish, because his skin was as dark as his sister's was fair.

"Not many families picnic here at midnight, that's for sure," he said, but tempered the remark with an easy smile.

"Speaking of family picnics, I thought you were supposed to be attending the big Sullivan barbeque bash this afternoon?" she said, trying not to sound wistful. Or worse, envious.

She'd always loved hearing the stories Faith told about her brothers and their family pub when they'd been at St. John's together. Faith's mother had died not long before she arrived at St. J's a year before Zelda, and Zelda suspected the stories had been a way for Faith to work through her grief. But in a strange way they'd helped Zelda work through her grief, too. Because just imagining herself as a part of that close-knit, loving family had comforted her as well.

Ty had always featured strongly in those tales, which had been whispered between their beds late at night. The big brother who had punched a local bully in the nose for stealing his sister's lunch money, or worked two jobs to help fund his way through college. Of course, when she'd finally been introduced to Ty that fateful day in the school foyer, she'd dismissed him as a judgmental, self-righteous prig. But she could see now her reaction had had more to do with her own envy—that Faith had a big brother prepared to fight her corner, instead of presume her guilt, and a family who would stand behind her and love her no matter what—than it did with Ty's judgmental glare. Why wouldn't he dislike her? Everyone had assumed she was the one who had stolen the wine. And normally they wouldn't have been wrong.

But now she felt guilty for dragging Ty away from important family business. As much as she had enjoyed his company last night, and as much as she appreciated watching the way his biceps strained the fabric of his polo shirt as he placed their cooler on the sand and spread out the blanket she'd packed—she would have been quite happy to come to the beach alone. Well, happy enough.

"How do you know about the family barbeque?" he asked, prizing the lid off the cooler to pull out a soda.

"Because Faith's been planning it for weeks. I don't want to be the cause of you missing it. You certainly don't have to babysit me." Which was what she was worried about. She had a feeling Ty Sullivan had an overdeveloped big brother complex. Something she definitely did not want to be the target of given last night's X-rated exploits.

"Faith won't mind if I skip it. She's cool about that stuff."

More like Faith would never tell him she minded, Zelda thought, because Faith loved him.

"She knows I have a life," he added, dipping into the cooler to pull out one of the sandwiches she'd wrapped in greased paper.

"Has it ever occurred to you that Faith might not have

much of a life?"

"How do you mean?" He bit into his sandwich, chewed and swallowed, apparently unfazed by the suggestion.

"Well, she's sort of tied to the pub because of your father's health. She used to want to be an artist when we were in school. She would draw all these amazing pictures in this sketchbook she took everywhere with her."

"I remember she got a place at Columbia to study art," he said. "But then Pop had his heart attack and she wanted to stay and look after him. And the pub."

"Yes, I know, but that was eight years ago now. I wonder what happened to her dream of becoming an artist and going to Paris?"

He shrugged. "Maybe you should ask her?"

"Maybe I will," she replied, trying not to be annoyed with the dismissive tone.

Who was she to get belligerent on Faith's behalf? Faith had never said she felt tied down, or disappointed with life. Well, except when it came to her nonexistent sex life. And what did Zelda really know about healthy sibling relationships? Given that her relationship with her only sibling had barely functioned for over a decade?

"You do that," he said, with easy confidence. "But I wouldn't worry about Faith. She loves the pub."

She pulled out her own sandwich, folded down the paper to take a nibble of the chewy rye bread, intrigued by the edge she had detected in his voice. "And you don't?"

He finished his sandwich, watching her, the intent stare tightening her skin. The way it had been doing last night. Interesting? His emerald green gaze still had the same potency hidden behind the lenses of his sunglasses.

"I didn't say that," he said at last, the hint of defensiveness in his tone more than enough to pique her interest. And make her fairly sure her assumption was correct.

"I go to Sully's once a month, to meet up with the girls," she said. "I've bumped into all three of your brothers there quite a few times. But I find it odd I've never seen you there. Not once. You didn't even show the afternoon Finn and Dawn got together," she added, remembering the impromptu celebration at the pub a few months ago. "And I know Faith tried to contact you."

He shrugged and concentrated on grabbing another sandwich and then unwrapping it. Yup, definitely defensive. Bordering on guilty. How fascinating. Did her white knight have a chink in his armor?

"I have a full-on job. It demands a lot of my time. I was on a case that afternoon. And I don't generally get much opportunity to hang out in bars."

The implication that she did was duly noted. And ignored. She happened to be an expert at handling the old offense-as-defense maneuver after the last few months of sharing a home with her brother.

"An interesting excuse, but let's examine the evidence, counselor."

He didn't speak, so she took that as her cue to continue.

"Your family has a regular time-honored tradition of having big family get-togethers every Labor Day weekend. Something you know your sister has been planning for weeks. And to which you are invited and have already agreed to attend."

"How do you know I agreed to go?"

"Do you deny it?" she shot back.

"Well, I guess I didn't exactly…"

"Interruption overruled, then," she interrupted. "For badgering the witness."

"Why am I getting the feeling you watch way too much Judge Judy?"

She grinned at the wry—and surprisingly accurate comment. "Judge Judy often makes some very good points."

"Judge Judy is an actual judge, whereas her viewers aren't. Even if some of them think they are."

"Right, that's definitely badgering the witness. Now, back to my evidence."

"Supposition and hearsay isn't admissible as evidence."

"It is if it's true," she continued, riding roughshod over his objection. "Now let me see, where was I? Oh yes." She popped up a forefinger before he could interrupt again. "You agreed to go and yet you're skipping out for very spurious reasons. And without even phoning your sister to let her know. Which makes me wonder if that Catholic guilt of yours might be in play again. And why would you feel guilty about not going, unless you don't want to go but don't want to admit it?"

"I don't consider having a picnic with you on Manhattan Beach a spurious reason."

"You should. You don't even like me."

She took another bite of her sandwich, savoring the sharp, creamy flavor of the cheese—and the odd glow in her chest at the thought that he didn't consider her a spurious reason.

Progress.

"What makes you think I don't like you?" He put down his sandwich, and picked up her hand. His thumb stroked down her fingers, and she felt it all the way to her toes.

Uh oh. A bit too much progress.

She snatched her hand back, knowing when she was being sidetracked. Even if she was enjoying being sidetracked. "Now you're adding misdirecting the witness to badgering."

"I thought you were the prosecutor?" he countered, the lopsided smile doing funny things to her insides.

Yup definitely misdirection.

She needed to get this cross-examination back on track before he misdirected her right into a kiss. "Okay, misdirecting the prosecutor then."

"You know, you're the cutest prosecutor I've ever come

up against."

Leaning forward, she tipped up his sunglasses, assessed the gleam of amusement and something hotter in his eyes and then dropped them back on his nose.

"That's an underhanded tactic and you know it," she all but purred.

"Didn't you know, all's fair in love and fantasy prosecutions?"

She did now. A lot of good it did her. Her mind scrambled to engage having been somewhat misdirected by the fireball of lust spreading up her torso. "Just answer me one question."

He'd picked up her hand and began nibbling her fingertips. Misdirecting her even more. "Hmmm?"

"Why did you really ask to go to the beach with me? Was it to avoid going to the pub?"

"I agreed to go to the beach with you so I would stop thinking about jumping you again. I needed a distraction."

"Surely going to the pub would have been a better distraction," she said, her voice more breathless than she wanted it to be. "Seeing as I wouldn't even be there."

"And miss seeing you in a bikini? And quite possibly wet? I love my family. I don't love them that much."

"I don't have a bikini. I was going to swim in my underwear."

"And get another citation?" He sounded outraged. But she wasn't convinced, because the grin only got more wicked. "Boy, am I glad I didn't let you come here alone."

"But surely there's nothing wrong with swimming in your underwear in broad daylight? Especially as you really can't tell this bra and panties isn't a bikini."

"I don't think we should risk it, you're already into me for two hundred bucks."

"What do you suggest we do then?" she asked. "It's way too hot to just sit here in the sun." *And getting hotter by the second.*

"How about we go back to the barge and investigate exactly how much that bra and panties looks like a bikini when wet. If we find them innocent we can come back in a couple of hours."

She swallowed the next bite of her sandwich, with difficulty, past the lump of lust in her throat. "Are you saying you want to cross-examine my underwear, counselor?"

"Any objections?" he said, the grin positively devilish now.

Endorphins careered round her body at a rate of knots. "I suppose not," she said. "As long as you promise to be thorough."

He balled up the sandwich paper and dumped it in the cooler. Grasping her hand, he stood up, then dragged her close, to plant a kiss on her lips. "When it comes to cross-examining hostile underwear…" His mouth curved and her breath gushed out in a staggered gasp. "I think you'll find I'm extremely thorough."

✦

IT HAD TAKEN them nearly twenty minutes to find a parking space in the crowded roads near the beach. It took them less than ten to find the car and race back to the marina.

He took her hand as they headed through the security gate to the dock. The barge was cool inside, the air conditioner unit working overtime. But her flesh felt hot and sticky nonetheless. They'd hardly spoken on the ride back.

This probably wasn't a good idea. She flattened her hands against his chest as he hauled her into his arms. He stilled, although she could feel his chest vibrating with tension.

"Problem?" he asked.

"Not necessarily, as long as we both know this is just an endorphin fix."

Not something she would normally bother to point out. But Ty Sullivan wasn't like the men she usually screwed around with. He was an upstanding guy; he was one of Faith's brothers. And she doubted he was as well versed in the etiquette of the anonymous hookup as she was, because very few people were.

"I just thought I should clarify that," she added, feeling mildly idiotic when his brow creased in a curious frown.

"Got it." He dipped his head to nuzzle the pulse point in her neck, his hands settling on her waist and cruising up under her new T-shirt. "Are we good to go, now?"

She could feel the ridge in his pants, pressing into her tummy. "Um, yes, very good."

He chuckled, the sound deep and gruff. Working off her top, he surveyed her bra, brushing his thumb across the satin cup until her nipple ruched into a hard point.

"Then let the cross-examination begin." He licked at the satin-covered tip before sucking it against the roof of his mouth.

She grasped his head, sinking her fingers into the soft silky strands, the wet suction both too much and not nearly enough.

Lifting her onto the kitchen counter, he stood back to survey the damage. "Nope, don't think that looks decent when wet. Definitely guilty as charged." His eyes twinkled with mischief. "You might as well be naked."

She unclipped the bra's hook, let it hang down, caught on the tips of her breasts. "If you say so."

He slid a finger under the strap and lifted the swatch of satin and lace away, leaving her naked to the waist. Her breathing became ragged, her breasts swollen and heavy, the hint of wetness left by his kiss chilling her already sensitive nipples in the stream of air from the unit. Grabbing her hips, he lifted her into his arms. She hooked her legs round his waist, holding onto his shoulders as he carried her into the barge's bedroom, her breath too ragged now to contemplate conversation.

Dropping her onto the bed, he closed the door, sealing

them into the small room. He stripped off his shirt as she kicked off her Converse. The daylight glimmered off the water, flooding into the space to highlight the firm contours of muscle and sinew.

She'd had nooners before, back when she would wake up at midday and yearn for a drink while she tried to remember who the hell was sprawled out beside her—and what the hell they'd been doing the night before. But she'd never had one sober before. And now she wondered why she'd missed out on the wicked treat. He looked glorious in the sunlight. The dark whorls of hair on his chest tapering down through the ridged muscles of his six pack.

For a desk jockey he was certainly ripped.

Her heart leapt into her throat at the sight of the thick erection as he dropped the cutoffs and boxers. He grabbed a box of condoms from the nightstand. She watched as he rolled one onto the hard length, the teasing light in his eyes darkening with determination.

The throbbing ache between her thighs became unbearable.

"Now to test those panties," he said, his voice husky as he joined her on the bed.

He inched her zipper down, then edged the pants over her hips and down her legs, until the only thing left protecting her from his intense gaze was the thin satin of her panties. Angling her knees up, she lay back still watching him. Anticipation and excitement built to fever pitch as he pressed his nose to the fragile gusset, already soaked with her juices.

"You smell glorious," he said.

A staggered purr of pleasure choked out, but what had been playful a moment ago, seemed suddenly serious.

Nudging the gusset aside, he blew on her heated flesh.

She jerked, the teasing contact too much and still not nearly enough. "Please, you need to…"

The plea cut off as his tongue explored her folds, then flicked over the straining nub.

She bucked, arching into the delicious caress. "Yes, just exactly there."

The rough chuckle was both temptation and torture. "You sure? How about here?"

He circled and licked, taking her to the brink of completion, then drawing back to tease and torment.

She panted, the coil tightening like a fist, her heart swelling up to hammer at her ribcage.

"Don't stop, please don't stop…" she urged him on, getting closer and closer to the edge but not close enough. Then he captured the swollen nub, and suckled hard.

A keening cry ripped from her as she flew over that final peak, the pleasure cresting in a never ending wave. She clung to him as he rose over her, stunned by the intensity of her orgasm and the fierce approval in his gaze.

"Again," he said, those deep green eyes fixed on her face. "I want to see you do that again."

Ripping away her panties, he pulled her up until he sat on the bed and she straddled him. Large hands bracketed her hips, encouraging her, directing her, as she sank down on his thrusting cock.

Her mind reeled, the fullness stretching her unbearably, his penis impossibly large inside her. She gripped his shoulders, firm with muscle and, using her knees for leverage, rose up to impale herself again.

He swore, his fingers digging into her waist, and began pumping up to meet her. Going further, forcing her to take even more of him as they established a furious rhythm.

Shock warred with sensation, the rub of his cock making the heat build again.

The wave rose towards her like a tsunami, destroying everything in its path.

"I can't come again," she cried, sure she couldn't because she never had before.

"Yes, you can," he demanded, his thumb locating her clit to caress the very heart of her.

The second climax hit like a freight train, hard and fast and unstoppable. She sobbed, shattering into a million tiny pieces.

She heard his yell of completion, her pussy clenching on him as he followed her into oblivion.

He felt back onto the bed and she flopped on top of him. Exhausted, spent, and a little shaky. Her cheek nestled against his neck, the salty scent of his sweat a potent accompaniment to the funky smell of sex.

"Damn," he murmured, the tone awestruck as his arms folded over her and gathered her close, his hands stroking her back to soothe and caress. "That wasn't just an endorphin fix it was a freaking endorphin apocalypse. You're amazing, Zelda."

She pushed out a laugh, aware of the strange weight pressing under her breastbone at the compliment. She pulled out of his arms and lay on the bed beside him. The roll and sway of the water made the boat creak as she stared at the ceiling fan, stirring the muggy air and pebbling her flushed skin.

She shivered, the heavy weight still sitting on her chest, the unsteady beats of her heart punching her ribcage. How had he known just how to touch her, and tease her, and why had he held her like that afterwards. As if she mattered to him?

She lifted her arm above her head, letting it lie on the bed as she turned to him.

It's just the sex talking. The seriously amazing sex talking.

"That was quite a work out, counselor," she said, keeping her voice flippant.

But then he reached out to trace his fingertip over her cheek and her heart bobbed into her throat.

"Zelda, you really are incredible. Who knew bad girls could be so damn gorgeous?"

She captured his finger, to draw it away from her face, the weight starting to crush her. Sitting up, she scooted off the bed.

"Where are you going?" he asked.

"I need a shower." She threw the words over her shoulder, scared to look back at him as she rushed into the bathroom, her legs trembling.

She closed the door and locked it, just in case Ty had any ideas about joining her. Then leaned on the sink and locked her knees to keep from falling on her arse.

Bloody hell, Madison, stop freaking out. You've had seriously amazing sex loads of times.

Maybe not an endorphin apocalypse. Not that she could remember anyway. But there was a lot of stuff from her drinking days she didn't remember.

But who would ever have guessed there could be so much more to Mr. High and Mighty than just a sexy glare? The tender smile. The wry humor. His unexpected naughty streak. Not to mention his inventive fingers and phenomenal cock. Even that glimpse of vulnerability about his attachment to his family.

It was just the surprise. That had to be the cause of the boulder on her chest, because this was only a sex thing. It was not a caring thing. Or a liking thing. Because that could lead to a *thing* thing. And she didn't do *thing* things. Ever. Especially not with men like Ty, who were sure and steady and idealistic and probably took *thing* things far too seriously.

She turned on the shower and stepped under the lukewarm spray, trying to steady herself. And make the panic go away.

So what if Ty Sullivan was a lot hotter and more complex than expected. That was no cause to freak-out over a bit of pillow talk.

She wasn't an emotionally crippled, wild child anymore, frantically seeking attention by whatever means necessary. Five years of staying clean and sober—and resisting the urge to knock back a bottle of champagne or snort a line of coke whenever she wanted to bolster her confidence—had seen to that.

She might like Ty, but she didn't need Ty to like her, because she'd learned a long time ago not to let the opinion of others matter.

Every time Seb looked right through her and didn't see her. Every time a new headline splashed her inadequacies across the front page of a tabloid rag. Every time she faced down her demons in a meeting, had taught her to ignore the sneers, the disapproval, the open hostility, and to keep the desperate desire to be loved kept securely under lock and key and move on.

Spending a couple of days enjoying the company of the likeable and very shaggable Ty Sullivan wasn't going to change that. So there were no freak-outs required.

She squirted a generous dollop of Ty's shampoo into one shaky palm and massaged it into her scalp. And the crushing weight on her chest finally eased up enough to allow her to draw a decent breath.

Even if she did like Ty Sullivan, he didn't mean *that* much to her. He was just a handy port in a storm, a short-term friend with exceptional benefits, a good guy who had a weakness for bad girls and knew his way 'round a clitoris.

And she would certainly never mean that much to him.

She rinsed off the last of the shampoo.

A guy like Ty might find a bad girl irresistible for a weekend fling, but he would never consider hooking up with someone like her for the long haul.

But just to be on the safe side, she ought to establish a few simple ground rules before they took this any further. After all, Ty's speciality was following the rules. And she'd become pretty good at it too, in recent years, when she had to be.

✦

So what the heck happened to no more surprise booty calls with supermodels?

Ty listened to the rattle of the shower unit he needed to replace, the heady feeling of afterglow fading as he tried to figure out where his good intentions had gone wrong.

Zelda had started teasing him about the barbeque he'd skipped out on. He'd started flirting back to distract her and then, bam! They'd been racing back to the barge and getting naked.

But what had been a sexy game at first, light and flirtatious and fun, hadn't stayed that way.

She'd captivated him and surprised him, and responded to him without holding one single thing back. He'd watched her eyes go glassy with stunned pleasure, seen her skin flush pink, heard her sobbing breaths as she came and he'd turned into a fucking caveman again. And for a moment there, while he was bucking his hips to get as deep inside her as he could, and she was riding him with her pussy muscles clamping down on his cock, he'd had the insane urge to stay inside her, forever.

Tugging on his shorts, he walked into the boat's main living space. Noting the time, he headed for the fridge. So what if it was only three in the afternoon, he needed a damn beer.

This could never be more than a weekend booty call—because their lives would always be way too far apart, both socially and economically—so why couldn't he shake the feeling this was already more than sex?

Zelda emerged from the bathroom in a puff of steam, one of his towels wrapped around her slim body. And the hollow feeling in his gut sunk down to tighten around his ball sack.

Relief shot through him. The panic retreating back where it belonged.

He and Zelda had a sexual chemistry that went all the way to eleven—and his life had been boring as hell for months now. An endless grind of long hours and limited recreation. If all work and no play had made Jack a dull boy, it appeared to have turned Ty Sullivan, attorney-at-law, into a sex maniac.

So maybe he needed to get a life. And what better way to do that, than to take a time-out this weekend, indulge the insane sexual chemistry between him and Zel, while discovering the fascinating woman who lurked behind the bad-ass sass?

"Hey." He tipped the bottle at her. "You want a beer?"

She stiffened and shook her head, but he saw the flash of something in her eyes. The flash of something he recognized, because he'd seen it before in the people he was representing who had something to hide.

"No, that's okay. I'm good. I need to get dressed."

What was with that?

She gave him a tantalizing glimpse of one flushed butt cheek as she shot off towards the bedroom. And the knot of panic returned to tighten around his larynx.

Was she leaving? Had he done something wrong? Was that why she'd run off to the bathroom so fast after he'd screwed her like a caveman?

"Zelda, wait." He placed the beer bottle onto the counter with a solid thunk and shot after her. "Where are you going?"

✦

"NOWHERE, I'M JUST getting dressed." Zel yanked the T-shirt on and turned, keeping her gaze fixed on Ty's face instead of the wide expanse of muscular chest dusted in dark hair. "Is there a problem?"

Was he already regretting their endorphin apocalypse? Or worse the sweet stuff he'd said afterwards.

Her heartbeat punched her throat like a rabbit on speed. Not that him regretting it would be bad. Because, of course, he hadn't really meant it, and she definitely didn't need him to mean it. Because this was not and would never be a *thing* thing.

"No problem," he said, looking relieved. "It's just… You seemed kind of spooked."

Bugger, did he know his sweet, make that cheesy, compliments, had sent her into a tailspin of panic? Because that would definitely be bad.

"You're sure everything's all right?" He asked again, the tinge of color high on his cheekbones. "I didn't hurt you, did I?"

"Ty, why would you even think that? Of course you didn't hurt me."

Good grief, his white knight complex was worse than she thought. How on earth could he look at her, after she'd ridden him like a bucking bronco, and still see a damsel in distress?

The tinge of color went a dull red and raced up to his hairline. The man was actually blushing.

Ty Sullivan really was one of the good guys. Which was exactly why she mustn't let this get any stickier.

"That's good." His lips quirked. "I just didn't want you to think…" He shrugged, obviously struggling. "That I was taking anything for granted. With you. While you're here."

"Actually I'd be more than happy if you took as much as you liked for granted."

"All right, then." He thrust his fingertips through his hair, sending it into haphazard tufts, the smile still a little unsure, but heating up considerably. "So we're still good?"

"I'd say we're exceptional." She stepped towards him, to wrap her arms round those broad shoulders and enjoy the feel of his hands, settling on her waist.

His lips curved, so close now she could smell the yeasty scent of the beer. She rolled her bottom lip under her teeth, tamping down on the urge to lick across that sensual mouth. And taste him again.

"Actually, I was thinking, maybe we should renegotiate the sleeping arrangements for the weekend," she said, seeing her opportunity to stave off any more potential freak-outs.

His hands slipped down to cup her buttocks, firm and warm and more than a bit possessive. "I guess there's no sense you sleeping on the couch. All things considered."

"Exactly…" she said. "But I think we should establish some ground rules first."

The man was seriously addictive. Something she needed to keep in mind given that she had always had an addictive personality.

"I thought you were a bad girl who didn't follow rules," he teased, the assured smile making her pulse pummel her throat in double time.

There was bloody Bugs Bunny again, mainlining coke now.

"I do, if I'm the one making them," she said.

"Who said you get to make the rules?" The cocky grin spread across his face making him even more gorgeous. "Last time I checked this was a democracy not a dictatorship."

The rabbit punching her throat went insane.

Piss off, Bugs.

"I get to make them because I happen to be an expert on them." She needed to be practical and persuasive now, without getting intoxicated by those industrial strength pheromones ahead of schedule. "Because I've broken pretty much every rule there is in my time." He didn't need to know that these days she couldn't afford to break the rules.

"I look forward to hearing all about that," he said, the naughty streak back. "All right, let's hear your rules," he murmured, pressing a kiss into the hollow of her throat. Day-old stubble rasped across delicate skin, and a low groan escaped her lips. "But I should warn you I'm a tough negotiator."

She didn't doubt it for a second, adrenaline shooting through her as he carried on nibbling.

Thrusting her fingers into his hair, she dragged his head back, and sent him her best 'don't-mess-with-me' stare.

"Behave yourself, counselor." She prodded her index finger into his breastbone, to press him back further and stop any more extracurricular nibbling from occurring before the rules were agreed upon. "Rule one. We share your bed for the duration of my stay."

"That rule I can abide by, one hundred percent."

"Don't be too sure, rule one comes with a but."

"A butt, huh?" The wicked tilt of his lips sent the heat south to throb between her legs as he caressed the naked butt in question. "I'm a big fan of your butt."

"That would be a but with one 't' you pervert." She knocked his hand away. "Which is that if we share the bed, it is strictly for the purposes of down and dirty sex and sleep. No cuddling or canoodling or snuggling or lovey-dovey looks allowed."

A muscle jumped in his jaw, the naughty twinkle in his eyes going feral. Exactly the way she wanted it.

"What's your position on spooning?"

She pushed out a laugh, her throat dry with lust. "Spooning is permitted, but only when erections are involved."

"Understood." His thumbs glided back down to the slope of her backside. "I can guarantee that when spooning against this butt with two 't's…" He gave her butt cheeks another squeeze making the throbbing heat settle in her clit. "Erections will definitely be involved."

"Excellent. We have an agreement on rule one." She

stretched, rubbing herself against the hard ridge growing in his shorts. "Rule two." She raised a second finger against his chest. "This is a three-day fling, tops. No bargaining for extra days, from either one of us."

Not that she would want to. She hadn't gotten past three days in the past five years. But she wasn't taking any chances.

He nodded. "I've got a court date on Tuesday morning, so three days tops works for me. No exceptions." He smiled. "Or buts."

"Rule three." She had to do this, even though it felt kind of sneaky. "We don't tell Faith now or in the future. If she asks, I'll say you helped me out with the citation and that's all."

Faith looked up to her brother. And Faith was a romantic who had always believed the best in Zel, despite all the evidence to the contrary. Maybe it was selfish and dishonest, but Zel didn't want Faith to know she had used her big brother for down and dirty sex—it might make Faith, and by extension her other friends, uncomfortable. And that she couldn't bear.

Faith and Dawn and Mercy had been there for her when she'd needed them the most at St. J's. Then Mercy had dragged her out of the pit five years ago, Faith had always been on the end of a phone line with words of support and encouragement during the most painful days of her recovery and now Dawn was back in all their lives.

The four of them were just beginning to rebuild the unbreakable bond that had been her salvation on the day they'd all been hauled in front of the Mother Superior. The bond which she was sure—if she hadn't been kicked out of St. J's that day and exiled from them in the years that followed—might have stopped her from going off the rails so spectacularly. She wanted to help make that bond strong again. As strong as it had once been. And she certainly wasn't going to put a possible dent in it over something that would mean nothing a week from now.

She edged back, a horrifying thought occurring to her. "Assuming of course you haven't told Faith already?"

"I don't generally brag to my sister about my sex life," he said, wryly. "But I've gotta say I'm not great at lying to her either."

"Really? So what exactly did you tell her about missing the Sullivan Family barbeque today then?"

His darkly tanned skin flushed again. "All right. Point taken. White lies I can do. But if she asks me a direct question…"

"She won't, why would she? Especially if we abide by rule four."

"Rule *four*? Seriously? How many rules are there? This is beginning to feel more like a contract negotiation than a weekend booty call."

"This is the last one, I promise." She took a steadying breath, knowing this rule was the most important. She couldn't cut loose with Ty Sullivan unless she knew she could control the fallout. And she really, really wanted to cut loose. "No contact after we're through."

His eyebrow lifted. "Define no contact?"

"No texts, no emails, no phone calls, no chance meetings. No extracurricular booty calls for old times' sake after our three days are up. No nothing. Once I leave on Tuesday morning, we go back to being strangers. Our worlds don't exactly collide," she added. "So it shouldn't be too hard to pull off, logistically speaking."

"Except at the pub. You and Faith and Dawn and…" He clicked his fingers a couple of times. "The other girl, whose name I can never remember…"

"Mercedes, or Mercy for short," Zel added helpfully, wondering where he was going with this.

"Mercy!" He said, exasperated. "That's the one. You guys hang out at the pub. I can't guarantee I won't ever go there."

"I don't hang out there on a regular basis," she said, knowing this was another golden opportunity to apprise him of her recovery. She never hung out in bars to socialize casually, because it would open her up to temptations she might find it hard to resist. She only went to Sully's when she had a specific reason to be there—namely the monthly meet ups with her friends and the odd celebration, such as Dawn and Finn's party. But somehow she couldn't bring herself to tell him. It was too personal. Too revealing. And still way too much information for a casual fling. "We have a scheduled girls' night out there on the second Thursday of every month. That's the only time I'll be at Sully's. So as long as you make a point of steering clear of arranging family time on that day, we're good."

His eyes narrowed. "You're serious about never wanting to see me again? Even accidentally?"

"Yes, I am."

"I don't know whether to feel hurt or used." He didn't sound hurt, more like astonished.

But still she nodded. This bit was non-negotiable. Ty Sullivan was going to be a hard habit to break. Thanks entirely to his phenomenal cock, she added hastily.

"Actually, you should feel flattered." She spread her fingers on his chest and ran her hands over his shoulders. Sinking her fingernails into the curls at his nape, she noted the compelling twists of gold in the deep green of his irises, and inhaled the delicious scent of soap and man. "These rules are for your benefit as well as mine." She pointed out. "I have an addictive personality. And I could become seriously addicted to sex with you." That much was certainly true. "Neither of us wants to get distracted by this for more than a long weekend, though. So cold turkey is the only way to go once it's over. If that doesn't work for you, say so. And I'll leave now."

She waited for his reply, convincing herself that the only reason Bugs had begun to punch her throat like a heavyweight champ was because she really didn't want to miss out on all the hot, recreational sex they still had in their immediate future.

✦

TY LOOKED INTO Zelda's upturned face, trying to halt the flames licking up his torso from melting the last of his remaining brain cells. He was pretty sure he'd never met a woman who said exactly what she wanted and how she wanted it—without an ounce of hesitation or prevarication. And on one level that was extremely hot, because he knew for damn sure he'd never met another woman he wanted as much.

And on a purely practical level, he didn't have a problem with Zelda's rules.

They made total sense. While he didn't have an addictive personality, he could imagine himself getting addicted to Zelda. And as she was the opposite of his Miss Right, a weekend booty call *was* the only way to go.

But even so, he hesitated. Disturbed by that hollow sensation under his breastbone again. Why did he get the feeling there was a whole host of stuff she wasn't telling him? And what the hell was wrong with hugging after sex? Or letting Faith know about their hookup? It wasn't as if his little sister would care? Was Zelda ashamed of him?

He dismissed the knee-jerk reaction—a layover from his time at Columbia, when he'd walked around with a chip on his shoulder because he was the first person in his family to make it to college. Zelda wasn't a snob, he'd already established that much. So if she wasn't ashamed of him, what was she so scared of?

He shook off the thought. Why was he overthinking this? A Labor Day hookup was what they both wanted. So there was no point overcomplicating stuff, or worrying about Zelda and her motives? She didn't need to be rescued. Especially not by him.

It was just the attorney in him, always trying to calculate all the angles, be the devil's advocate. He gazed at her, the flush of arousal riding high on those awesome cheekbones as she waited for his answer. The ache in his shorts became painful.

Fuck it, if there was ever a time to take something at face value, this had to be it. No need to question the rules, if he was happy to follow them. And there was no rule against them getting to know each other better during the next three days.

Enough soul-searching.

Closing his hands over her hips, he tugged her into his embrace.

"I'll agree to your rules on one condition," he murmured, sinking his face into her neck and licking from her collarbone all the way up to her earlobe, the hollow feeling burned away by the rush of lust as she moaned.

"What condition?"

"We can stop talking about what we're going to do to each other and actually start doing it."

She laughed, the smoky purr making him imagine all the wicked things he wanted to do to her. His dick shot to full attention and strangled in his shorts.

"But you're so good at talking." She teased.

Drawing back, he yanked the bedroom door closed, so no one walking past the barge would see them. If he wasn't careful, she was liable to get him a citation for disorderly conduct.

"True, but right now my mind is on other stuff."

"Other stuff? That doesn't sound very articulate for a qualified attorney."

Anticipation made his throat dry up to parchment as he backed her toward the bed and then whipped her T-shirt over her head.

She crossed her arms over her naked breasts, but the bold, flirtatious look on her face made a mockery of the modest gesture.

"Was that a grunt I heard, counselor?" she said. "My goodness, you're becoming less articulate by the second."

He gave her a soft shove, toppling her onto the bed. Her breasts bounced, the large, cherry red nipples begging to be sucked. Climbing on top of her, he stretched her arms above her head, so she couldn't hide herself from him again.

"You want articulate?" He licked around one thrusting

peak, smiling when she bucked off the bed. "You're gonna have to hire some other lawyer. Because this one is now officially off the clock."

He captured the nipple between his teeth and tugged, all the thoughts crashing out of his head bar one—as that smart-ass laugh turned into a thready moan.

Why had he always strived to be a goddamn gentleman, when bad guys got to have this much fun?

Chapter Seven

ZELDA FELT THE soft sway of the boat, her body slightly sore but mostly pleasantly numb after a second day and night of raw, energetic sex—during which all the rules had been carefully observed.

Well, apart from the rule about snuggling, because she could vaguely remember drifting off to sleep with Ty's arm wrapped around her midriff at midnight. She sighed. Fine, she'd give him a pass on that one. At least she hadn't woken up in his arms. She spread her hand over the rumpled sheets on Ty's side of the double bunk, inhaling the scent of him that lingered. Then frowned at the sunshine blazing through the shutters on the back of the barge, lighting the dust motes. It had to be well after noon.

It was Monday. They only had today left to spend together, and she'd already slept half of it away.

She pushed off the flicker of melancholy. The Labor Day weekend couldn't last forever and she needed to get back to Manhattan tomorrow. Not only was that one of the rules, but she would have to face her brother sooner or later and explain her disappearing act on Thursday night.

Not that he seemed to care.

As expected, Sebastian hadn't bothered to check on her whereabouts. If he'd been informed of her no-show at the foundation gala, it obviously hadn't surprised him enough to make him pick up the phone and break his usual no contact rule.

At least the press attention had died down already.

She'd spotted a headline on the cover of the Post, when she and Ty had ventured out to the Seven-Eleven to get some supplies during their all-day sex fest on Sunday, but hadn't given it much thought. It was only the second lead, featuring a blurred picture of her taken a month or so ago with the headline: 'Not So Model Behavior From Fantasy Girl.' If she didn't even warrant a name check anymore, that could only be good.

The last two days had gone by in a rush of great sex and not too much conversation. She'd ventured out to phone her sponsor first thing on Sunday morning while Ty was still fast asleep. But there hadn't been anything too confusing to work out with Amelie. Zelda had explained about Ty, about their weekend booty call. But when Amelie had quizzed her about him, she'd dismissed her concerns.

It was okay, there was nothing serious between them. Certainly nothing for her to need to work through with Amelie. One of the few weaknesses she'd never had as an addict was relying too much on the men in her life. Her brother had taught her that lesson at thirteen and she'd never forgotten it. She'd had that minor freak-out before establishing the rules with Ty, but that was two days ago and there hadn't been a single wobble since.

Scooping her T-shirt—correction: Ty's T-shirt—off the deck, she threw it on and padded into the main living area following the sound of tuneless whistling and the luxurious scent of melting butter. She paused in the doorway to appreciate the view. Ty's dark head bent over a mixing bowl as the pan sizzled on the two-ring burner. Naked to the waist, his lean, tanned back glowed bronze in the sunlight, the bare feet and the low-slung button-fly jeans adding to the picture of super sexy domesticity. Seriously, was there anything more mouthwatering than a hot guy cooking pancakes?

He dumped a dollop of the mixture into the pan, looking as focused and competent as he had the day before while bringing her to orgasm. The aroma of freshly fried batter drifted towards her and her stomach rumbled.

God, the man looked delicious. His unruly hair falling across his brow as he concentrated on the task at hand, the two-day stubble making him look rough and ready and dangerous. Drool collected under her tongue—and not just for the pancakes.

She glanced at the clock on the wall, the melancholy spiking under the lust at the realization that it was already two in the afternoon.

"You must be the only Sullivan Brother who can't carry a tune," she said.

The off-key whistling cut off as his head whipped round. His wide mouth tipped up in a self-deprecating grin, the lazy once over he gave her making heat glow like a hot coal in her belly.

"True enough." His eyebrows wiggled, the smile decidedly suggestive. "Luckily, I have other much more useful talents."

She smiled back, the glow sinking low. "Such as cooking pancakes, I see."

"Among others things." He gripped the pan. "Pancakes happen to be one of the three things I can cook without killing anyone. I hope you're hungry because I've made enough for a football team."

"I'm starving." Her belly flipped over with the pancake. She blinked away the stupid sting of emotion.

Get real, Madison. He's making you pancakes. This is not a big deal.

"What are the other two things?" she asked, as she walked to the table which was already set with syrup, plates and cutlery, and a carton of OJ.

"Oatmeal and Lucky Charms." He slid the finished pancake onto the stack by his elbow and set up another. "I did the breakfast shift every Sunday before Mass when I was a kid, so my mom could have a couple of extra hours in bed."

"That's sweet." Zelda grabbed a mug from the shelf and poured herself some of the freshly brewed coffee, trying for sarcastic but not quite pulling it off thanks to the melting sensation in the center of her chest.

"How old were you?" she asked, trying to concentrate instead on the play of his shoulder muscles as he handled the pan with proficiency.

She knew Faith's mother had died when she was still a teenager; that was why her father had packed her off to St. John's. She also knew how much Faith had missed her brothers, especially Finn. But how much she had also depended on Ty's support. And over the last couple of days Zelda had begun to see why. The man was a natural-born nurturer, despite all his big talk about being a workaholic. The care and attention he paid to her during sex matched the care and attention he paid whenever she spoke to him. She'd had to be fairly careful the day before, when they'd been having the evening meal they'd put together from the leftovers in his fridge on the roof of the barge, not to spill any secrets. He listened, and asked questions, as if he were genuinely interested in the answers. And her. Luckily though, she had been cautious, managing to steer him away from anything other than the vaguest of conversations about her modeling career and her reasons for leaving. And it hadn't been too hard to distract him with sex.

But it occurred to her now, that while she'd been distracting him, he'd also been distracting her. And she was wildly curious now, to return to the topic of his family. She'd always been so fascinated by Faith's closeness to her brothers and her pop. While she and Faith had the connection of shared grief, she'd always felt that Faith had this bedrock of support which Zelda had always lacked. So it fascinated her now to realize Ty seemed to have a much less rose-tinted view of his childhood. The problem was, he also seemed as reluctant to talk about it as she was to talk about her family life. Which of course just made her all the more curious.

"How old was I when I started doing the breakfast shift?" He shrugged, stacking the last of the pancakes and transferring the plate to the table. "Around seven, I guess."

"That's young," she said as she forked up a pancake from the stack and smothered in it maple syrup. "To be handling a frying pan on your own."

"The first couple of attempts weren't too pretty. I'm not a natural when it comes to kitchen chores. But I wanted to do something to help my mom out, so I kept working at it till I had it." He smiled, but his gaze remained focused on his plate.

Had she embarrassed him? She tried to erase the thought. Before the melting sensation got any more gooey.

"The effort paid off. These are delicious." She hummed with pleasure. "Why was it so important to you to help your mother out?"

He jerked his shoulder, the shrug carefully nonchalant

this time. But the flags of color hit his cheeks. She *had* embarrassed him. How intriguing.

"She worked so hard for all of us and she was always so exhausted, especially after the…" He stopped, the smile on his face flatlining as he concentrated on dousing his own pancake.

"After the what?" Zelda probed.

He swallowed, before his gaze finally met hers. "She had a miscarriage the summer I was seven. I was the only one there. Faith was asleep in her basinet and my brothers were out in the yard playing baseball. I came in to grab some lemonade for us all and went to take a leak. And there she was in the bathroom, sitting on the floor, with tears on her cheeks, her teeth gritted against the pain." His voice had become so low, Zelda almost couldn't hear it. "I'd never seen her cry before. And then I noticed the blood, spreading over the linoleum. She was six months gone, already big with the baby, but I knew it was way too soon."

"That must have been hideous." And terrifying, she realized, for a seven-year-old to see his mother in that much distress.

"I thought she was dying. She gripped my hand so hard the bones ground together. After the contraction finished she told me to call Pop. But I knew there was nothing he could do, so I disobeyed her for the first time in my life and called the paramedics instead."

"Surely your father would have called an ambulance?"

she asked, surprised by the edge in his voice. The same edge she'd heard two days ago on the beach when he was talking about the pub.

"I guess so, but I didn't want to leave it to him."

"Why not?"

He looked up from his plate, his expression neutral. "Because I figured it was his fault she was so tired all the time. They had to work such long hours to keep that damn place going."

She heard the raw resentment in his tone. So that was where his dislike of the pub came from? Borne out of a little boy's fear for his mother.

"And I knew it was his fault that she kept having babies." He added. "Because he wouldn't leave her alone."

"Wait a minute; you knew about the facts of life when you were seven?" She asked, unable to hide her shock.

She'd loved her parents both a great deal. But they had always been so unattainable, more like celebrity icons than parents—glamorous and ethereal and so perfect. She and Sebastian would get a few precious hours with them each evening, after high tea in the ambassador's residence, before her parents would be whisked off to another charity gala or diplomatic soiree. Her father would look handsome and debonair in his tux, her mother stunningly beautiful in some gorgeous designer gown, while Zelda would be ushered to bed by the nanny and Sebastian would either go to his room to read or head out for the evening with his friends.

What she'd always thought of as a fairytale childhood, though, suddenly seemed very sheltered, and carefully orchestrated, in comparison to Ty's.

His mouth hitched up on one side in a lopsided grin. "I had three little brothers and a baby sister, and we lived in a three-room apartment. What I didn't know, I had pretty much figured out by the time I was seven. My parents were both demonstrative people and they loved sex. Hence the five kids. And there wasn't a heck of a lot of privacy in that apartment." He leaned back in his chair, smiling now. "Damn, don't tell me that I've shocked the unshockable Zelda Madison."

"I'm not shocked, just…" She paused, suddenly realizing she sounded hopelessly prissy. Worse, she actually felt a little prissy. Which hadn't happened since she was about seven herself. "Surprised. I don't think I ever even saw my parents kiss."

They had been far too polite and well-bred for public displays of affection, especially in front of their own children. This was the first time though, it had occurred to her that polite might be a euphemism for passionless. She had always idolized her parents, probably because of the shockingly sudden way in which she'd lost them. But she could see now maybe they hadn't been quite as perfect as she had always believed.

"Count yourself lucky," he said wryly. "My parents

couldn't keep their damn hands off each other. When you're twelve years old and just starting to figure out how much you like girls, there's nothing more horrifying than catching your father necking with your mom over a barrel of Guinness a half hour before opening time."

Zelda snorted out a laugh. "So if they both enjoyed sex so much, why did you blame him for all the pregnancies? It sounds like they were both to blame."

He shrugged, looking suddenly sheepish. "I guess you're right. I was a kid. If you know anything about Irish boys and their mammies, you'll know that my mom meant the world to me. I wanted to look after her and protect her, because as far as I was concerned, she was the next best thing to the Virgin Mother… So, of course, I blamed him."

"How very Oedipal of you."

"Oedipus had nothing to do with it. I was a good Catholic boy with a healthy terror of sex drummed into me by the nuns at St. Patrick's. It's a miracle I've turned out so well-adjusted."

It was her turn to laugh. She got up from her seat and pushed his shoulders until he moved his chair back. Hooking her leg over, she sat down in his lap. The denim of his jeans felt deliciously rough against the soft skin of her inner thighs as she met his sheepish grin with one of her own.

"I hope you don't mind, but I suddenly have a devilish compulsion to corrupt you. And damn you to eternal damnation. It must be the militant anti-theist in me."

He slid hot hands under the T-shirt she wore, the thick ridge under his button fly becoming more pronounced as she squirmed.

"Ah, well, I guess I can be a martyr to the cause," he said, putting on a perfect Irish accent as he stood up, holding her in his arms.

He hefted her into the bedroom as she locked her legs around his waist and thrust her fingers into his hair to slant her lips over his. The sweet taste of maple syrup mixed with the heady taste of lust as she sucked on his marauding tongue. Callused hands cupped her bare buttocks, her swollen clitoris already aching for his touch. She let the endorphin rush wash over her, hoping it would sweep away all the sentimental thoughts of that young boy who had thought the world of his mother, and been determined to do anything to protect her.

What would it be like to have a man like this willing to protect you? Not as a son, but as a lover?

Her pulse jumped and she released the thick erection from his jeans, suddenly desperate to feel him hot and hard inside her. Raw, sweaty sex would have the desired effect and keep those disturbing thoughts at bay.

She didn't need anyone to protect her.

Especially not Tyrone Sullivan. It would feel cloying and claustrophobic and far too intimate.

But as she chased another endorphin high, determined

to prove to herself and him she didn't need Ty for anything other than sex, the look in his eyes as he drove her to orgasm didn't seem cheesy or sentimental or claustrophobic. It felt tender and affectionate and completely, bloody terrifying.

Chapter Eight

"IT'S TIME TO haul ass, Madison. Let's clean up and get off the barge."

Zelda stretched and yawned, her butt smarting from the light slap that had woken her up from a perfectly pleasant doze in Ty's arms.

"You haul ass." She pouted. "I'm still recuperating from your pussy-eating skills."

Ty whisked back the sheet and, ignoring her shriek of protest, hauled her up and over his shoulder.

"What the fuck do you think you're—"

Another slap landed on her naked backside. "Watch out or I'm going to wash out that potty mouth with soap."

"*You* watch out," she grumbled as he dumped her naked in the barge's tiny bathroom and flicked on the shower. The rest of her outraged protest was drowned out by a deluge of cold water from the showerhead.

Dunking her under, he continued chuckling as he soaped her tired body and doused her head with his piney shampoo. She released a low groan and stopped struggling as his clever fingers massaged her scalp, then drifted down to untie the knots in her shoulder muscles. Her nipples squeezed into tight peaks as rough palms slick with soap suds, skimmed down to cup her breasts. Throwing her arms round his neck, she dragged him under the spray.

"I'll forgive you for your outrageous treatment if you come back to bed," she offered, feeling relaxed and playful.

She'd had a moment while they made love. But only a moment. They were still good, still fine. Maybe she'd dozed off in his arms again, but that was only because she'd been too comfortable to move out of them.

And that lovey-dovey look she thought she'd seen on his face while they pounded each other into oblivion must have been an apparition, too, brought on by the echo of sentiment after thinking of her own parents while he'd been talking about his. She hardly ever thought about her parents now. Having mourned their loss too deeply as a teenager, she'd learned to lock the grief away.

His thumbs flicked her nipples, making the ache pound in her sex, before he wrapped his arms round her hips, the fierce arousal on his face a joyous vindication.

Nope, this was still just a sex thing. They'd made love two times already today before she'd dozed off. But still she wanted him again, even though she felt tender from their last sex-capade.

"Nothing doing," he murmured, contradicting himself

somewhat as he nuzzled the sensitive spot under her chin. "We need to get the hell off the barge for the rest of the day."

She glanced out the steamed glass of the bathroom window at the gathering twilight, and ignored the prickle of anxiety. They only had tonight left. "But it's practically bedtime?"

"Bullshit, the night is still young." He pulled out of her embrace, shut off the water and grabbed a towel. Sending her breasts a regretful look, he looped the fluffy white cotton over her shoulders and held it closed. "And I need some damn recovery time. We've hardly been off the barge in three days, and there's such a thing as too much hot sex. I'm not fifteen anymore."

"But I like hot sex." And while they were preoccupied with it, it generally avoided conversations about stuff that might give her more insights into Ty Sullivan the man, instead of Ty Sullivan the sex machine. She cast a salacious glance at his already thickening cock. "And that looks surprisingly perky for a guy who isn't fifteen anymore."

He lifted another towel off the pile she'd laundered for him on Friday, and hooked it round his waist. Covering up the growing erection. She reached for the towel to yank it off, but he snagged her wrist.

"Nuh uh." He lifted her hand to his lips and kissed her knuckles. Her heart bounced into her throat. "That can wait till later. I want to take you out, on a date."

"A date? What for?" She grinned, determined to tease him and ignore her erratic pulse. "Please don't tell me that Tyrone Sullivan, the big bad attorney and all around super stud is a romantic?"

He chuckled, despite the strain on his face. "It's not romance, it's self-preservation." Turning her 'round, he gave her bottom a light pat. "Now go get dressed. We're getting out of here before you kill me."

She felt that odd bounce again as they got dressed together in the small bedroom. She didn't need Ty Sullivan to take care of her. But it wouldn't do any harm to let him do it for a few hours. He seemed to need it. Probably all part of his Catholic guilt/shining armor routine. Ty couldn't help caring for women, for people. It was why he was so good at his job. It wasn't significant that he seemed to need to care for her. It was simply part of his personality—after spending his formative years minding his younger siblings, and trying to protect his mother.

As long as she didn't need him to do it, it didn't really matter what he needed. And a date seemed charming. And would be something new to explore.

Because she was fairly sure she'd never actually had a date before. She'd been far too wayward and self-destructive after her parents' death to ever do anything as quaint as let a boy take her out. What harm could it do letting Ty take her out now? It wouldn't be a real date, because they already knew she was a sure thing. And that lots more hot sex would be involved when they got back to the barge. Also, she'd come perilously close to breaking her no-cuddling rule. Having an audience for the next couple of hours might not be a bad thing.

Once they'd gone through the marina security gate, she strode off across the parking lot, having figured out where he was probably taking her.

He grabbed her hand, tugging her to a halt. "Hold up, where are you headed"

"Aren't we going to see a movie?" The marina parking lot backed onto a multiplex, so she had assumed a movie would be the obvious place for their date. And she was in the mood for something violent and dark and edgy, preferably without any lovey-dovey bits.

Drawing her towards the SUV, he clicked open the locks. "I've got a better idea. How about we go to Coney Island?"

"The amusement park?" The buzz of excitement hit her unawares.

"Yeah. We could grab a couple of Nathan's Famous, ride the Cyclone, neck on the Wonder Wheel and then take a stroll along the Boardwalk, maybe take a turn on the karaoke. What d'you say?"

The buzz peaked. "That sounds wonderful, as long as you promise not to sing." A bit too wonderful really, but she would deal with that later. Right now she was itching to find out what Nathan's Famous were exactly. "I've never been to an amusement park before." Her heart kicked under her ribs, at the childish anticipation in her tone. "It's been on my bucket list ever since I was six."

"You're kidding? Not once? How come?" He sounded so astonished, she felt hideously gauche and a little embarrassed that she'd revealed so much. Here was the evidence she was the pampered little, rich girl everyone—including him—had accused her of being.

"Don't look so surprised. It's not my fault I had a hopelessly posh upbringing. The nanny would take Seb and I to all the museums and galleries while we lived in London, but my parents wouldn't have been seen dead in an amusement park. I remember Seb tried to persuade them once to let him take me to Disneyland when we were in Paris for the Easter holidays." She hesitated, the long forgotten memory of Seb before the accident, when he had been her adored fun-loving, big brother instead of the cold, forbidding stranger he had become, bringing with it the sharp pang of grief. "But they said no, because they felt it wouldn't be suitable, or particularly educational."

Her entertainments as a child had been so carefully vetted and always so cerebral and sophisticated—the few family outings her parents had time for invariably part of their official duties—a garden party in the grounds of Buckingham Palace; the opening night of a play at the National Theatre; a performance of Bizet's Carmen at the Paris Opera House; even a pre-Christmas shopping trip with her mother to Harrods one year had been to open the newly refurbished Food Hall. How funny to think, she had once been so good at being on her best behavior.

"It all sounds so ludicrously pompous now, doesn't it," she added. "Especially when you think of the sort of things I got up to after they'd died."

"It doesn't sound pompous. It sounds sad. And kind of lonely. What about after they died? Why didn't your brother take you to Disneyland then?"

Zelda shielded her eyes against the dying light, trying to assess Ty's reaction. Why did he sound so serious?

"Seb packed me off to a succession of boarding schools not long after the funeral, where I proceeded to behave so badly I was never permitted to go on any outings. And once I was finally free of school, I was tempted towards the sort of amusements that you don't find in parks. Does that answer your question?"

"He sounds like a selfish bastard."

"Who?" she asked, puzzled by the spike of anger.

"Your brother."

Zelda frowned, dropping her arm. She didn't need to see Ty's face anymore. And she really didn't want to see his anger on her behalf. Because it might bring back the pointless yearning that had dominated so much of her adolescence, to have someone like him, someone older and stronger, care about her. To shelter her and protect her, and protest her innocence when the Mother Superior and her evil minion Iggy accused her of stealing the wine when she hadn't.

And it was far too late for that.

Maybe Seb had abandoned her emotionally, at a time when she had needed him. But she was all grown up now. And she'd had to force herself to stop using all the things she'd lost that fateful day thirteen years ago as excuses to explain the mess she'd made of her life since. Ultimately, you had to own your mistakes, or you couldn't correct them. All Ty's sympathy and anger would do now was make her feel like that lonely, isolated, defenseless child again. When she wasn't.

And anyway, Ty's anger wasn't really about her. This was just his white knight complex talking. It had to be.

"Seb can be a beast. You won't get any argument from me there. But he isn't selfish, he's damaged. The accident damaged him. He was driving the car, and I think he blamed himself. Maybe that's what messed him up, because something certainly did. But frankly, I don't really care anymore." Because she couldn't afford to care—because trying to hold on to her brother, trying to understand why he didn't care about her anymore, had damaged her, too. "So I guess if anyone is selfish in this scenario it's me," she added defiantly.

Ty took her arm, tugging her round to face him, his expression illuminated by the gathering dusk.

"He abandoned you, Zel, when you were just a little

kid and he was the only family you had left. You do know you're not to blame for that, right?"

"Of course, I do." She jerked her arm free, suddenly afraid that he would be able to feel the jittering pulse under his thumb. And see through the lie to the fear beneath, that she *was* to blame for Seb's abandonment, because she'd been so difficult and so unlovable in the years after their parents' death.

She forced a smile to her lips. The sultry, sexy, couldn't-give-a-shit smile she had perfected over the years to hide the great big gaping wound in her heart. The smile that told everyone she was a bad girl, and that's the way she liked it.

"Now can we please stop talking about Seb? I thought you were going to take me to Coney Island? Not bore me to death with a conversation about my brother."

His frown arrowed down, and a muscle twitched in his jaw. She braced herself for a blast of temper at her failure to give this discussion the gravity he probably thought it deserved. But to her surprise, the blast of temper never came. Instead, he looked away, his face rigid, but when he turned back, he'd pasted an easy smile on those sensual lips. The muscle in his jaw was still twitching, though.

"Fair point." He opened the passenger door of the SUV. "Climb aboard, princess. We better get you to Coney Island before your chariot turns into a pumpkin."

She beamed her bad girl smile back at him, before placing a light, teasing kiss on his lips. "Let's hurry, it's not every day a girl gets to go on her first rollercoaster ride."

But as he climbed into the driver's seat and backed out of the lot, it occurred to her even her first rollercoaster ride was unlikely to leave her feeling as giddy as Ty Sullivan had managed with one far too perceptive conversation.

✦

"HOT DOGS! NATHAN'S Famous are hot dogs. And they're delicious." Zel's eyes lit up, much as they had done most of the evening, the dark blue sparkling with enthusiasm as the light from the Ferris wheel a block away illuminated her flushed skin.

Ty watched as she consumed another huge bite of her Nathan's Famous, enjoying the way she devoured it, the way she'd devoured every new experience tonight—with an infectious enthusiasm at discovering new things, and without an ounce of the snobbery he would have expected from her three days ago. Before he'd come to know her.

He didn't think he'd ever forget the earsplitting shriek she'd let out when their car had arrived at the top of the Cyclone, the vintage wooden structure creaking ominously before they swooped down into the night. She'd held her arms above her head like a pro and screamed her lungs out right next to his ear.

And he'd loved it.

The woman was wild and untamed and all the more

beautiful for it. There was a danger to Zelda, a sort of unstoppable joy about the way she consumed experiences, the same way she consumed sex. As if she were scared that it might be her last chance, so she was bound and determined to make the most of it.

She was easily the hottest woman he'd ever dated. Not just in bed but also out of it. She made him feel alive in a way he never had before. He'd always been so damn cautious. Careful not to get sidetracked by the little things in life, because it was only the big stuff that mattered—working hard, achieving his goals, and making sure he didn't step into the same trap as his parents, living a chaotic existence, with too many mouths to feed, in a tiny apartment running a business that sucked all the energy out of you.

But right now, all his caution didn't seem like such a great thing. Had he maybe been too cautious? Because how had his plan turned him into a workaholic who'd never made a real connection with any woman, who lived on a house barge that was little more than a pit stop and whose whole life had become a dull round of case files and plea bargains and trial dates?

He avoided his family, rarely took time off and when he did, it was usually to crash into bed and think about the stuff he had to do next. Somehow or other his carefully planned out life had become no life at all. And he might never have figured that out, but for these last three days with Zelda.

"Damn it, Zelda, that's a capital offense." He teased as she stuffed another huge bite into her mouth.

"Wot iz?" she said, her eyes wide as she talked round a mouth full of bread and beef frank.

"I don't care how long you lived in London, you were born in Manhattan, right?"

She nodded.

"Which makes you a freaking New Yorker. And every New Yorker should know hot dogs were created in Coney Island by Nathan Handwerker."

She swallowed. "What are you, the pop culture police?"

"Damn straight." He grinned at the snotty tone, then brushed his thumb over her lip, catching the drop of ketchup that hung at the edge of her mouth.

She watched him as he licked it off his thumb. The tart, sweet taste lingered in his mouth as she looked away, but he had spotted the flash of knowledge.

Jesus, he wanted her again. The hunger hadn't really gone away all night, even when they'd been playing the slots, or riding the Wonder Wheel, or joining in the karaoke dances on the beach. He had to be the only guy capable of getting aroused while busy shuffling his butt out of time to *Cha-Cha Slide Part Two* with a hundred other people. Or when she'd stood with her back against his chest, his arms wrapped around her as they watched the fireworks explode over the bay signaling the last day of summer.

The woman was like a drug, both potent and addictive. He dumped the last of his own dog in the trash as they headed back towards the parking lot, unsettled by the grinding weight in the pit of his stomach, at the thought that the weekend was nearly over.

Neon lights glittered in the night sky, the piped music hyperactive and discordant as it filled the muggy air with fake merriment. The scent of popcorn and freshly cooked donuts smothered the sea air as they headed past the food vendors and hit the main thoroughfare.

She finished her dog and he lobbed her napkin into a trash can, before taking her hand loosely in his. The soft skin felt cool in his, but she didn't draw away.

"I've had fun." Her hand squeezed his. "Did you come here a lot when you were a child?"

He could hear the wistfulness. And imagined her as a child. Lost and alone.

"Not often, no. My folks couldn't afford the time and money for vacations, and they were always stuck in the pub." He kicked an empty cotton candy carton, then bent to pick it up—hearing the bitterness in his tone. But as he threw the carton in the trash, he felt a little ashamed of his resentment. His parents had always relied on him as a kid to watch over his younger siblings, and they'd never been able to give any of them much in the way of material goods, especially in the early days, when they were working all hours to change a failing business into a going concern. But those family trips to Coney Island had been a high point of his childhood.

"But we used to come here once a year and it was a really big deal, because it was the only vacation we had," he continued, allowing the old joy to take the bitterness away. "Pop would put a couple of big, old mason jars in the kitchen at the start of summer vacation which we'd have to fill with nickels and dimes and quarters as fast as we could. Finn and the twins would play for change on the sidewalk. I had a couple of paper rounds and did deliveries for Mr. Zunicki at the grocery store, and Faith, when she got to be a bit older, would sell lemonade after Mass. Mom and Pop would put into it, too, tips from the bar, or spare change from the grocery shopping. The deal was, once it was full, Pop would break the jar and we could go to Coney Island for a whole day. But he used to keep us in suspense for weeks, while my brothers would moan and carry on, insisting the jars were full. And then usually, when we'd all given up hope, Pop would come into the kitchen one morning with a hammer. We'd start cheering and whooping because we knew what it meant. Today was going to be Coney Island Day."

"Please, will you tell me about it? I used to adore hearing Faith's stories about your family at school, but she never told me about Coney Island Day." Zelda's fingers squeezed his, her excitement an echo of the joy that had exploded in his chest when he was a kid and his Pop would arrive in the kitchen with the hammer. "And don't stint on the details," she added, her enthusiasm making her sound like a child on Christmas morning. Or even Coney Island Day.

He laughed, feeling strangely proud and humble that he had the story to tell. "Sure, if you want." He gripped her hand, set it swinging, realizing how long it had been since he'd thought of this—such a simple memory, but such a good one.

Why had he always found it so easy to focus on the tough aspects of his childhood, instead of the good stuff?

"Well, once Pop had smashed the jar, we'd run around laughing like loons while we scrambled into our clothes, and mom got Faith ready. Then Pop would send me off with my brothers, hefting the big bag of change 'round to Mr. Zunicki to get all the nickels and dimes changed into dollar bills. When we got back, there would be a 'closed' sign on the pub. And we'd all pile into the station wagon and Pop would tell me to count up the money and share it out between me and my brothers and, when she was old enough, Faith, too. But I always had to leave enough over to give myself an extra twenty dollars.'

"Didn't that piss off your siblings?" Zelda said, outraged as only a younger sister could be. "That you got more than them?"

"Are you kidding me? They pissed and moaned about it

every single year. All except Faith, who always stuck up for me, no matter what. But Pop would shut them up, saying I was the oldest and I did the most to help out, so I deserved the extra money."

How come he'd never remembered that either? That amongst all the responsibility he'd shouldered, and which he'd come to resent once he'd gotten older, there had also been all those small rewards and acknowledgements—which had made him feel ten feet tall when he was a kid.

"I suppose that's fair," Zel said, still sounding aggrieved.

"Hey, don't get too upset. I always ended up sharing the extra money with my brothers and Faith anyway. Who wants to ride the Cyclone on their own?"

"Not me." She shuddered theatrically. "So what else did you do? Did you spend the whole day on the rides?"

"No, eventually the money would run out, so we'd head for the Boardwalk. Mom would hound Finn and the twins into singing a couple of her favorite Neil Diamond tunes on the karaoke. Pop would stand in line to get us hot dogs for supper so we could eat them on the beach while we watched the fireworks. And Casey always threw up on the car journey home because he'd eaten too much candy."

Zelda laughed, the throaty purr rich and full. "It sounds like so much fun. What a wonderful family memory to have. I envy you." He caught the wistfulness in her tone again. And suddenly felt unbearably sad for her.

He'd been devastated when his mom died, the cancer diagnosis had been so unexpected, the swiftness of her death so shocking, and even though he'd been nineteen and just starting college, he'd felt the loss like a wound for years. And because of that, he'd been so mad with his pop, for not noticing how ill she was, for not doing enough to save her. And for falling to pieces when she'd gone.

He'd needed to have someone to blame. But the truth was, it had been nobody's fault. And while he'd missed his mother, he'd still had his brothers and his sister and even his old man—despite the fact the guy had been hollowed out by grief. What must it have been like for Zelda, who'd lost both her parents when she was so much younger and had nobody to take their place? Least of all her older brother?

Did that explain all the dumb choices she'd made? The wild behavior and reckless misdemeanors? Had it all just been a plea for attention? For affection?

He let go of her hand, and slung his arm round her waist, pulling her round to face him in the darkness. The urge to hold her, to kiss her and keep her safe, overwhelming. "Yeah, I guess it was pretty amazing," he said.

He looked back across the lot towards the pulsing neon in the distance, the raucous sound of piped disco music carrying towards them on the breeze, and recalled the aching sense of loss he'd felt as a kid when the fireworks had finished and Pop would declare it was time to go home for another year.

Back then, the weeks and months it would take for the summer to come round again and the long days after that before they had managed to fill the jar with enough money to earn another trip had stretched ahead of him like an eternity.

Because he was the oldest, and he knew his parents needed him to set a good example for his brothers, he had never kicked up a fuss the way they did when Pop said Coney Island Day was over. Even though for him the longing to stay had been painful, because he knew once they got back to the pub he wouldn't be able to be just a kid again for another year.

"You don't seem too sure," Zelda said beside him.

He looked at her, the sharp sense of longing returning, but for something very different this time. Zelda had set her damn rules at the start of this weekend, but after everything they'd done together and how much they'd shared and how good she'd made him feel, he knew something now that he hadn't known as a boy.

Sometimes it was better to break the rules than stick to ones that made you miserable.

"No, you're right. It was amazing having my family with me back then."

Almost as amazing as it's been having you with me for the last three days.

He cradled Zelda's cheeks, lifting her face to his, and saw the wariness in her eyes as her palms settled over his.

"Ty, what is it? You look so serious?"

He shook his head, smiling at the concern in her voice. "Not serious. Just happy."

This *so* wasn't just a weekend booty call, for either one of them.

"Happy I can handle," she said, smiling as she relaxed.

If she knew what he was thinking, she'd probably freak-out again, the way she had on Saturday when he'd given her a simple compliment. So he decided not to tell her. Not yet anyway. But even if he couldn't tell her how he felt, surely there was no harm in showing her.

So he sunk his fingers into the short curls of hair, angling her head and placed his lips over hers.

She tensed for a moment, her hands covering his, but as he traced the seam of her lips, coaxing her mouth open with his tongue, she softened up again.

The tempting tug of hunger weighed down the pit of his stomach like a hot brick, as he poured everything he felt into the kiss—the ardent strokes of his tongue firm and seeking. At last her tongue danced with his and he wondered if she could feel the solid thumps of his heart beating against her ribs.

She dragged his hands down from her face, and drew back first, her eyes shadowed, her fingers trembling.

"Let's go home and fuck," she said, sending him that confident come-on smile which was supposed to make him think sex was all she wanted. All she needed. But her bottom lip quivered a tiny bit and he could see the flicker of need in her eyes.

She'd used the word fuck to shock him, to bring their relationship back to the level she was comfortable with. But Ty Sullivan had never shocked easy. And all he'd really heard anyway was the word home.

"Your carriage awaits, princess." He dipped into an exaggerated bow, opening the passenger door for her.

She hopped into the car and he slammed the door. He said nothing as they raced home through the night. Or as he fucked her hard and fast, then slow and easy in the moonlit bedroom, bringing her ruthlessly to climax before he found his own release.

He held her close afterwards, satisfied when she lay in his arms as docile and trusting as a child. Did she know she was breaking her own rules?

"It wasn't you, was it?" he murmured in the darkness, stroking her cheek with his thumb.

"Hmmm?" she said, her voice heavy with sleep, as she snuggled against him.

"Who stole the wine at that fancy boarding school."

It wasn't a question, because he already knew the truth. Zelda would never have stayed silent, if she had been the guilty party. No way would she have let Faith get suspended over a crime she had committed. Or Dawn or… That other girl whose name he still couldn't remember. Because under her bad girl exterior he'd discovered a woman who was smart-mouthed and strong enough to always own up to her mistakes, and far too aware of her own faults to ever judge others.

She stilled beside him. "Why does it matter now?" she said, not contradicting him.

He dropped his hand to her shoulder. Resisting the urge to hug her too tightly, he let his thumb drift backwards and forwards over her collarbone.

He didn't want to scare her. But he needed her to know this much at least. "It doesn't, I guess, except..."

She tilted her face up, those dark blue eyes wide with astonishment. And it crucified him. How could she not know how smart and strong and brave she was?

He pressed a kiss to her forehead, inhaled the pine-forest scent of his own shampoo on the blond curls.

"I just wanted to say how sorry I am," he continued. "For convicting you that day without a shred of evidence. For assuming you were the guilty one, because you were rich and privileged and I'd gotten it into my head that you were corrupting my kid sister, when you were just a kid yourself." A kid who had lost so much and had no one to stand for her, or support her, except his sister and her friends. "You didn't deserve that. I was being an asshole and I wanted to apologize." He smiled, his Adam's apple swelling to the size of a boulder in his throat. "Even if it is ten years too late."

She gave a half laugh and tucked her head back under

his chin, her cheek resting against his chest. "That's sweet, Ty, but entirely unnecessary." She yawned, her cheek rubbing his sternum and making the hairs stand to attention. "Even if I didn't do that, I was guilty of pretty much everything else. And it gave me a massive thrill when you noticed me, so we're all square."

He chuckled but her confession only made him feel sadder. For that rebellious girl who had used her defiance to protect herself from being hurt. He held her, listening to the solid thunks of his heartbeat in his ears, the creaking of the boat as it settled into the tide, and the murmur of her breathing, as her body softened into sleep. He wanted to say so much more. But he forced himself to hold back.

They'd moved on from a weekend booty call, surely she could see that? So what if their lives were worlds apart? They could make this work, if they were both willing to try. But he needed to put the case to her properly. And he would have more than enough time to do that before she left in the morning.

✦

HE WOKE UP to the beep of his iPhone alarm refreshed and alert the next day, the case he'd planned out in his head still clear in his mind, to find the bed beside him empty and Zelda gone. The only trace she had ever even been there were the two T-shirts she'd borrowed, that still carried her scent, neatly folded on the couch, and the note stuck to his coffee pot written in a looping blue scrawl which read:

Thanks for everything, counselor. You're a prince.

Zx

He scrunched up the note in his fist, as all his carefully rehearsed arguments wadded up in his throat. She hadn't even stuck around to say goodbye? But as he showered and shaved and got ready for his next day in court, the last thirty-six hours reeled back through his head and hope blossomed under the hurt.

This was fixable. He'd call Faith, get Zelda's cell number, and contact her, to arrange a date to meet up. All he needed was a chance to make his case.

If she wasn't interested, if he'd read her all wrong and made a mistake about her feelings, he would respect the rules they'd agreed to and he wouldn't contact her again.

But until she told him that to his face, as far as he was concerned all bets were off. Because he wasn't a prince, he was just an ordinary guy. And unlike when he was a kid and his Pop told him he had to leave Coney Island for another summer—there was no freaking way he was going to do as he was told this time, without putting up a fight.

Chapter Nine

ZELDA ENTERED THE comforting half-light of Sullivan's pub on a Thursday night ten days later, not feeling at all comfortable. She scanned the bar and the tables at the back by the stage, where Faith's twin brothers, Ronan and Casey, were warming up the small Thursday night crowd with an old, rebel ballad on accordion and guitar. She sent the two of them a quick wave, then headed towards the last booth opposite the bar where she knew her friends would be waiting. She spotted the posters of Faith's younger brother Finn's illustrious career as a concert violinist which Faith had tacked up during the party at the pub a couple of months ago. She passed the fireplace and the portrait of John F. Kennedy which hung above it, letting out the breath she'd been holding, and ignored the jabbing pain, that might just be regret, under her left breast.

It was good that Ty wasn't here. She didn't want him to be here. Skipping out on him while he slept on Tuesday morning over a week ago had been tough enough. Not to mention letting the succession of calls from him the next day and the day after on her mobile go to voicemail. It was cowardly, she knew that, but they'd had an agreement. And he'd broken it. And she wasn't sure she would be able to do and say what she had to say if she heard his voice again.

She blinked away the emotion as she made her way past a group of city workers, remembering the hushed apology Ty had given her their last night together. A hushed apology that had moved her in a way she couldn't allow herself to be moved.

There were reasons why she couldn't contemplate a relationship with anyone, but she especially couldn't fall for someone like Ty. A guy who was genuine and kind and nurturing. She'd heard him hesitate, while she lay listening to his heart beating, her body still humming from afterglow and the sweetness of his apology, as if he were debating whether to say something more. And for one foolish moment she had yearned to hear him say he wanted her to stay, that things had changed, that the rules didn't matter.

That what they had was more than a sex thing.

Recalling that bit of foolishness had terrified her once she'd woken up the next morning, still snuggled against him.

Thank goodness he hadn't said it. And when she'd woken up with his arm around her, her flight instinct had finally kicked in. The way it should have done the night before.

Of course, she could have simply told him the truth. That she was an alcoholic in recovery—and as a result, she would never be able to make a commitment to any man, because her commitment must always be to her recovery. But she hadn't wanted to say it, hadn't wanted to shatter the illusion he had of her. Or watch the affection in his eyes die. She didn't care if it was dishonest, or delusional, she'd wanted to keep that one memory sweet. Telling him the truth would have killed it altogether, and felt like too cruel a price to pay, if she didn't have to.

As she edged past the last of the city slickers at the bar, she had another wobble when she noticed a tall, broad-shouldered guy with his back to her, his dark hair curling against the collar of his blue, pinstriped suit. But then he turned and winked at her and it wasn't Ty.

"How about a drink, hot stuff?" he said.

Instead of delivering the flirtatious slap down that would usually have popped out of her mouth, she simply broke eye contact and walked on.

She spotted Mercy in their designated booth, her luscious hair gleaming ebony in the low lighting. Mercy dropped her head back, the rich throaty laugh carrying over the plaintive melody of Ronan's accordion and the hubbub of Thursday night conversation.

Dawn sat beside her, sleek and professional in a crisp blouse and pencil skirt to go with her neat and efficient chignon, probably completely oblivious to the way her smile drew the eye and held it. Like Mercy, Dawn's face could have put her on any catwalk in the world. But her friends hadn't taken the easy way out like she had. They'd followed their brains instead of their looks—with Mercy currently taking a break from running her parents' wine empire to do an MBA at Stern and Dawn heading a medical research company that benefitted the world.

Tucking away the sting of inadequacy as she approached the booth, Zelda inhaled the scent of yeast and cigarettes that clung to the woodwork despite New York's smoking ban. She'd always loved the smell of stale smoke, polished wood and hard liquor—a bit too much for a while. But despite the emotional upheaval of the last week and a half, as she had struggled to wean herself off her addiction to Tyrone Sullivan, the temptation to drink had been noticeably absent. Plus, she'd finally begun to take the first steps on a career path that would give her life real meaning. She could be proud of that.

She was somewhat less proud of the fact she'd seriously considered skipping out on the monthly meet-up with her friends, just in case Ty showed up, but was glad now she hadn't. Ty wasn't here and Faith, Dawn and Mercy were her lifeline, her support network. The only family she had that was worth having. Ronan went into a riotous reel joined by his twin brother Casey on the Irish flute and Zel's spirits lifted out of the doldrums they'd been in ever since she'd left Ty's house barge.

She couldn't tell them about Ty, because of his connection to Faith and Dawn's relationship with Faith and Ty's brother Finn, it was way too close to home. Virtually incestuous. But just seeing her friends, hearing their voices, sharing whatever stupid stories they had to tell since the last time they'd met up a month ago ought to help blast her out of her present funk. Hopefully. Maybe.

Mercy spotted her approaching first and gasped as she leapt out of the booth. "*Dios*! Zelda, your hair!"

Zelda laughed and touched her fingers to the boy cut she'd all but forgotten about. Fantasy still hadn't done a press release on her departure as their 'it girl' and when she'd arrived back at the Mausoleum there had been no paparazzi in attendance—so her new look had yet to hit the newsstands.

Seb's response when she'd finally gotten up the guts to visit his study on the townhouse's top floor at the weekend had been to flick his glance up to her hairline and then say nothing. He'd been equally dismissive of her apologies for not showing up at the Foundation Gala the previous Thursday, saying simply, "I find if I expect nothing from you, Zel, I'm rarely disappointed."

The cutting remark had stung, as it always did. But she'd tucked the hurt away with more ease than usual, because her misery over Ty had felt a lot more immediate.

"What do you think?" She slid into the red-leather booth opposite them as Mercy took the seat beside Dawn.

"I had a radical hair rethink over Labor Day weekend."

Dawn whistled. "Not that I know much about current hair trends, but I'd say it totally suits you."

Mercy clapped her hands in glee. "I love it. It makes those cheekbones look even more incredible. Although…" She paused, her expression sobering. "You've given up your modeling career, then?"

She nodded. "Yes, I'm finally free of Fantasy. No more ivory tower for me, it's time to get a proper job." The mention of her ivory tower brought with it thoughts of Ty and the way he'd sneered the words at her the night he'd come to rescue her from her own stupidity. Which suddenly felt like several lifetimes ago, instead of just a fortnight. She swallowed the lump in her throat.

Good grief, Zel. Now you're even getting sentimental about his sneer? Seriously?

Mercy grinned, and leaned across the booth to squeeze Zelda's hand. "That's wonderful; it's the right thing for you."

"Yes, it is."

Dawn toasted her with the Guinness glass in her hand. "That's terrific, Zel. I'm so glad you finally took the leap. Have you thought about what you're going to do for your new career?"

"Actually, I have. The only thing I'm any good at—other than looking good with hair—is my language skills. So I've been checking out classes—I'm thinking of becoming an interpreter." The truth was, she'd never even thought of it until she had checked out the site for the Legal Aid Society—because she'd had an insane urge to look at Ty's picture—and seen an ad for volunteer translators. She wouldn't consider working in the same office as Ty, but it had made her think about how much she admired him for what he did, and how she could be useful, too. Maybe not as useful as him, but certainly helpful. Of course, she'd had an awkward moment, when it had occurred to her that even though she'd broken it off she might be looking for his approval, but had discarded the idea. After all, she was never going to see him again.

"Wow, you look amazing, Zel. Love the cute and sassy new do." Faith arrived at the booth, toting a jug of the virgin mojitos she always made up especially for Zel. "When did you get that done?"

"Um…" Zel wrapped her hand round her neck, to cover the burning sensation at her nape. "Over the Labor Day weekend." *At the barbershop next to your brother's house barge, before I screwed him to within an inch of his life.*

Faith poured Zelda a glass of the fizzy apple juice and lime and mint concoction. The pub didn't usually sell cocktails, but Faith had learned how to make this one for Zel, so she didn't feel left out during their girls' night. Guilt made the blush on Zel's neck spread across her collarbone.

"How did everything work out in Sheepshead Bay? Did Ty manage to bust you out of jail?" Faith said, grinning.

"Zelda was in jail?" Mercy sounded more amused than

shocked. "What for this time?"

"She went skinny dipping on Manhattan Beach and got arrested," Faith supplied, a little too helpfully.

"I did not," Zelda managed, the blush going radioactive. "I had underwear on and it was only a citation. Ty paid the fine, so I need to give you a check to pay him back." Stupid she hadn't done that already, but somehow it had felt too final. Too much like the end.

"I told you he'd help you out," Faith said, her voice thick with pride. "He can be an awesome big brother when he's not being too overbearing."

"Unlike the one Zel got stuck with," Mercy said, the caustic edge in her voice surprising Zelda. She knew Mercy didn't have much time for Seb, even though she'd once had a huge crush on him at school. But it wasn't like Mercy to be too critical of anyone. She usually saw the best in people.

Then again, Seb didn't really have a lot of redeeming features. There was that.

"Hey, by the way, did Ty manage to reach you?" Faith cut in. "He called me a week ago for your number. Said he needed to talk to you about something. I guess it was to do with your midnight skinny dip," Faith added, still teasing.

"Um, yes, he did. It's all sorted," Zel lied again, the guilty blush incinerating her neck and working its way into her cheeks. Thank God for the low lighting in the shadowy booth. Even so, she raised the icy mojito glass to roll it across her brow before she caught fire.

Faith looked at her quizzically. "Are you okay? I could turn up the air conditioning in here. You look a little hot?"

"Maybe you need another midnight swim?" Dawn said, not at all helpfully. "Then again, two arrests in one month would be a record, even for you."

"Ha ha, so glad you guys can see the funny side," Zel hissed, because she was not seeing the funny side, at all. "I told you, it was only a citation. And Officers Kelly and Mendoza only fined me so they would have a good excuse to take me back to the station house. They were worried about my safety."

"Ah, New York's finest." Faith heaved an exaggerated sigh. "I hope they were both really hot."

"They were both almost as old as your pop, actually,' Zel said, trying to redirect the conversation away from the extremely dangerous topic of hot men.

"Silver foxes, then? Maybe?" Dawn asked.

"Behave yourself," Mercy said. "You don't need a silver fox, now you're cohabiting with the scorchingly hot Finn Sullivan."

"Do you mind if we don't talk about how scorchingly hot my brother is?" Faith said, plaintively.

"As the woman who had her hands on your brother's exceptionally hot nekkid butt this morning, I'm afraid I do mind," Dawn piped up, sending Faith a cheeky grin.

"Gee, thanks, Dawn," Faith grinned back, taking the

familiar teasing in stride.

Zelda bit her bottom lip to hold in her groan of distress.

How the bloody hell had the conversation gotten out of control so quickly? One minute they'd been talking about college classes for translators and the next they'd been discussing Finn Sullivan's naked butt. Which she would hazard a guess wasn't a patch on his older brother's naked butt. Not that she was thinking about Ty's naked butt. At all.

Just as she was trying to get that inappropriate thought the hell out of her head, Mercy piped up again. "Talking about Faith's hot brothers, another one of them just walked into the pub."

Dawn craned her neck to get a better look. But already Zelda's heart was slamming into her ribcage with the force and fury of a sledgehammer—equal parts horror and euphoria. It couldn't be? Could it? He'd promised he wouldn't come into the pub while she was here? Then again, he'd promised not to contact her, too. Or hug her and cuddle her and spoon with her, unless erections were involved.

Don't think about his bloody erection, are you nuts.

"It's Ty," Dawn said, and the last of the blood drained from Zel's head, to crash into her already palpitating heart. "And it looks like he's headed this way."

So much for Ty Sullivan being a law-abiding citizen. The man couldn't even follow a simple set of rules.

"That's weird." Faith swiveled round to look through the crowd, as Zelda shrank into the corner of the booth. "He hardly ever comes into the pub."

Maybe he wasn't even here to see her? It had been over a week since he'd contacted her. This didn't have to be bad.

"Hey, Ty, how's it going?" Faith said.

"Hi, sis," came the clipped response in that deep, Brooklyn accent which detonated all over Zelda's body.

She concentrated on her mojito, the blush now setting light to her scalp. If she didn't look at him, maybe he'd go away. She wanted him to go away.

"I need to talk to Zelda."

She could hear the barely leashed temper. She carried on staring at her mojito. She could feel four pairs of eyes on her. But only one set of them, the deep emerald green ones with flecks of gold in the irises, were making her feel as if it the top of her head was about to blow off.

"What do you need to talk to Zel about?" Faith said, cutting through the tension now crackling in the air.

"That's between me and her."

Zelda risked a glance and wished she hadn't. He stood at the end of the booth, his eyes locked on hers. With his tie gone, and the shirt unbuttoned at the neck to reveal his tanned throat, he looked tall and dark in his rumpled business suit and completely and utterly gorgeous.

"Go away," she managed, but the demand came out on a mortifying squeak of distress. "You promised you wouldn't come here."

"Fuck that. We need to talk."

"We do *not* need to talk."

"Is this something to do with Zelda's citation?" Faith's head swung back and forth between the two of them.

"Butt out, sis. This is between me and Zel."

"Don't talk to Faith like that." Zel found her voice at last, the guilt consuming her.

"Forget it, Ty. No way am I butting out," Faith said. "Until someone tells me what the hell is going on?"

"I'd say it was fairly obvious what's going on," Mercy observed, only the tiniest hint of her native Argentina still present in her flawless English. "Zel and your brother are lovers."

Zelda shot a horrified look at Mercy. "How did you know that?" she blurted out, then realized she'd revealed exactly what she had intended not to reveal.

"Simple," Mercy replied with unshakeable pragmatism. "There are enough sparks flying between you two to give an innocent bystander an orgasm."

"For the love of Christ, Mercy," Faith groaned. "That's my brother you're talking about."

"Faith, your brothers are hot," Dawn jumped in, sending Zelda a sympathetic smile. "Deal with it."

"Okay, enough of the chitchat, girls," Ty cut in, not sounding amused. "Get the hell out of the booth, Faith, so Zel can come out of there and talk to me in private."

"I'm not going anywhere." Zelda clamped her hand on Faith's arm, in case her friend decided to obey her big brother's surly command. "And neither is Faith."

Ty leant into the booth past his sister, his eyes fixed on Zelda. The familiar scent of him enveloped her and sent a blast of need to her already overwrought senses. "You want to have this conversation here, in front of my sister and your friends? Or in the basement, in private? It's your call. But we *are* having this conversation, you owe me that much."

She could still hear the spike of temper, but behind it was the echo of hurt. The hurt she'd caused, by being a coward, and not telling him the truth when she had the chance.

She let go of Faith's arm. "It's all right, Faith, you can let me out now."

"Are you sure?"

She nodded, and her friend stood up.

Ty took her arm as soon as she had edged out of the booth after Faith. As if he were scared she would run off again.

"Thanks, sis. Goodbye, ladies," he said, his voice tight.

Before any of her friends had a chance to reply, Zelda found herself being drawn towards the back of the bar and out into a narrow alleyway. Slamming open a side door, Ty hauled her down a flight of stairs into a vast, cavernous cellar room stacked to the ceiling with kegs. Dimly lit by a single bulb at the far end of the space, lines of tubing snaked upwards, siphoning the beer and stout and lager from the tapped kegs to the bar above.

She tugged her arm out of his grasp. “You can stop manhandling me now, thank you very much.”

Shoving the door closed, he flicked the lock. “Damn it, Zel. Why did you run off like that, without a word? And why didn’t you answer any of my calls or texts?”

“I left you a note,” she protested, the energy firing through her system at the sight of him, the smell of him, clean and male, above the cloying scent of alcohol. “What more did you want? I told you the rules and you agreed to them. And now you’ve informed Faith of our liaison, you’ve finally managed to break every single one of them.”

“Fuck the rules. I don’t give a shit about them, because this became more than that. And you broke those damn rules, too, so don’t deny it.”

“If I did, I regret it now,” she lied, her gaze fixating on the strong column of his throat, the bob of his Adam’s apple, the firm sensual line of his lips, flat with displeasure.

“No you don’t.” He grasped her arm again, pulled her towards him.

But this time, she couldn’t find the will to pull away, to pull back. She’d missed him so much. But even as the sharp rush of longing consumed her, she assured herself it was nothing more than endorphins. This was chemistry, biology. The instinctive desire to mate. It was an addiction she would have to break, but as the answering desire sparked in his eyes, and his fingers pressed into her bicep, she took in the tortured rise and fall of his chest beneath the creased shirt. And knew he wanted her, too.

Why not have one more fuck for old time's sake? Before she had to go cold turkey. Did the hair of the dog theory work for sexual addictions?

And if they jumped each other, there would be no time for talk.

Her fevered mind clung to the insane logic, as his fingers plunged into her hair, and lifted her face to his.

"Damnit, I've missed you so much," he murmured, his lips hovering so close, promising so much. "Now tell me you haven't missed me, too?"

"I can't." She grasped his face, pulled his mouth down to hers and shoved him back against the stacked barrels.

Insanity gripped her as she ripped at his shirt. Buttons popped, pinging against the concrete floor. Her hands found warm solid flesh and felt the quiver of muscle and bone, the leashed power in him like a racehorse at the starting gate. She sucked in a lungful of his scent. Fresh male sweat, pine shampoo, the spicy hint of cologne. Then fastened her lips over his and thrust her tongue into his mouth.

He sucked on her tongue, groaning, and then swung her round, until her back hit the damp brick, cool against her heated flesh. His large hand gripped her thigh, to hook her leg over his hip. The solid ridge of his erection felt glorious, as he ground his length against her aching clit through their clothing.

Reaching down, she grappled to find his fly, to tug down the zipper and work her hand into his shorts.

He swore, letting out a low groan as she found him firm, and long, and so wonderfully hard.

"I want you inside me," she begged.

His fingers located the damp gusset of her panties, nudging the satin aside to plunge into the wet heat. His thumb brushed her throbbing clit and she bucked.

"You're so wet." He pressed his forehead against hers, the groan wretched with longing. "I don't have any condoms."

"I'm on the pill." She stroked his length, felt it leap against her hand. "I'm safe." But this wasn't safe. If she took this plunge again would she ever be able to pull back?

But even as the sane thought pierced the feverish longing, she knew she couldn't say no. Not this time. Not to him.

She glided her thumb across the head of his erection, spreading the bead of pre-come. The magnificent shaft bobbed in her hand, but he shifted back, to cradle her face. "Are you sure, Zel?"

"Yes, now shut up and do me."

His eyes narrowed at the vulgar tone and she wondered if she'd pushed him too far. But then he swore under his breath and lifted her, wedging her thighs further apart to rip at her panties.

The sound of satin tearing echoed in the cavernous space and then his fingers were digging into soft flesh as he positioned himself to thrust hard. Her head dropped back, the brutal swell of desire tempered by shock as he impaled himself to the hilt, her slick flesh stretching to receive him.

He buried his face in her neck, pulled out and plunged back. She held onto his shoulders, anchoring herself as best she could against the stunning pressure, the punishing pleasure. His grunts and her sobs sounded raw and primal as he drove into her. Again and again. Flesh slapped against flesh, the spiral of heat yanking tight, surging up from her center, threatening to tear her apart. The feeling of loss and longing and regret burned away on the savage swell. Brutal, tumultuous, unstoppable.

She fisted her fingers in his hair, urging him on, crying out as the orgasm overtook her at last, exploding through her senses. His yell rang in her ear, his seed flooding her.

She floated down on the wave of afterglow, her heart thundering right out of her chest. But as her fingers relaxed in his hair, her palms brushed the rough skin of his cheeks, the day-old stubble, and she had the sudden yearning to cling to him forever.

He slipped out of her and lowered her to the floor. She felt raw and too open like a seeping wound—his semen wet against her thighs. The sense of loss overwhelming. She locked her knees, to keep from collapsing, the last of the pleasure chased away by the wave of horror. As realization dawned of what they'd just done. And what she would have to do and say now. To push him away for good.

She would have to pay the price for her recklessness. Because Zelda had discovered long ago that if there was no such thing as a free fuck, there was certainly no such thing as a free fuck-up.

✦

TY'S BREATH SAWED in his lungs as he shoved his cock back in his pants, surveyed the tattered remains of his shirt. Had that actually just happened? Had he just taken Zelda against a wall in Sully's basement? And come like a freight train? He stared at the familiar stacks of beer kegs, inhaled the musty smell of damp brick and stale Guinness.

She looked blank, shaky, her lips pursed in a thin line as if she were trying to hold onto control. Was she in shock? Because he thought he might be.

"Jesus, Zel." He cupped her cheek, brushed his thumb across the delicate skin, so soft, so fragile. "I didn't come here intending to do that. I just wanted to talk. But you do something to me. Something I can't control. Something I don't want to control. Not anymore."

She wrapped her fingers around his wrist, and drew his hand away from her face. "Well you're going to have to, because that's all there is."

"No, it's not," he said, her dismissive tone, the flat acceptance in her eyes scaring him.

She was so precious, so special. Why couldn't she see that?

"Something happened last weekend." His voice sounded small and far away. He paused to take a breath, and push the confidence into his tone he used when presenting evidence to a jury. "Something important. And it was never just about the sex. It meant something to me. *You* mean something to me. I don't want this to be over."

She stepped away from him, her face flat and expressionless and his panic careened up another notch. "Don't be ridiculous, Ty. This can't go anywhere. Our worlds are too far apart."

The barb was well-aimed, hitting him right where it hurt the most, at his pride. And that niggling doubt underneath, that told him he would never be good enough for someone like her. She was beautiful and cultured and rich and aristocratic, the daughter of an American ambassador who had probably been to every major city in the world, while he'd never been outside the US. She lived in a townhouse on the Upper East Side twenty times the size of the apartment above them where he'd grown up. She probably earned more disposable income in a week than he could earn in a year.

But she didn't look at him when she said it and the chip that had ridden on his shoulder all through Columbia

Law, because he couldn't afford to join a fraternity, and didn't want to have a corner office in some pricey, mid-town law firm, toppled off. Zelda wasn't a snob. She didn't judge people by their hourly income. She was simply feeding his own prejudices back to him. He knew an unreliable witness when he saw one.

"Don't do that." He grasped her chin, forcing her gaze back to his, and he saw that flicker in her eyes that he had seen once before. "Don't play the Park Avenue princess when I know you're not. If there's a reason why you don't want to explore this thing further, tell me straight what it is. And I'll back off. But you have to give me a reason I can believe."

He was through being on the defensive, through playing this game by her rules. If she had secrets, he wanted to know what they were. He was entitled to know, because he'd told her every one of his.

She slapped his hand away. "Fine, I'll give you a reason. I don't do relationships."

"That's not a reason, it's a platitude. Tell me why you don't?"

"Because I'm no good at them."

"How do you know if you won't even try? I'm not asking for anything more than a chance here, Zel, to see where this is going, without putting obstacles in our path."

"There's no point, when I know I'll screw it up."

"Why would you think that? Is this something to do

with your jerk of a brother?" That had to be it. She needed someone to show her exactly how precious she was. And he could be that guy. If only she would believe in herself enough to let him in. "Can't you see his neglect has made you think you're worthless?" he continued. "That you can't do this, when you can."

He tried to gather her close, but she struggled free and shoved him back.

"Who the hell are you to tell me what I can and can't do? You arrogant bastard. We fucked for three days. You don't know anything about me."

The cruel words felt like a slap, but he could see the terror in her eyes, and knew she was pushing him away because she was scared. She was hitting out at him, playing the bad girl to hide her fear, the way she had all those years ago at that pricey convent school.

"I know enough, Zel," he said, refusing to let the bad girl act distract him, the way it had a decade ago. "I know you believe the worst of yourself. But that's not who you really are. Because I also know you're the kind of woman who would take the blame for something she didn't do, rather than let down her friends. Who would get torn away from the only people who cared about her, rather than speak up in her own defense."

"I'm not one of your charity cases. I don't need you to rescue me."

"I don't want to rescue you. I want much more than

that. Don't you get it? I'm falling in love with you, for fuck's sake."

He saw shock, followed quickly by panic. It wasn't the way he'd intended to say it. This was the first time he'd ever told a woman he loved her, and he'd messed it up. But the truth of it still stood. He didn't care if it was too quick.

And yeah, maybe it was supremely arrogant of him, but he didn't think he was having these feelings all on his own.

"You can't love me, you don't know me," she said, the panic rising in her voice. "You don't know the things I've done. I've screwed up all the way down the line. This isn't about bad choices, it's more than that, just read any headline about me and you'll see."

"Do you think I give a damn about what the press says about you?"

"It's not just the press, they didn't make it up."

"I don't care."

He tried to hold her arm, but she jerked free. "I'm an alcoholic, Ty. Now do you get it?"

"Bullshit, I've never seen you take a drink."

"Because I'm in recovery," she said, exasperated. "I've been sober for five years. But I'll always be an alcoholic."

She looked devastated at the admission. He almost laughed. Did she really believe he was so shallow and insensitive, that he couldn't see that made her even more heroic? Because she'd faced her demons and overcome them?

"That's your big confession?" he said. "That you're an alcoholic and you've fought to control your addiction for five years?" He reached for her again, and this time she let him pull her into his arms. "It doesn't matter, not to me. If that's what's stopping you from admitting how you feel, I don't care." He brushed her hair, cupped her skull, felt her cheek rest against his collarbone. "I can give up drinking, too. I want to help. I want to be there for you. Don't you see? We can fight this thing together."

✦

ZELDA STRUGGLED FREE, wrapping her arms around her midriff to hold in the hollow hurt, the trembles of reaction. And forced her anger to the fore to cover the crippling feeling of loss, of yearning that she could never let him see.

Tyrone Sullivan wanted to be her knight in shining armor. He wanted to protect her and care for her, and maybe he really was falling in love with her. But what he didn't realize was she could never take that leap, because she'd lost the right to take those kinds of risks, years ago.

"No, you're the one who doesn't see," she said. "This isn't about you, or me, or whether we can give this relationship a chance." She spat the words out, filling them with as much contempt as she could to hide the pain. "I have a fucking disease, Ty. A disease for which there is no cure. A disease which would happily kill me if I let it. And fighting that disease has to be my only priority. Not you. Or any relationship I might have. It's not that I can't admit my feelings, it's that I don't want to. Because then you'll think that we can be a normal couple, when we can't. We had three great days together. I told you there couldn't be more right from the start. That you chose not to listen is your problem. Not mine."

He flinched, clearly shocked at her outburst. But she could see the knowledge finally dawning on his face. That she wasn't who he'd convinced himself she was. Not the romantic wild child, worthy of his sympathy and support, but something damaged and desperate, seedy and ugly, who would have to spend the rest of her life atoning for the mistakes she had made before she had ever met him. Someone who would forever have those mistakes hanging over her, waiting to drag her back down.

She had to be strong. She couldn't let anything weaken her. So needing him, wanting him, believing he could rescue her when she had to be able to rescue herself could destroy her.

"Zelda… Don't throw this away…" He reached for her again.

"No." She yanked her arm out of his grasp. "Please just leave me alone. I don't want this. I…" She gulped down the ball of tears wedged in her throat. "I don't want you."

Because I can't have you.

He said nothing as she turned and walked to the door on unsteady legs. Nothing as she unlocked it and ran up the cellar stairs and out into the alleyway.

Tears streaked her face as she rushed into the Brooklyn night and called a cab. Foolishly, she cast a glance at the back door of the pub as the cab sped away from the curb, willing him to appear, to chase after her. But even as a part of her wanted him to be willing to take her, broken and damaged as she was, wanted him to be willing to fight for what they might have had together, and take on her burdens, another part of her knew it was a selfish and destructive pipedream that would only destroy them both. Neither of them could turn back the clock to a time when love would have been enough to conquer all. The realist, the pragmatist, the cynic inside her, which had been forged in fire during five years of fighting her addictions, knew she had to fight her battles alone. That she couldn't afford to believe in fairy tales.

And the foolish, romantic unrealistic part of her that wanted to believe in happy ever afters also knew she couldn't shackle Ty to a person who could never give him everything he deserved.

Because every part of her cared for him too much.

Chapter Ten

TY STABBED THE buzzer to apartment D and prayed his brother's voice would come over the line. He hadn't texted, or called ahead, because he hadn't known he'd been heading to Finn and Dawn's loft apartment in SoHo, until he'd found himself walking towards the subway after work.

"Who is it and what the hell do you want?" Finn's muffled voice rumbled out of the intercom, the clipped surly tone almost making Ty smile, for the first time in close to three weeks, ever since he'd woken up in the barge to find Zelda gone. His brother had never been one to hold back, unless he was trying to charm a lady, but right now the gruff response fit Ty's mood.

"It's Ty. I was in the neighborhood doing a deposition." He lied. "You want to go grab a beer to celebrate TGIF?" Not that he had a damn thing to celebrate, and not that he felt like drinking, but he'd rehearsed the casual request for the last twenty minutes, while walking past all the loved up couples, dating up a storm in the upscale neighborhood on a warm Friday evening in Manhattan. In fact, he hadn't had a drop of alcohol since Zelda's revelation over a week ago at Sully's, because for some dumb reason just the thought of drinking made him feel guilty, as if it were a betrayal of the struggle she'd waged—and won—for five years.

Why hadn't she told him sooner? When he'd accused her of being drunk in the station house? When he'd offered her that beer on the barge? Before he'd fucked her like a mad man next to the kegs of Guinness in Sully's basement?

But of course she hadn't told him, because they'd only known each other for ten days by the time he'd jumped her that night at Sully's. And while he'd been losing his head over her, and holding nothing back, she'd been holding everything back.

"Sorry man," Finn said. "I'm working on a violin concerto and it's killing me."

That would explain the pissy attitude. When Finn was in the zone, you couldn't blast him out of it with a stick of dynamite.

"No problem. I'll take a rain check," Ty said into the intercom, as his spirits plummeted even further into the pit of doom at the thought of returning to the house barge alone. And spending another night trying not to see Zelda in the shower, or lounging on the couch, or hurling potato salad at him. It was as if the scales had been ripped away from his eyes. He'd gotten one shining glimpse of what his life could be like—richer, fuller, more real—and now everywhere he looked the memory of that moment was torturing him. He couldn't sleep, was struggling to eat, and his work was suffering, too.

He still spent hours every evening reviewing cases, checking precedents, writing notes for court appearances, but somehow he'd lost the drive, the ambition, and, most of all, his optimism, the unshakeable belief that if Ty Sullivan was on the case, he could make a difference. How could he have been so damn arrogant? The truth was the poor would always be there, struggling against unscrupulous landlords, exploitative employers, punitive bureaucrats, and anything he could do to help was like pissing in an ocean.

And however much he might want to help and protect Zelda, he couldn't undo all the crap that had happened to her, or make her want him back.

"Hey, hold up, Ty. Why don't you come up? I've got some Sam Adams in the fridge. I've hit a snag with the damn concerto and Dawn will be home soon anyhow."

"That'd be great," Ty replied.

He shoved the heavy security door open as Finn buzzed him in, pathetically grateful for his brother's change of heart. He bypassed the elevator and made his way up the metal stairwell to the sixth floor loft apartment. If he could stretch this beer out until Dawn appeared, he could stave off returning to the house barge alone for at least another hour.

✦

"SO WHAT'S GOING on?" Finn cracked open the bottle of beer and handed it to Ty. "You look like shit."

"Thanks," Ty said ruefully, and took a swig of the beer. But the cool lager tasted sour on his tongue.

"Hard day at the office, huh?" Finn said, the smug smile an acknowledgement of the running joke they'd had for years about which one of them had chosen the better career path.

"It's been a long day, that's for sure." As they all were these days.

Ty took off his tie and tucked it into his pants pocket, not in the mood for his brother's friendly mockery as he followed Finn out of the state-of-the-art kitchen and into the loft's huge open living space. Polished, cedar wood floors flowed to a wall of floor-to-ceiling French doors that afforded a dramatic view of the downtown skyline, and the bridges of the East River, framed by the 1920s building's fancy ironwork. The place was all clean lines and luxurious designer accents that had to be down to Finn's girlfriend, because as far as Ty could remember his brother had never had an opinion on interior design. He spotted the vase of fresh flowers on the sideboard, sunny yellow buds he couldn't name in a profusion of spiky green leaves. No way were they Finn's doing either.

"Tough case?" Finn asked as he settled onto one of the green suede sofas parked on top of a deep pile rug.

"Something like that. How's Dawn?" Ty asked, keen to change the subject.

He might have needed company for this evening, but he'd rather suck out his own eyeballs than let his brother know how low he'd gotten over a woman who didn't want him. He was the big brother in this relationship. He didn't lean on his siblings, they leaned on him.

"Dawn's good." Finn placed his beer on the low occasional table and Ty noticed the upright piano behind him, tucked into the corner of the huge space, which had once been jammed into their bedroom above the pub. The battered instrument should have looked out of place in the five million dollar apartment, but it somehow seemed as comfortable here as his brother. "In fact, Dawn's great," Finn added. "We're thinking of trying for a kid."

Ty stifled the cruel stab of envy at the cautious optimism in Finn's voice. What the hell was he jealous of? He knew this was a big step for Finn, after finding out Dawn had miscarried ten years ago—and all the other drama involved when she had come back into his life. Plus, Ty had made a decision years ago he probably wouldn't want kids of his own. Kids were a lot of responsibility and he couldn't see himself wanting to interrupt his career. And he could hardly ask the woman he married to interrupt her career, because he believed wholeheartedly in gender equality.

But the thought of that meticulously detailed blueprint

for his life and that of the fictional Mrs. Tyrone Sullivan, which he'd designed before he'd ever met Zelda, felt like so much self-serving bullshit now. Jesus, had he actually believed that he could just plan out his life cleanly and efficiently and that everything would simply slot into place the way he wanted? Life was messy, emotions were messy, people were messy. Real people that was, like Zelda with all her faults and flaws. *But that's what made them fascinating and exciting and unique.* And as hard as he was finding it now to move on and forget her, he wouldn't have changed the short time they'd had together for anything. Because he'd discovered in those precious few days, it was better to face the curveballs life threw at him, than spend his whole damned life watching the game from the bleachers.

"That's great, man." Ty tried to inject some enthusiasm into his tone as he leaned across to clink the neck of his bottle with Finn's. "Here's to the next generation of Sullivans." He was happy for Finn and Dawn, they'd had a rough time and they deserved the good stuff now.

Finn laughed, and took a long swig of his beer. "Yeah, well…" He sent Ty a smartass grin, the same smartass grin Ty remembered from when they were kids, which usually meant Finn was about to talk them all into a whole heap of trouble. "It's a tough job, but someone's gotta do it, because we all know you're dead set against following in Mom and Pop's footsteps and fathering a load of little Sullies."

It was a familiar jibe, one Ty had deflected a thousand times before with a self-satisfied smirk, because he'd once boasted about how immune he was to the kind of love that left you struggling to raise five kids above a rundown pub in Brooklyn. But after a week of feeling the huge loss in his life just get bigger, of what he might have had with Zelda, the self-satisfied smirk refused to come. In fact, he couldn't even muster the smallest smile.

He placed the beer on the coffee table, and sank his head into his hands, the misery he'd kept so carefully at bay for the last week, ever since Zelda had walked away from him, rushing towards him like a runaway train.

"Fuck." He thrust his fingers through his hair, and bit into his lip to stop the misery engulfing him. If he started bawling like a baby in front of his kid brother, he'd have to kill himself. "Why didn't anyone ever tell me what a major league asshole I was being?"

"Hey, man, what gives?" Finn patted Ty uncomfortably on the back. "I was only kidding around. I didn't mean anything by it."

"Yeah, but I wasn't kidding around." He gazed at his brother, whose face had gone ashen beneath his tanned complexion. And who looked a lot less relaxed and carefree than usual. Ty would hazard a guess Finn hadn't expected to be handling his brother having a breakdown on a Friday evening. "I thought I was better than them. That what they had wasn't real," he said. "Wasn't important. I was going to make something of myself and find the perfect wife and be who I wanted to be and never end up letting my emotions turn my life into the chaos our lives were." He leaned back, and Finn's hand dropped away.

"What's wrong with that?" Finn said, jumping to his defense, because when the Sullivan brothers had their backs against the wall, they always stood up for each other. "You're a planner," Finn added. "You've always been a planner. That's just who you are, Ty. No one ever felt worse of you for that," he said, one hundred percent earnest for once.

Wow, he must really look like shit if his brother was actually being serious for a change.

"Yeah, but I felt worse of Pop. When he went to pieces after Mom died. I thought he was weak, that I would never be that weak."

"That was a tough time for all of us," Finn said, looking confused and wary now, as well as earnest. "Especially for you. We all knew how close you were to Mom, how much witnessing her miscarriage screwed you up."

"Wait a minute, you knew about the miscarriage?" How could Finn have known, he'd only been three years old?

"I didn't know the particulars, not until years later, but Pop told me and the twins not to tease you about the nightmares."

"What nightmares?"

"You had nightmares, for years afterward. Don't you remember? You'd wake up sweating and crying. And mom would have to come in and hold you until you calmed down."

Ty shook his head, but he did remember, vaguely. The night terrors that had haunted him for years. And his mother's cool hand stroking his brow, the soft crooning lulling him back to sleep. '*It's okay Tyrone. I'm okay, we're okay. You're my hero, my sweet boy.*' And the ones that had returned for months after his mother had passed and the aching pain because she had no longer been there to soothe him and tell him everything would be all right.

Somehow he'd blanked the nightmares though, or blanked them enough never to have to acknowledge their significance. "And Pop told you not to tease me about them? And you didn't?" This was new, too.

"You know Pop, he was usually a pushover. Mom was the one with the evil eye that could spot mischief a mile away and a smack which could keep your butt hurting for weeks. But he put the fear of God into us over that. And it scared us all so much when you had them, we never did mention it in the morning."

"I never knew that," Ty said. How many times had he sold his father short? Found him wanting? When he'd been a devoted husband, a loving father. Probably a better man than Ty would ever be. "I guess I owe the old guy an apology."

"If you do, I owe him about fifty, so let's not go there," Finn said. "What's going on Ty? Because you're freaking me out a little here."

He could have lied, he really wanted to. If he confided in Finn about Zelda, it would change the complexion of their relationship forever. He'd always been the older brother, the one who knew best, the one who had all the answers. And he'd liked lording it over his brothers. The way he'd tried to lord it over Zelda.

But he didn't have the answer to this. And maybe Finn did. Finn had fallen for Dawn when he was still a teenager. And somehow or other he'd figured out a way to get past all the bullshit and rekindle the flame over a decade later when Dawn had returned.

And maybe it was about time Ty got off his high horse and asked someone else for help. Because if there was one thing Zelda had taught him, you couldn't solve a problem until you admitted you had one.

"You know Faith's friend Zelda?" he began.

"Sure, the model, right?" Finn replied. "With all the hair?"

"Not anymore. She cut off the hair," Ty said. "She spent the Labor Day weekend on my house barge and we..." He hesitated. How did he explain the unexplainable? That while banging her senseless he'd fallen in love with her? In the space of a long weekend? Finn would think he was nuts. He probably was nuts.

"You what?" Finn prompted.

"We got together. At first, I thought it was just exceptionally good sexual chemistry, because the sex was awesome. But then we talked and I discovered stuff about her that made me realize she wasn't at all what I thought she was… She's been hurt so badly, lost so much when she was a kid, and even though she's made a lot of mistakes in her life, she came out the other side a stronger and better person. She's smart and funny and sassy and unconventional. She made me feel alive when I was with her. And I didn't want it to end. I wanted to see more of her. A lot more."

He stopped. Shit, he was babbling. What was wrong with him? He made a living out of his skills as a litigator and now the one time he had to explain something as succinctly as he possibly could, so his brother wouldn't think Ty needed to go to the nut house, he sounded like freaking Oprah.

"Okay." Finn didn't look stunned or astonished. In fact he didn't even look particularly surprised.

"Okay?" Ty asked, annoyed at the low-key response. His whole life had been turned upside down in the space of a weekend and that was all his kid brother had to say on the matter. Finn had always been laid back, but this was insane. "That's all you've got?"

"Well, it sounds pretty intense, if you fell in love with her after only three days. But that can happen. It happened to me and Dawn after one night."

"Yeah, but you were like seventeen and full of rioting hormones. I'm thirty-two, a graduate of Columbia, and a licensed attorney."

"When it hits, it hits. Your age, your SAT scores, and your professional qualifications don't have a hell of a lot to do with it. And it sounds like you had a few rioting hormones going on, too."

A blush warmed Ty's cheeks, mortifying him.

"So what's the problem?" Finn said, being more perceptive than Ty had expected, but at least not ribbing him about the blush. "Because I'm assuming there's gotta be a problem or you wouldn't be wasting your time with me on a Friday night?"

"The problem is, she doesn't want me. I told her I was falling in love with her…" And had been arrogant enough to believe that was all he needed to do. "And she told me she didn't do relationships because she's an alcoholic in recovery. And then she told me to get lost."

"How did you respond? When she told you she was an alcoholic?"

"I told her it didn't matter to me, that I still wanted to try." He picked up the beer, ran this thumb down the perspiration on the glass, still not sure what he'd said that had made her so mad. "That I wanted to help her."

"Ty Sullivan to the rescue, huh?" Finn said, the sympathy in his voice making Ty feel like a bit of an ass.

"I guess it sounds arrogant, but I was in shock, and feeling hurt that she hadn't told me already."

Finn shrugged. "It doesn't sound arrogant; it sounds exactly like you, Ty. You've always had an overdeveloped superhero complex."

"What the hell does that mean?"

"Come on, Ty, remember when we used to play superhero super-soaker wars when we were kids and you always wanted to be Batman?"

"So what?" Ty said, getting annoyed. He'd already been given the third degree about this by Zelda, he hardly needed to take another hit from his kid brother.

"Do you remember why you always wanted to be Batman?"

"Sure, because Batman had all the cool gadgets and he was real."

Finn's eyebrows popped up in ironic amusement.

"You know what I mean." Ty qualified. "He didn't have special powers, he was smart, and he worked for it. And that's how he saved people. What's that got to do with anything?"

"Here's my point, Ty." Finn leaned forward, earnest again. "You wanted to be Batman, because he was a real guy. You never wanted to take the easy road. You planned and you worked hard and, because you wanted to help people, you carried on arming yourself with cool gadgets—like your law degree and your bar certificate. That's just who you are and I figure it goes right back to that little kid who found his Mom bleeding out on the bathroom floor and had nightmares for years afterwards because he couldn't save her from that."

"I still don't see why that's a bad thing," Ty said, feeling surly and defensive. What was so wrong with wanting to help people, wanting to protect the ones you loved?

"It's not a bad thing. It's a good thing. And it totally stands to reason that if you're falling for Zelda, you would want to be able to help her and protect her, too. But sometimes people have to save themselves, Ty. I know guys who've been through the twelve-step program and an important part of the recovery process is knowing they can save themselves. They need their autonomy. You probably scared the crap out of Zelda, coming on strong like that with your superhero routine as soon as she told you she was an alcoholic."

"But I didn't mean it like that. I know how strong she is, how smart, how real. I would never want to take that away from her. Or undermine her."

"Then maybe you need to tell her that?"

The tiny spurt of hope was squashed like a bug. "It wouldn't do any good. Not if she doesn't have any feelings for me. To her it was just a weekend hook up; she made that pretty damn clear."

"Did she? Are you sure about that? Isn't it possible that you just spooked her, Ty? This thing between you has happened fast and I'll bet being in the program also means she has to be cautious about making drastic changes in her life. So you coming on strong like that was bound to spook her even more. But did she actually tell you she didn't have feelings for you, or did she just tell you all the reasons why it wouldn't work?"

It's not that I can't admit my feelings, it's that I don't want to.

The surge of hope felt almost painful as he recalled Zelda's words, the one phrase that he'd gotten stuck on the million or so times he'd relived the conversation they'd had in the taproom. "I guess you could be right. She didn't tell me she didn't have feelings for me, she just told me she didn't want to tell me what they were."

"Okay, then maybe you need to find out what those feelings are before you give up on her?"

"But how will that help? If we can't have a relationship because of her recovery?" he said, trying not to let the surge of hope blind him to the reality of the situation. "If us being together messed that up for her, I could never live with myself." Thinking Zelda didn't care for him had been tough enough, but forcing her to admit her feelings and screwing up her recovery in the process would be far worse.

Finn nodded. "I'll admit I'm not an expert on this stuff. But if there's one thing you're good at, Ty, it's coming up with a plan. I happen to know that because when you were Batman, Casey and Ro always got to be Superman and Spiderman, which meant I always had to be

Robin."

"Yeah, and as I recall you used to whine about it every damn time, so I don't see how it's relevant."

"The whine was just for show. I loved being your sidekick, because while Ro and Case were busy running around like loons wasting all their ammunition on each other and Mrs. Zigler's tomcat, you always came up with a cool plan to ambush them. Remember that time we soaked them both half an hour before their Holy Communion?"

"How could I forget it," Ty said, unable to resist cracking a smile at the memory, despite the dull pain in his chest. "Mom nearly murdered all four of us."

"Uh huh, but you managed to argue our sentence down from outright murder to a missed supper, no TV privileges for a month, and a couple of stinging wallops on the butt. So don't tell me that guy can't come up with what to say to the woman he loves, so she can see he could be the best thing that ever happened to her. Instead of the worst."

The blast of fiddle and pipes had them both reaching for their cell phones.

Finn grinned when it turned out to be his. "Cool ringtone." He lifted the phone to check the caller. "It's Dawn. I better take this. I won't be long."

Finn got up and walked towards the kitchenette, for privacy, but Ty could still hear the affection and easy domesticity in the hushed tones. Who would ever have thought that Finn would be the first of them to settle down?

The stabbing pain in his chest got worse, because he wanted to make things right with Zel. He wanted to give them both another chance. But what if the obstacles were too great? And the stakes too high? Even for him?

"Yeah, I'll see you later." Finn clicked off the phone as he walked back.

Ty drained his beer, feeling like a fifth wheel. "I should scram if Dawn's on her way home. You've got the next generation of Sullivans to start creating." Plus he had a lot of thinking to do.

Finn dropped his cell on the table. "Actually she's on her way to Zel's for the evening. Apparently the shit has hit the fan and the press is camped outside her place on the Upper East Side. Couple of the tabloids have printed a story saying she's off the rails again."

Every protective instinct Ty had went on high alert. "Why the hell would they say that?"

"The shampoo company released some bullshit statement saying they'd ditched her because she cut her hair. That she's a liability they can't afford to have fronting their brand any longer."

"Those sons of bitches, they didn't ditch her, she ditched them." He protested, outraged on her behalf. "She should sue the bastards for defamation." But he knew Zelda would never defend herself against the accusation—because she had never apprised anyone but her closest friends of the struggle she'd fought and won for the last five years.

"I know." Finn agreed. "Dawn said the same thing. But apparently the shampoo company has gotten hold of a photo of her at Coney Island, in a clinch with some mystery dude on the beach that they say proves she got her hair cut before they dropped her." Finn lifted his eyebrows, making it clear he knew exactly who the mystery dude was. "The thing's gone viral. The girls are heading over there after work to give her moral support."

"Shit." Ty jumped up from the couch. "I should never have taken her to Coney Island. I might have guessed someone would spot her. She warned me she was always getting this sort of negative attention from the press." And he knew how much she hated it, but he hadn't taken that seriously enough, any more than he had her revelation about being an alcoholic. "This is all my goddamn fault." Gathering up his suit jacket he headed for the door.

"Where are you going?" Finn asked.

"Over to her place, she may need my help." He could offer her his expert legal advice. She probably wouldn't want it, but damn it, if nothing else, it was a reason to see her again. "And I can offer myself up to the press to take the heat off her."

Finn unlocked the deadbolt, but paused before he pulled the heavy steel door open. "Would you take some advice before you go?"

"What advice?" Ty said, impatient to get going.

"Don't go dashing over there half-cocked. Take some time and figure out what you're going to say to her first. You don't want to scare the shit out of her all over again."

"But she needs my support now." He protested. He didn't want to wait. If she needed his protection, he wanted to be there for her, because he knew for damn sure her brother wouldn't be.

"She's got support. The girls will be there in a half-hour or so. They can hold the fort until you get there. And you said yourself she's a strong lady."

Ty rested his forehead against the door and took a steadying breath. And then took another, forcing back the panic, and the need to ride to Zelda's rescue. Damn it, his brother was making sense. He couldn't afford to screw this up.

Faith and Dawn and … His mind snagged on the name of the other girl until a vision of the exotic-looking girl sitting in the booth at Sully's came to him. Mercy! That was it… Would be there watching out for Zelda for the next couple of hours. He had time to go back to the boat and change, and do some vital research, so he knew exactly what he was going to say, and how he was going to say it. He had to gather all the evidence and make a persuasive case; a case that would prove to Zelda giving this thing between them a chance—whatever this thing was—didn't have to be bad.

Once he'd done that, the decision would be Zelda's.

But whatever happened, he was not about to fuck up presenting the most important case of his life a second time.

"Okay, you're right." He straightened away from the door and nodded at his brother. "I probably should have told you this before, Finn, but you were a great Robin."

His brother gave him a high five as he hauled open the door. "Holy heck, Batman, you got that right." The smartass grin spread across his face. "Now go figure out a plan to capture Catwoman."

Chapter Eleven

ZELDA STARED OUT of the library window at the gauntlet of photographers and journalists. They had been camped outside the townhouse all day like a pack of ravening wolves, but she felt oddly detached from the chaos her latest screw up had caused.

Not that she was actually guilty of the 'reckless' behavior the press had attributed to her. She hadn't cut off her hair during a drink- and drug-fuelled weekend spree in Brooklyn over Labor Day. But defending herself would only draw more attention to the story—and make them more determined to identify Ty. She'd already caused him enough trouble. If she didn't give the story any oxygen, the press would be gone tomorrow, to go hound some other celebrity screw-up—and Ty would be spared another reason to regret the misguided declaration he'd made a week ago.

He hadn't contacted her again. As she'd known he wouldn't. And even though her sponsor, Amelie, had assured her that a committed relationship didn't have to be a threat to her recovery as long as she managed her expectations, she had decided her knee-jerk decision to push Ty away was for the best.

She had no experience of making relationships work, especially not intimate ones. And even if starting something serious with Ty didn't have to threaten her sobriety, it was still scary, new territory, which she had no guarantees she would be able to negotiate. Handling the problems she already had was a full-time job. How could she risk having Ty in her life, when that could mean the possibility of losing him?

Of course, using her recovery as an excuse not to admit her feelings had been cowardly and dishonest. But Ty was an optimist, who, for all his pragmatism and intelligence, believed he could fix things if he tried hard enough. But he couldn't fix her.

Then again, now he knew exactly how broken she was, he probably had no desire to fix her anymore anyway. Which just made it all the more pathetic that losing something she had never really had still hurt so much.

She picked her mobile up from the library table and keyed in a text to Seb. She needed a distraction from the hopeless thoughts which kept circling around in her head like vultures hovering over a rotting corpse. Unfortunately, her brother was the only distraction on offer.

Can you join me for dinner tonight? Zx

She pressed send, not caring how needy it sounded. Even her brother's monosyllabic company would be more appealing than spending another night eating alone in the townhouse's cavernous dining salon while the memory of the meals she'd shared with Ty—sitting on the roof chatting over their ad hoc picnic supper, or watching him cook her pancakes—made the loss seem all the more acute.

She waited for a reply, but nothing came.

Perhaps Seb had stayed late at his office on foundation business, or he might even have a date. How would she know, when she knew virtually nothing about his personal or professional life because he refused to share details about anything?

She noticed Mrs. Jempson, their housekeeper, walking past the library door and called out to her. "Mrs. Jempson, do you know where my brother is this evening?"

The housekeeper nodded, because she was clearly permitted to know more about Seb's life than his own sister. "He's in the roof garden, working on the new trellis he's designed for the roses."

Trellis? What new trellis?

"I see," she said, but she didn't see.

Since when did Seb care about the rose garden? Their mother had adored roses. One of Zel's earliest memories was of her mum kneeling in the embassy garden, her beautifully manicured hands covered in dirt, as she planted the cut-offs she'd brought to London from the garden upstairs. Zel also recalled Seb getting into trouble once for kicking a football into the growing bushes—which only made the thought of him designing and constructing a trellis for the plants now all the more absurd.

Mrs. Jempson excused herself as Zelda keyed in another message. She'd give him one more try. Maybe he didn't have his phone with him. But instinctively she knew he did. He was blanking her, the way he always did, because the futility of trying to reach him felt all too familiar.

> *How about coming down to dinner, then I could explain what the press is doing outside the door? Zx*

Maybe that would get a reaction. He must have noticed the paparazzi besieging the house again. She should explain to him what was going on. Not that he'd asked for an explanation, but her pride demanded she supply one.

The reply popped onto her phone.

> *Can't do dinner. Busy tonight. And I don't care why the press are here, I'd just like them the hell off my doorstep.*

She hadn't really expected him to accept the invitation. But even so, her fingers began to tremble, and the air squeezed out of her lungs as she read the typically blunt text.

And suddenly an incandescent anger was surging up her chest like hot, viscous lava, searing everything in its path. She felt it exploding in her heart, and charging through her bloodstream, as she slammed down her phone.

She marched out of the library, into the oppressive grandeur of the hallway and took the main staircase two at a time, her heels sinking into the Aubusson carpet. The fading summer day shone through the mullioned windows but the dusky light was hard to distinguish from the red haze descending over her vision.

After racing up four flights of stairs, she flung open the door on the top landing that led past Seb's suite of rooms towards the back stairs. Rooms she hadn't been invited to enter since she'd returned to New York months ago.

She supposed he didn't bother to lock the door, because he would never expect her to enter his inner sanctum without his express permission.

Well, bugger that.

She strode down the corridor, and headed up the staircase that led to her mother's old roof garden, the volcano of fury burning up her torso. She knew the anger was irrational. That it was spurred on by the brutal pain of losing Ty. And the thought of all the lonely days, which hung like thunderclouds over her future and would be that much harder to bear now she knew what she would be missing.

And in that tiny corner of her brain that was still rational, she also knew it wasn't fair to transfer that pain and anger onto her brother.

But fuck it. She was through being fair and reasonable and rational and bloody polite with Sebastian. And blaming herself for the crappy way he'd treated her all these years—as if she were an embarrassment, or a burden, or worse, simply an inconvenience.

Just because she couldn't take what Ty had to offer, she could bloody hold her useless brother to account. For all the times he'd failed her. For all the times he'd shunned her and dismissed her and refused to see her pain because he was too busy wallowing in his own. He'd made her feel like nothing for so long, and she didn't want to feel like nothing today.

She stepped into the palatial roof garden, and stopped dead, stunned for a moment by the heady fragrance and the sight of the beautiful twisting vines, clinging to the garden's latticed ironwork in riotous profusion. Seb stood in the sunlight at the end of the terrace, his dark hair tinged with gold, his face for once devoid of its usual brooding scowl, a tool belt slung low on his hips as he hammered the trellis against a wall.

The fury surged back. What right did he have to be so content, when she was so miserable? And then the volcano in her chest erupted right out of her mouth.

"You cold, heartless, son of a bitch."

Sebastian jerked round, his hand plunging into a clump of roses, then swore and yanked his hand back to suck on his thumb.

Good, she was glad he'd pricked himself, because he'd been a total prick to her for far too long.

"Zel, what are you doing up here?" The nickname that he hadn't used since they were children, plus the complete astonishment on his face, made her hesitate for a second. But then she gathered her strength and her fury and marched towards him to jab a fingernail into the center of his shirt.

"So this is why you're too busy to have dinner with me."

"I have work," he said, but she could see the lie in his dark shuttered eyes. "I was taking a short break."

"Bullshit. You'd rather spend your evenings here than spend any time with me. I'm your sister, Seb, and we've been living in the same house for months and you know how many times we've dined together?"

He didn't answer, his brows lowering in the familiar frown.

"Twice. And both times you spoke approximately twenty words to me. Why do you find my company so excruciating? I'm not drinking anymore. I won't get hammered or high and make a spectacle of myself or start gushing uncontrollably. I just want to be able to talk to you. Occasionally, like a normal human being. Like your sister. Instead of being treated like someone who has the plague."

She wanted him to care enough to be interested in what she had to say. All those mundane details of her life. The way Ty had been interested.

"I know we can never be a normal brother and sister." She continued when he remained stoically silent.

Or rather, she'd spent the last five years forcing herself to come to terms with the fact their family could never be as warm and loving and supportive as the Sullivans.

"But why can't we at least talk to each other? You're the only family I have left, Seb?"

"I'm well aware of that," he said, turning away. But she noticed the fine lines round his eyes, the tension in his jaw, the scar that bisected his lip going white with stress. He was hating every second of this.

Seb didn't do confrontation. He didn't do soul-searching. He had never even admitted he had a problem. So it had been far too easy for him to make her think that all their problems had been hers alone.

Why had she let him have his way for so long? She wasn't nobody. Or nothing. And she wasn't the only one to blame for their estrangement. Ty had noticed that, why hadn't she?

"Did you even know I've given up my modeling career?" she tried again.

Even if going postal on Sebastian could never make up for losing Ty, she needed to at least try to sort out this area of her life one last time.

"I could hardly fail to know it," Seb said, his expression rigid, his voice tight. "Given that those bloody parasites have been besieging us since five this morning."

She heard accusation in his tone and her pride kicked in. "What they're saying isn't true. I didn't go on some alcohol-induced weekend jolly and shave my head. I made a conscious decision not to sign another contract."

"It makes no difference to me," he said, the brooding expression back to hide his discomfort. "What you chose to do with your life, Zelda, is your business. I've never interfered."

"Didn't it ever occur to you that I wanted you to make it your business?" she said, forcing herself to say the words that had been buried inside her for so long—and had come out in so many self-destructive ways.

She'd made a decision five years ago during rehab to stop trying to attract Seb's attention. To stop caring about what he thought of her, because it had only made her think less of herself. But Ty was right; she didn't deserve to be treated this way, not anymore.

"When they kicked me out of St. J's? I would have loved you to interfere then. But you didn't say one word in my defense. They tore me away from the only friends I had. Mercy and Dawn and Faith were so important to me, and yet you didn't do a single thing to stop them."

"If you'd wanted to stay at the school, you shouldn't have stolen the bloody wine," he said with unswerving certainty.

But I didn't steal the bloody wine.

She wanted to scream the truth at him. But the futility of protesting her innocence, ten years after the fact was obvious. And it would only make her remember the man who had been convinced of her innocence after knowing her for only three days. Not that she was ever likely to forget him.

"You wouldn't have defended me anyway," she said, seeing it all so clearly now. "Because it would have meant actually bothering to see me."

"That's a little melodramatic, don't you think? Even for you."

The droll comment sliced to the bone. But she could see it for what it was now. A distraction technique. One that Seb had used countless times before.

"Really?" She shot back. "It's melodramatic to want your support, to need some small sense that the one family member I have left at least cares enough about me to be there when I need him?"

The problem hadn't been that she felt too much. It had been that he refused to admit he felt anything at all.

"I survived the accident," he said. "What more do you want?"

"Much, much more," she said. "I wanted you to hold me, when we stood by their graves together. I wanted you to stay with me instead of running off to join the French Foreign Legion weeks after they died. I wanted you to let me come home for the holidays without making me beg. I wanted you to welcome me back a few months ago and I wanted you to accept a simple dinner invitation tonight without making up some pathetic excuse."

He flinched, his whole body going rigid. And for a

moment she thought she might have pierced the armor plating he had worn around his emotions ever since he had regained consciousness in the emergency room all those years ago. But within seconds, the inscrutable expression had returned.

"At least I didn't get lost in a haze of booze and pills and God knows what else," he murmured.

"No you didn't," she said. "And you're right, I did. And it's true that wasn't your fault, it was mine." Because blaming him for her addiction issues would be as damaging as blaming herself for his emotional withdrawal. "But I did eventually face my demons, Seb. And I'm prepared to spend the rest of my life making sure they don't beat me again." Even though it meant letting go of the one thing that could have made her truly happy. "What I'd like to know is when exactly are you planning to face yours?"

He stared at her for the longest time, but his dark eyes remained blank, his expression revealing nothing, until he finally said. "I don't have any demons."

"Yes, you do," she said, even though she already knew the argument was pointless. "The accident changed you. I don't know how or why particularly, but maybe you need therapy to get over that?"

One eyebrow rose in cynical disbelief. "I don't need therapy. I'm absolutely fine."

She threw up her hands. "Right, yes, of course, you're absolutely fine, Sebastian. Silly me."

He didn't respond, but then she hadn't really expected him to.

She walked back through the rambling bushes, refusing to let the foolish, self-indulgent tears fall.

The lush blooms and vibrant colors seemed to mock her, a testament to how much care and attention her brother had lavished on them. He'd obviously nurtured their mother's old plants, coaxed all this fragrant beauty out of them with a patience and tenderness he'd never been able to show her.

As the anger drained away, it left the hollow sense of loss in its wake. Not just for the brother she'd once had, but for the man who might have been able to love her—if only she had been able to turn back the clock.

She took the staircase back to the second floor landing and walked into her own rooms. Fabulous, well that had been a staggering success, now she felt even less worthy of affection than a bunch of bloody rose bushes.

The sound of a commotion from outside had her peering out of the window to see Dawn, Mercy, and Faith piling out of a cab. And the surge of joy and surprise eased the hollow loss, at least a little.

Her friends were here. The women who had stood by her no matter what.

She had lost Seb's affection through no fault of her own all those years ago and killed Ty's stone dead eight days ago. But she had this, she had them, and right now, she needed them, more than ever.

Sucking in a careful breath, she rushed out of the room and headed down the stairs, determined not to give in to her pity party and fall to pieces in front of them.

The bell rang and the housekeeper appeared from nowhere to check the peephole in the door.

"Let them in, Mrs. Jempson." Zelda called out, countermanding the order she'd given that morning.

The flash of bulbs, the whirr of shutters and the shouts for a statement burst into the quiet entrance hall as her three friends spilled through the door as if propelled by a hurricane. Mrs. Jempson slammed the door shut behind them.

Zelda raced down the last few stairs as Faith lifted the large flask she had stowed under her arm. "We have virgin mojitos!"

"And Bridget Jones *and* Eliza Bennett," Dawn chimed in, holding a selection of classic DVDs aloft.

"And enough truffles to sink the Titanic." Mercy finished, brandishing a bag from Zelda's favourite chocolatier.

Zelda smiled as tears of gratitude clogged her throat.

Bloody men, who needs them anyway? When you have handmade chocolates. Faith's delicious virgin mojitos. Colin Firth's Mr. Darcy.

And girlfriends to die for.

"Then it must be slumber party time," she said, but her voice broke on the words and the traitorous tears slipped down her cheeks.

Mercy rushed forward to gather her close. “Zel, it’s okay. We’re here now. We’ll keep you safe from those pigs.”

“I know.” She eased back, furiously scrubbing away the tears. “It’s not them; I’m used to them saying crappy things about me. I know it doesn’t matter.”

“Then what is it?” Faith asked, sounding concerned. “Because you look devastated and that’s not like you.”

“It’s silly. Stupid.” She shook her head, struggling to come up with a convincing reason for her pity party, because she couldn’t tell them about Ty. She just couldn’t. “It’s just… I had a row with Sebastian,” she said, deciding to throw her brother to the wolves.

“That beast! What has he done now?” Fire flashed in Mercy’s eyes.

“It doesn’t matter.” She laid her hand on Mercy’s arm, her friend’s reaction more volatile than the sympathetic looks she was getting from Dawn and Faith.

“It *does* matter,” Mercy said. “What did he do?”

“I asked him to join me for dinner, and he came up with some lame excuse,” she continued. “So I confronted him about it. But it was a disaster, as usual. He looked right through me, the way he always does. And I let it hurt me, when I know I shouldn’t.”

“Is he upstairs?” Mercy asked, the fire still blazing.

“Yes, but…”

Before Zelda had a chance to say more, Mercy pressed

the bag of chocolates into her arms. "Take these, and don't eat all the butterscotch walnut ones. I shall be back shortly."

Mercy swept past her to charge across the foyer towards the staircase.

"Where is she off to?" Zel asked, bemused, as her friend's heels cracked like rifle fire on the parquet flooring, the waves of ebony hair bouncing on her shoulders with each defiant stride.

"My guess…" Faith piped up. "She's gone to give your beast of a brother a taste of the Spanish Inquisition."

Chapter Twelve

"I STILL CAN'T believe they'd lie like that… in a freaking press release. It's unreal…" Faith trailed another of the strawberries Mercy had stashed away in her Godiva haul through the white chocolate dip, looking relaxed even though she would have to return to the pub soon, because she'd only managed to get a couple of hours cover. "You should sue."

"And I think we all know who she should get to do the legal work," Dawn added.

Zelda took a long gulp of the chilly drink, Dawn's teasing making the blush fire across her cheeks and her throat close. Of course her friends had seen the photo of her and Ty watching the fireworks at Coney Island. She'd expected them to comment on it, eventually. And she thought she'd been prepared for it.

But she wasn't prepared. She couldn't talk about him. Even with her friends. She'd avoided calling them all week, ever since disappearing so abruptly with him during their monthly meet up at the pub. And apart from a text from Mercy the next morning, which read—*If you need to talk about a certain hot attorney, call me*—her friends hadn't contacted her about the incident, because they were being thoughtful and giving her space. And perhaps they were being discreet for Faith's sake.

They knew how close Faith was to her brothers. And they also all knew about Zelda's less than stellar track record with men. And they had probably concluded Ty was just another of her many, many fuck-and-forget flings. And she hadn't wanted to disabuse them of that fact. She'd told herself it was because she didn't want to upset Faith. But that was just a cowardly excuse to protect herself, because the truth was talking about Ty was the same as thinking about him, it only made her more aware of how much she missed him.

Keeping her silence now would probably be best, but despite those good intentions, try as she might she could not stop the ache in her throat forming into a huge boulder.

"Shit." Tears welled again, and she brushed them away with her fist, but it was already too late.

"Oh hell, I'm so sorry, Zelda." Dawn wrapped an arm round her shoulders. "You're under a lot of pressure because of that dumb photo. I shouldn't have kidded you about it."

"No, you should have." She sniffed.

Mercy offered her the tissue dispenser, her face still flushed from her earlier showdown with Seb—which she'd refused to elaborate on, except to say 'your brother is a disaster.'

Zelda took the tissue and blew her nose, and quashed the cowardly urge to use her argument with Seb to deflect attention again. No doubt he had blanked Mercy, too, which was probably why her friend didn't want to talk about what had happened upstairs.

Poor Mercy, she was such a loyal friend, and such an optimist about people. And always so determined to face any problem head on. But even she would now finally be forced to admit Sebastian was a lost cause, if she couldn't make an impression on him in all her glorious Argentinian fury.

But as the four of them lounged on an array of colorful pillows in the living room of Zelda's suite, and Zelda observed her friends' expressions, all shadowed with concern for her, she knew she couldn't pretend Seb was the real cause of her distress. Any more than the jackals still amassed outside her front door.

"The press stuff doesn't bother me," she said.

"But they flat out lied about you," Faith said. "They shouldn't be allowed to get away with it."

"If I wanted to sue them, I'd have to prove I have a reputation to protect. And I don't. And that's my fault, not theirs."

Faith opened her mouth to protest again, but Dawn interrupted. "So what is bothering you, Zel? And don't tell us it's because of what happened with Seb, because he's been a lost cause for a long time…"

Mercy swore softly in Spanish in agreement.

Zelda stared at her mojito, blotting away another tear. Even if she wanted to confide in them, was there really any point? This thing between her and Ty, whatever it was, was already over, and she'd never been one to pick through the wreckage. Not that she'd ever actually had any wreckage worth picking through before.

"You looked very happy in that photo with Faith's hot brother."

Zelda's gaze met Mercy's at the quietly spoken observation. Mercy had seen through her lies and evasions. Just as she had once before, when she had come to Paris for a flying visit five years ago and found Zelda living in a squalid unheated apartment in the Pigalle, strung out on quaaludes and vodka.

Mercy was the one who had made her see what a mess she was making of her life. And made her acknowledge how low she had allowed herself to sink. Not with angry words or accusations, but with the exact same expression she wore now which simply said: *I am here for you, and I will help you, but only if you want to be helped.*

Guilt assailed her. She should never have used her friend's passion and loyalty against her, pretending Seb was the problem, when he really wasn't.

"Did Ty do something to upset you?" Faith asked. "He's one of the good guys, I swear, but he wasn't behaving like himself last Thursday. If he's done something dumb, you can tell us. He's my brother and I love him, but he's still a guy."

Zelda shook her head. God, how much worse could she feel about this? Now even Faith was willing to stand by her, to trust her and support her. She couldn't keep silent about this, and let Faith believe that Ty was at fault, when she was the one who had messed up.

"He didn't do anything wrong. He *is* one of the good guys." Which was precisely why he was too good for her. "All he did was tell me he was falling in love with me."

The silence could only be shock, Zelda decided. Not that a guy would say he was in love her, because she'd had tons of half-assed declarations of undying love over the years. It was the hazard of being a supermodel with a very liberal attitude to sex. But that a guy like Ty would say it. A guy who was brave and honest and sincere and always meant what he said.

"And this is bad because…?" Dawn asked, pouring another virgin mojito and handing it to Zelda.

Zelda swallowed, easing the dryness in her throat. "I hadn't told him the truth about me. Now he knows the truth and he knows we can never be together and I hurt him and I wish I hadn't, but I did."

"What truth are you talking about?" Mercy probed.

"That I'm an alcoholic, of course," she said.

"And this means you can't be together because… Why exactly?" Dawn asked.

"Because my recovery has to be a priority. And who wants to live with someone that can't ever fully commit to a relationship? He deserves better than that. I could never make him happy."

"Umm, excuse me," Dawn interceded again. "Surely it's up to Tyrone to decide what he deserves and what will make him happy."

"And knowing Ty, he won't be shy about telling you," Faith chipped in. "Because he overthinks every damn thing. He's had a five-year plan in place since he was about ten years old. So if he's decided he wants you…?" Faith let the question hang in the air.

"I think now he knows the actual extent of what he would be taking on, he's reconsidered." Zelda countered.

"What makes you say that?" Mercy asked.

"He hasn't contacted me again, since last Thursday. We had one final fuck in Sully's basement. He told me he loved me. I told him I was an alcoholic and that was the end of it." Okay, maybe she had also told him to leave her alone, or words to that effect—and maybe she had banged on rather loudly about the importance of her recovery. But even so, he hadn't exactly put up much of a fight, once her secret was out. She felt a tiny prickle of irritation at his instant capitulation surfacing beneath the hurt. Which had to be about as insane as her stealth attack on Sebastian while he was building his trellis. But she'd take insane over devastated any day.

"I don't think I needed to know about the final fuck, thanks," Faith said.

"Sorry," Zelda mumbled, contrite.

"Oh, I don't know, for those of us not getting any, it creates a rather compelling visual," Mercy said.

"For you, maybe." Faith rolled her eyes in exaggerated patience. "He's not your brother."

"Enough you two." Dawn held up her hands, acting in her familiar role as adjudicator. "Can we just focus here for a minute on something other than the compelling picture of Zelda and Faith's hot brother bumping ugly in Sully's basement?"

"Yes let's," Faith said, sounding relieved.

"Moving swiftly on." Dawn smiled at Faith. "I just want to ask you one question, Zel. Did you at any time give Faith's studly brother reason to believe you returned his feelings?"

"No, of course not."

"Why not?" Dawn shot straight back. "When it's blindingly obvious to everyone here present and anyone who has seen that photo, you are completely nuts about the guy."

Was she? Was that why she felt so miserable? Was it possible to fall for a guy who was totally wrong for her in every conceivable way, in the space of three fricking days, when she had never fallen for anyone before? With the question came a wave of panic, very similar to the wave of panic that had assailed her the first time he'd said it.

"It doesn't matter how I feel," she said. "Or how he feels. My recovery has to come first. Always."

"That's true, and that's laudable," Dawn said. "But seriously, Zel, why does there have to be a conflict between the two?"

"Because there just is. I can't make those sort of changes in my life without thinking it through carefully, knowing what I'm getting into, anticipating all the pitfalls."

"Which would totally explain why you panicked when he told you how he felt. But does not explain why you're still panicking," Dawn commented, with razor-sharp logic and intuition. "Surely those are all things you can talk through with your sponsor Amelie? Or us? Or in your meetings? Or even with Ty?"

"Don't sell Ty short," Faith added. "Believe me, there's no one better qualified to debate every nuance of your relationship in minute detail than my big brother. He lives to pick apart people's problems and then figure out ways to solve them. It's what he does best."

"I know." And she had been bound and determined to see that as a failing, when she could see now it had never been the real reason she'd flipped out. "I just… I can't tell him how I feel…" Zelda stumbled to a halt, her throat thick with tears.

"Why can't you?" Dawn asked. "Really?"

Dawn had her totally busted. And from the looks on her other two friends' faces, so did they.

"I can't because I'm scared. I'm terrified. Because I know I'll fail. Because I'm rubbish at this stuff, and I always have been, just ask my brother. And I'm not sure I could cope if I screw this up, too."

"Zelda, you mustn't judge yourself because of the way your brother has failed you." Mercy covered Zelda's hand, and held on. "He is a deeply cynical man, who has problems of his own which he has never dealt with." Mercy's comment sounded heartfelt and sad, making Zelda wonder what had actually been said between Mercy and her brother upstairs.

"Seb has never appreciated your worth. If Ty does, you should give him a chance," Mercy said, the mention of Ty's name making all thoughts of her brother fly out of Zelda's head. "No one's saying it will last forever," her friend continued. "But never underestimate how much you are capable of. You've proved that with everything you've achieved since I found you in the Pigalle five years ago. If you can do that, you can do this. It'll take time and effort and it will be tougher for you because your recovery has to be paramount, and maybe it won't succeed. But you're strong enough to survive if it doesn't. Because you've survived so much more. Your parents' death, your brother's carelessness, your addictions, the constant lies about you in the media… Don't you see?"

The wave of gratitude overwhelmed Zelda, because for the first time, she did see. She saw herself the way Mercy and Faith and Dawn saw her. Not as a fuck up, but as a friend. And she could also see now that she'd panicked, not because Ty was a threat to her recovery, but because she had fallen so hard and fast for him, too. And because inside her still lurked that terrified, lonely child who had convinced herself all her losses were somehow her fault. And that rebellious teenager, who had believed if she stopped caring, bad stuff would stop happening.

But Mercy was right. That scared child, that reckless teenager didn't exist anymore. Because she'd stopped running five years ago. And she did care. Enough to repair the mistakes she'd made.

Unfortunately, she could hardly tell them it was already too late to repair this. That she'd already fucked it up too much, because she'd been too scared, and too insecure to tell Ty the truth a lot sooner. And in the process she'd destroyed what chance they might have had to make their relationship work before it had even really begun.

"Thank you, Mercy. You guys…" She huffed, the pain achingly bittersweet. "I don't know what I'd do without you guys."

Mercy picked up a truffle, popped it in her mouth and swallowed. "That's simple." Her lips curved. "Without us, you'd be even more disgustingly thin."

Chapter Thirteen

TY SHOVED THE ball cap down as far as it would go and pushed through the press gang on the sidewalk, who were cutting off access to the steps leading up to the Madison townhouse. His insides knotted with frustration and anxiety.

This could well be the defining moment of his life. And it looked like he was going to have an audience, because there was a good chance he wasn't even gonna get through the door.

"Hey, buddy, who the fuck are you?"

He ignored the shout from the photographer he'd just shouldered aside.

Someone flipped up his ball cap and he slapped it down. Too late.

"It's the Coney Island mystery dude, hot damn."

Flashbulbs started going off around him, but the sea of photographers had stepped back to take their shots. He charged up the steps to the huge, oak door which stood before him like the entrance to a fairy tale castle. The townhouse's gothic red brick frontage as intimidating as the thought of what lay behind it. Rose vines grew around the columns on either side of the doorway reminding him of the ring of thorns tattooed on Zelda's arm.

It all seemed mighty symbolic all of a sudden.

But symbolic of what, he had no clue. Was he the guy who was going to be able to hack through those thorns and rescue her, or were they there to tear peasants like him to pieces?

He'd done his research, spent the better part of an hour on the phone to a very nice lady from Al-Anon, who had explained to him a few of the challenges facing people in relationships with those in recovery. All of which had convinced him that Finn had been right, and he'd probably scared the shit out of Zelda by coming on so strong, so quickly.

But hell, he knew what that felt like, because he was scared, too. He hadn't exactly planned for this to happen either. But his research had also given him hope. If he could just convince Zelda this was a one-day-at-a-time proposition, not necessarily a forever-after deal, yet, then maybe, just maybe, they could have a chance.

But those thorny roses weren't filling him with a whole lot of confidence at the moment.

Ignoring the shouts for a statement, and the whirring clicks of cameras, he rang the large, brass bell on the side of the door. And spotted the small eyehole in the center go dark.

The oak slab edged open and a middle-aged woman peered out.

"I'm sorry, sir, but Ms. Zelda and Mr. Sebastian are not receiving visitors at the present time unless you have an appointment." He could just about make out her crisp British accent above the noise.

These bastards were scenting a story, but he didn't plan to make things worse for Zelda by giving them one. So identifying himself would not be smart.

"I think my sister's here, visiting. I need to see her, it's urgent." It was a low blow; Faith would assume it was something to do with Pop's health. But hopefully he'd be in the door before she found out about the lie.

Unfortunately, this woman was up to those sorts of tricks. "Your sister, sir? Do you think you could give me a name?"

"Yeah, buddy, why don't you give us a name? Not every day Her Highness screws a regular guy. She must have been totally wasted this time."

The sneering words had Ty swinging round, even though he knew the comment had been made to arouse his anger and get a reaction. The part of him that believed in truth and justice and the rights of the disadvantaged rose up anyway, to defend the honor of the woman he loved.

"What the hell do you know about it, buddy?" He

snarled as the flashbulbs fired at him and camera phones were lifted to his face. "Zelda Madison's been sober for five years. She's been fighting to stay sober, fighting a heroic battle against her addictions, and yet every time she turns around she has you guys on her ass waiting to kick her back down."

Somebody whistled, more shouted comments went off in his ear, but he only heard one. "That's some speech, coming from a guy who's too ashamed of his association with her to even give us a name."

"My name's Tyrone Sullivan. I'm an attorney for the Legal Aid Society. And I'm not ashamed to say I love her."

It was the worst possible thing he could have said. He knew it the second the words were out of his mouth. The chuckles of derision and the pitying looks as the jackals photographed him scoured at his pride. But worse was the thought he'd let Zelda down again. By declaring himself to the press before he'd got things straight with her. But fuck it, he'd wanted to take the attention off her and now it was squarely on him.

The door opened behind him. And the noise level increased tenfold, the photographers and reporters pressing forward in a phalanx of flashes and shouts.

"Ty, get the hell in here."

He dived through the door as Zelda stepped aside to let him in.

The door closed behind him and he found himself on

his butt being stared down by five sets of female eyes.

"Is there something wrong with Pop?" Faith sounded anxious. With the housekeeper standing next to her, it was obvious what she'd assumed.

"Pop is fine, sis." He got up off the floor, dusted off his jeans, to give himself a moment. "I came here to talk to Zelda."

Zelda stood behind the others, her hands wrapped round her waist, her face downcast. "I can't believe you said that to the press." She didn't sound pleased about his declaration. "What the hell are you trying to do? They'll stalk you now, like they've stalked me."

He walked past his gaping sister, her two gaping friends, and the gaping housekeeper, to grasp Zelda's elbows, and force her to look at him. "Do you think I care about that? All I care about is you. Is us."

She jerked out of his grasp. "Please don't say that Ty, when you don't know what you're asking."

"But I do know what I'm asking now. Better than I did. And I know it's a lot."

Her midnight blue eyes sparkled with unshed tears making fear rise up his throat and strangle the speech he had prepared on the subway ride from Brooklyn. Had he screwed it up again? Already?

"I know I'm asking you to trust me, and it's not easy for you to do that, because so few people have been worthy of your trust," he said, the speech forgotten as he went with his gut. His tangled, twisted, terrified gut. "But all I'm asking for is a chance. A chance to see if we can go somewhere with this. I've spoken to a lady at Al-Anon, and she said new relationships don't have to threaten your recovery. I'll go to their meetings. I've already ordered all the literature I could find online. I'm not going into this blind. I'll do the homework so I don't mess this up for you. I'm great at homework assignments, just ask Faith. I used to help her with hers when she was a kid..."

He stopped, seeing the watery smile lift Zelda's lips, and wondered if she thought he was as nuts as he sounded. He was talking nonsense. He wasn't making any sense. He made a living at negotiating, at advocacy, at litigation. He had a graduate degree from Columbia Law, a framed certificate that said he had passed the New York State Bar Exam and a license confirming his right to practice as an attorney in the Empire State—and yet he didn't know what to say to make this right.

"Please, just give me a chance," he continued, his voice gruff with desperation now. "I know it was only a weekend. But it was the best weekend of my life. If you don't feel the same way, I'll leave now. And stick to the rule about never contacting you again. I swear." He placed his hand over his heart, scared to touch her, because she suddenly looked so fragile, so unsure. He mustn't push. This was her decision to make. It had to be, but he wanted to give himself the best possible chance. "But I can't back off, not until I know for sure you don't want to try."

✦

ZELDA FELT AS if her world had tipped on its axis and everything she'd thought she knew about herself had turned inside out with it.

She'd never believed she could fall in love. She'd never believed she could have a committed relationship. And she'd never really believed that she deserved to be happy. Not truly, one hundred percent, all the way happy. Not since that fateful day when the Embassy housekeeper had come to tell her there had been a terrible accident. But most of all, she'd never really believed she could be loved for herself, with all her flaws and weaknesses and all the mistakes she'd made.

Until she'd gone swimming at midnight on Manhattan Beach and climbed out of her ivory tower into the waiting arms of her very own knight in shining armor.

And now this strong, handsome, caring, and courageous man was standing in front of her and offering her everything she had ever wanted. Because he was willing to try. Because he was prepared to go that extra mile, just for her. And because with him, she knew he meant it.

But before she could accept his offer, she had to know one more thing.

"I can't let you rescue me, Ty. I have to be strong enough to save myself."

He titled his head to one side, his dark hair falling across his brow in haphazard disarray before he pushed it back impatiently.

"Are you kidding me?" he said. "You're the strongest woman I've ever known. If anyone's doing the saving here, it's you who's saved me. From a lifetime of boring goddamn plans."

She placed her arms on his shoulders, ran her fingers into the curls of hair at his nape and grinned at her three friends who stood behind him grinning back at her.

"I'm not sure I can promise you a lifetime," she said, scared to hope for so much. All at once.

But instead of looking disappointed, or even surprised, the flat line of his lips, so serious a moment ago, curved into the captivating smile she adored. "That's cool, you only have to promise me tomorrow."

Lifting up on tiptoe, she felt her heartbeat skip as his large hands settled on her waist and he drew her close.

God, she loved that he was so much taller than her.

His head bent and he kissed her, the meeting of lips hot and exciting and yet excruciatingly tender.

He raised his head, peered down at her. "So do we have a deal, princess?"

"We have a deal on one condition, counselor."

His lips quirked. "Please tell me you don't have a whole new set of rules I'm now gonna have to negotiate?"

"Just one rule."

"Which is?"

"That I never have to live in my ivory tower again."

He chuckled, the sound rich and deep and full of

promise—for all the bright, shiny tomorrows that awaited her if she was strong enough to grab them. And with him by her side, she knew she would be.

"You're in luck." He nuzzled her cheek, and nipped her earlobe, sending a sizzle of heat to her center. "We're not real big on ivory towers in Brooklyn."

She laughed against his lips, the joy like a starburst inside her. Because she knew, that here was something and someone she could care about for a very long time.

And maybe even for happily ever after.

The End

If you enjoyed these Fairy Tales of New York romances, you will love the rest of the series!

Pursued by the Rogue

Kelly Hunter

Tempting the Knight

Heidi Rice

Taming the Beast

Lucy King

Seduced by the Baron

Amy Andrews

Buy now from your favorite online retailer!

About the Authors

Accidently educated in the sciences, **Kelly Hunter** didn't think to start writing romances until she was surrounded by the jungles of Malaysia for a year and didn't have anything to read. Kelly now lives in Australia, surrounded by lush farmland and family. Kelly is a USA Today bestselling author, a three-time RITA finalist and loves writing to the short contemporary romance form.

For more from Kelly:

Visit her website at KellyHunter.co

USA Today Bestselling and RITA-nominated author **Heidi Rice** is married with two sons (which gives her rather too much of an insight into the male psyche). She also works as a film journalist and was born in Notting Hill in West London (before it became as chi-chi as it is in the film starring Hugh Grant). She now lives in Islington in North London – a stone's throw away from where they shot Four Weddings and a Funeral... (She has asked Hugh to stop stalking her, but will he listen?!)

She loves her job because it involves sitting down at her computer each day and getting swept up in a world of high emotions, sensual excitement, funny feisty women, sexy tortured men and glamorous locations where laundry doesn't exist ... Not bad, eh.

For more from Heidi:

Visit her website Heidi-Rice.com

Thank you for reading

Fairy Tales of New York

If you enjoyed this book, you can find more from all our great authors at TulePublishing.com, or from your favorite online retailer.

Printed in Great Britain
by Amazon

65194335R00234